The Work Boyfriend

T0275014

REBECCA MARDON

TORONTO 2023

RE:BOOKS

www.rebooks.ca

Published in Canada by RE:BOOKS

RE:BOOKS
Brookfield Place
181 Bay Street
Toronto, Ontario
M5J 2T9
Canada

www.rebooks.ca

First RE:BOOKS Edition: December 2023

ISBN: 978-1-7389452-6-9
eBook ISBN: 978-1-7389452-7-6

Printed and bound in Canada.
1 3 5 7 9 10 8 6 4 2

Cover Design By: Jay Flores-Holz
Typeset By: Karl Hunt

For Carol

Now

DESPITE THE WICKED weather outside, the car was warm. The drive was long, but not dangerous, and the snow swirled, but it wasn't sticking. The route was clear, empty—no one else was crazy enough to be driving this late on Christmas Day. The girls were dead asleep in the back; even our twelve-year-old, who never usually conked out on long drives, was out, like her eight-year-old sister.

His profile was the same, older, more ingrained. We'd lost our youth, but we'd gained so much more—a whole life I never imagined. I never knew how deep feelings could run beneath the surface of our everyday: school, lessons, hockey, volleyball, piano, his work, my work, the house, the dog, this world we had created together, ours.

"Are you sure?" he asked me quietly as we turned off the highway.

"Yes," I replied. "I want to go, and we could see all the family back east too."

"All right," he said. "But only because I've missed your mom's cookies, and I bet she and your stepfather would take the girls for a few days, and we could side trip to Montreal."

"Now that's an idea."

We were silent the rest of the way home, with the snow and the sleet, the sound of the tires on the road. How had we gotten here, of all places? All these years later. Here. And now we were going back. School reunions, sure. I'd avoid those like the plague. But the years I spent at work in Toronto were different. I missed the friends I'd made, and we could afford the trip. So why not? Sometimes life doesn't go in a straight line and doubling back makes sense. Right?

Christmas 2005

Chapter 1

FRIDAY MORNING MEANT I was running late. Since it was the morning after the company holiday party, at least I had a good excuse. Still, it would be dishonest not to admit that I was always late, and managing to get out of my condo this morning had taken a herculean effort. My one chance to make it to the office on time was the streetcar approximately two minutes away. I had called the automated number, which was surprisingly accurate, and even though I couldn't see the car yet, it was on the way. Here was the problem: I was not at my stop, but three hipsters deep in line at the French café down the street from my condo.

Hipsters never ordered plain coffee. It was mixed, whipped, and then openly mocked before being poured into their stainless-steel mugs. My stomach churned and my hands trembled. I could blame the cold (December in Toronto is never kind, and I was stylishly underdressed), but the truth? I was desperately hungover. A caffeine fix was essential, so abandoning my place in line to race to the streetcar stop was not an option. Plus, I worked in the publicity department of an entertainment company, so the occasional late arrival was almost a rite of passage.

While waiting for my turn, I poked my head out of line and peered out the giant window to see if there was still a pile of people on the sidewalk. There was. If the streetcar was delayed by a stop or two, I was saved. I prayed for snow. A gale. Some unforeseen weather to throw the schedule off the tracks.

The line moved faster than expected. It was my turn to order, and I was still fumbling around in my purse for my wallet.

"The regular, Kelly?"

"Morning, Max," I replied. "Please."

The tall, heavily tattooed barista-slash-owner was the first person in the neighborhood I had introduced myself to after Rob, my boyfriend, and I moved in. I couldn't go ten feet without a coffee. Max was a very important person in my life.

"My mug was filthy. I didn't have time to wash it, so I'll have to pay for a cup today. And I've only got my bank card. Color me the jackass who holds everything up today. I'm sorry."

"No worries," Max said.

He turned his back to me to grab a dusty, slightly battered paper cup from the cupboard behind him. As he did, no lie, the entire line *gasped*. He poured in the morning blend, something fair trade and Ethiopian, and handed me the cup. For environmental reasons, he overcharged heftily for disposables. It was a dollar a cup, and all the regulars took it seriously. You can guess where this is going—I often paid for my cups, and it added up.

Last month, Rob had sat down with me to help me sort out my finances. He created a giant spreadsheet for me entitled "Kelly's Expenses" and showed me how to enter the information to keep track of what came in and what went out. Every. Single. Penny. Rob explained that budgets were the ice-cream cone holding up the treats in our lives. And since, after almost eight years together, he knew how bad I am with money, I finally caved and let him into the chaos. It wasn't the fact that Rob was good with money or that he came from a family that had it—it was more he was organized in ways I wasn't.

After I had handed over my bank statement and the little

notebook that he'd told me to note my daily cash spending in, Rob was shocked to see how much I paid for coffee each week.

"Why don't you make coffee at home?" he said. I asked him how much it would cost for one of those fancy espresso makers. "Thousands of dollars," he replied. "It's not that bad when you look at it that way. I can't make a latte at home."

"What about a reusable mug? In the last two weeks alone you've spent ten dollars at Max's in paper cups. That's one for every day of work."

"Look at it this way: that would mean washing it, making sure I haven't lost the lid, remembering to switch it over when I switch bags or purses, buying a backup mug or two, and then making sure *those* are clean, and soon our entire kitchen would be overflowing with mugs whose tops don't match."

He laughed. "Let's enter an extra twenty bucks a month in mad money for you, for coffee. At the end of the day, it's your money. Spend it how you want."

I lasted about six weeks remembering a travel mug before ending up in the same place—spending way too much money on coffee cups. Still, I carried around that damn notebook, even if I was always forgetting to write down what I'd spent. The perks of having a boyfriend who worked in finance meant that I was lucky he understood how to automate payments and the concept of pay yourself first. That meant my bills were covered, and my half of the mortgage was always sorted. But while I was paying my way, I wasn't making much headway in terms of savings—I was trying to go back to school, *in theory*, but never really making any progress because, well, coffee. And shoes. And new sweaters.

"Dude."

Max had noticed my hands shaking.

"Rough morning." I wrung them together. "Trust me, this will cure all that ails." I took a sip of the hot, rich coffee before putting it down on the counter and trying to find my bank card, which was, of course, not in my wallet. "Just a sec, it's in here . . ."

My BlackBerry buzzed, eliciting another audible gasp from the masses as I quickly checked it. No cell phones were allowed in Max's either. It was a text from Garrett: *I bet I know where u r. 2 choc croiss pls.*

"Sorry, Max, before you ring me up, can I take three chocolate croissants too?"

"Sure."

He stepped away from the cash register, and the pressure of the line hummed behind me—toes tapping, stern looks, the lot of it. Max bagged up the decadent, butter-weeping deliciousness for me as I located my bank card deep in the most inaccessible pocket of my purse. I swore under my breath that I'd make Garrett pay for the line being so mad at me. He was my closest work friend and, due to the nature of his gender, someone my sister, Meghan, was constantly teasing me about.

"You have a crush," she joked the twentieth time I brought up something Garrett had done that cracked me up or explained the cycle of lunch outings to her.

"I love Rob," I insisted. "And Garrett has a girlfriend. We're friends."

"He's your work boyfriend."

"He's not any kind of boyfriend."

After effectively pissing off the entire clientele of the café, I made it outside in time to see the streetcar trundling down Queen Street, saved by the terrible weather and the fact that schedules mean nothing in the face of snow, sleet, and shitty drivers. As I raced through the slippery streets in fashionable winter footwear to meet it, I swore the next time boots went on sale I was going to invest in something practical like Sorels that would allow me to meet this weather on equal standing. Maneuvering the takeout bag into my mouth, I barely had enough time to flip out my Metropass, hop in, and then hold on for dear life before the doors closed, packing me in like a paratrooper on D-Day, except without the comradery of *Band of Brothers*.

Stashing the food in my bag, I hooked my arm around a pole and took a deep breath. At least I was on the way. The cold had shocked my face back to normal under the residue of last night's makeup, which was buried somewhere under today's. My head hurt where I had tried and failed to unstyle an odd bump of hair, a result of the high bun I'd worn to the party and hadn't unspooled before crawling into bed around four-thirty.

Still, I had gotten dressed somewhat professionally and, by piling on the concealer, had managed to hide the fact that I had only gotten my head down for three hours of sleep last night. My lashes were laced with old and new mascara, which was muddled up with leftover and repurposed liquid eyeliner. I was happy to be pulling off a sort of upscale Edie Sedgwick chic without the heroin.

The streetcar pole was cool against my forehead as I rested it there for a moment. The car wobbled, and after righting myself, I wrapped the arm that was not holding my coffee tight around it for balance. The streetcar was packed to the brim, which meant that I was elbow deep in urban commuters with their earbuds tapped in, wearing the half-bored, half-irritated stare of every passenger on the TTC. The coffee was hot, soothing, and a piece of heaven.

"You look like you needed that."

There was literally nothing worse than someone trying to make conversation on a crowded commuter streetcar. The guy standing beside me had sleek, short hair and was wearing a rich deep-gray wool overcoat. His foot, encased in a sleek brown leather shoe, was inches away from mine. Garrett and I had looked at that very pair at Holt Renfrew last week when we were window shopping over lunch. When we flipped them over, the price tag said fifteen hundred dollars. Wearing them in this weather was a bold choice. The day could go either way—cold without snow or warmer but terrifically sloppy—and certainly ruin those shoes. Putting them on regardless of the whims of the weather seemed reckless even for a man who exuded the air that he *could* afford to waste expensive items.

"I did," I said, taking another sip to attempt to ward off the conversation.

Never talk to strangers. A rule for children and for people taking the TTC to work in the morning. Case in point: the minute I let my guard down, this dude saw it as an opportunity to chat. About how crowded the car was, about him taking up too much of my personal space, telling me the coffee smelled delicious, *boldly,* asking if he might have a sip (I declined). Then he went on for a good three stops about how the city planners should have looked ahead for the needs of all these bozos who own condos and taxed them up so they could build a subway line.

"I'm one of those bozos," I said. "My condo is right on Queen."

Then he started in on how amalgamation all those years ago was a death knell for the city and how Mel Lastman was the world's most embarrassing mayor. He laughed. "Those Bad Boy commercials alone are *ridiculous.* Thank goodness David Miller has turned things around for now. Transit in the city is awful."

"Are you a politician?" I asked. "Do you work for the city or something? Your opinions are, well, opinionated for an a.m. commute."

He replied that, no, he wasn't on the city council; he was simply a concerned citizen. I did my best polite nod and smile between sips of coffee and silently prayed that the trip to St. Andrew station was quick. The last thing I needed was a mess of taxicabs blocking the route because then I'd be stuck talking to this guy the entire ride. The car chugged through the Fashion District and, lucky for me, he stepped off at Spadina, but not before asking for my number. On the TTC. At eight-thirty in the morning.

"I'm flattered, but I've got a boyfriend," I said. "Hope the snow doesn't turn to slush for the sake of those gorgeous shoes."

"I had to try." He winked before squeezing by to step down and open the doors. *Winked.*

The streetcar emptied out at University Avenue, and this allowed me to take a seat and text Garrett: *Two for you. One for me. Be there in 20.* The rest of the ride passed calmly, and I had a chance to finish my coffee in relative quiet, no booming headphones beside me, no nosy neighbors checking out what I was reading. After hopping on the subway at Yonge and Queen, I opened my wreck of a purse, and the novel I was reading, *Alias Grace*, wasn't there. The only thing I could find buried deep in my bag was an old Harlequin of my mother's. My sister had stuffed it in there as a joke last weekend when I was at home and complaining about the titles that littered the bookshelves in the family room—all Maeve Binchy and endless rows of romances. I must have left the novel on my desk before heading out last night for the holiday party. Who knows? I'd find out when I got to work. In the meantime, I spent the rest of my commute engrossed in the story of a single woman turning forty who found out she was pregnant only to discover her beast of a husband was cheating on her the whole time. Abandoned by him, she leaned on his best friend and then struggled with the idea of letting him into her life. I texted my sister after almost missing my subway stop and surfacing back up to ground level.

Okay, this book is actually good.

Ha! she messaged back. *I told you.*

The habit of my job was something I enjoyed more than the work itself these days. The practical nature of the day to day got me out of bed in the morning, and my paychecks provided a basis for a very nice life with Rob—we had our condo, took vacations, were saving for a rainy day. But there are moments, like today, when I wished I didn't have to grind it out nine to five, Dolly Parton excepted. Three years have already passed by without my making any meaningful effort to research grad school. Each New Year's Eve I make a list, order my transcripts, try again, and January drifts into February, February into March, and suddenly half the year has elapsed, and I'm still working a dead-end job. Maybe this New Year's Eve will be different. Maybe this year I'll put myself on a strict money diet, give myself an exit strategy re: my job and finally get myself out of this rut. Where there's coffee, there's hope. But as the wind blasts me halfway across Yonge and Bloor, and the snow's already turning to slush with another gray day on the horizon, I'm not filled with hopeful, sunny optimism.

Chapter 2

B Y THE TIME I got to my desk, I was only forty-five minutes late. Not bad considering. Half the floor was empty. Co-workers smarter than me had taken the day off—they had clearly understood the nature of the massive post-holiday party hangover and had acted accordingly.

After booting up my computer, there were only sixteen new messages, and none urgent. This gave me time to settle in, properly hang up my coat, and swap my heeled boots for a pair of sleek Michael Kors pumps. Grabbing the pastry bag from my purse, I left my computer on with the desktop set to wait a half hour before switching over to the screensaver. I put my empty coffee cup in the middle of my desk, right beside my missing book in case Siobhan, the manager of our department, passed by and wondered why I was not actively engaged in, well, work. I headed off to find Garrett and deliver his pastries.

We worked at a large cable-television conglomerate in downtown Toronto. The company owned a bunch of so-called specialty networks: channels filled with programming about homes and gardens and cooking, and a few more "serious" stations like history and documentary channels. I worked in the publicity department. Garrett was in programming—a far more fascinating job. Every time I sat down to write a press release about another show that would tell you how to rebuild your house properly or what kind of wallpaper might work with your drapes, that line from *Bridget Jones's Diary* echoed in my head. You know, when Hugh Grant's character tells Bridget that she wouldn't know the first thing about the company being in trouble, blah, blah, blah, because she bandies about with press releases all day?

While it wasn't challenging work, I liked most of my co-workers, and I got to see Garrett every day. Plus, every now and then there was a cool event that we got to plan or an actual, bona fide superstar to set up media for (her name might start with *M* and end with *A*, just saying), and I was busy, not bored out of my tree. This wasn't the fault of the job—it was fine, it just wasn't for me. But that meant admitting that I wanted something different, something more, and, well, I couldn't quite get there either. It paid well. I was lucky to have it. These were facts I needed to remind myself when I was falling down an internet trap after I'd finished all the day's tasks, and there were still four hours left in the day.

Since it was the holiday season, there wasn't a lot going on. There was busywork—making sure the listings were correct, wading through the usual amount of customer complaints—but as of the next day, Christmas Eve, our offices would run on a skeleton staff for a week. Only those actively pressing the buttons to make the network go needed to be here. I felt bad for the engineers, but not bad enough to switch over to their department.

Downtime was dangerous, though—long days punctuated by the fact that I'd have to come back in the new year and begin my "new me" by starting in the exact same position. No job change. No commute change. No timetable change. Nothing "new," actually. I call bullshit on all the New Year, New You promotions that promise inner growth and eventual happiness. I'd spent enough of my measly bonus on books from the gorgeous store in the building kitty-corner from work. Yoga to balance me out. Getting in touch with my feelings to counter what I'd consider to be a dead-end job. Doing endless online quizzes to determine what personality traits have led me here. Searching for answers I should probably have in myself but haven't quite got the hang of yet in this whole adulting stage I'm in.

Sure, I could move up to manager or over to the marketing department, but this was still so far removed from the dreams I'd had after finishing my film degree. I love television. I could spend all day watching decorating shows, but I'd always dreamed of creating the programs, not simply publicizing the work of other people. I'm adjacent. My dreams were never to be in front of the camera but behind it—making the decisions, framing the shot, understanding what went into the storytelling.

Garrett's job as a programmer made me jealous. He was a member of the team who chose what went on air, and sometimes worked to bring important shows to broadcast. His work wasn't without its struggles either—budgets were slashed, hours were cut, network directions changed—but at least he was on the right side of the camera.

We'd been friends ever since we started on the first day and went through two rigorous weeks of onboarding. Endless meetings with the various other departments. Tours of the studios. Chats with the CEO. Teamwork, everyone explained, was the backbone of each decision made. Garrett's eyes sparkled as he cracked joke after joke, his slender frame always folding into the available seat beside me. If I wasn't with Rob, and he didn't have a long-term girlfriend (Jen), there's no doubt I would have been convinced he was flirting. And maybe he still was—but it was low-key, with no stakes. I'd never cheated on Rob, and I wasn't planning on doing it any time soon. But as my time with the company progressed, so did our friendship. And now we spent almost every lunch hour together, alongside texts, instant messaging while at the office, and hanging out at every work event. The details I kept to myself. And I downplayed all the time I spent with Garrett to Rob. That didn't feel great, if I was being honest. Still, the guilt didn't make me stop. Case in point, bringing Garrett pastries from my favorite coffee shop.

The elevator was slow, and by the time I got upstairs, Garrett wasn't in his office. He'd probably wandered off to collect some tapes, or else he was in a production meeting. I dropped off his pastries and made a pit stop before heading back to my desk: the coffee machine on his floor had the best brew in the entire building. The programmers had complained the loudest to senior management on one of those employee happiness questionnaires we had had a few months ago, and they were rewarded with a state-of-the-art machine that spewed out designer swill. The programmers needed it. After all, they spent most of their days sitting at their desks watching reel after reel with their feet up on their desks, headphones on.

Cup of scalding hot coffee in hand, I headed back down to my floor via the stairs, relishing the cool air of the concrete hallway before I was hit with the stifling, half-dead air on our floor.

I had barely put on my headset when my phone rang. The call display read GOV OF ONTARIO, which made me panic for a moment before answering. "Kelly Haggerty speaking, how may I help you?"

"Dude." Meghan's voice piped into the earpiece. "You sound so professional."

"Why are you calling me from the government?" I asked. "I worried someone might be taking me to task for my sloppy taxes or something."

"Rob does your taxes, and they are always impeccable. I'm in the travel office in the same building as the daycare. It's an Ontario Tourism thing. They let me use the phone sometimes."

"You never call me at work," I said.

"Are you sitting down?"

"That's a silly question, Meg."

"I have huge news, and I don't want you to freak out."

"I am too hungover to freak out," I said. "It was our Christmas party last night."

"I'm pregnant."

"You're what?"

"With child."

"Shut up."

"Nope. Confirmed this morning by the blood test. Mom said I should wait to tell people, but I can't keep a secret from you."

The phone line crackled as we both went quiet. I listened to my sister's breathing on the other end, knowing she was waiting for me to say something. "I'm incredibly happy for you."

"Honestly?"

"Yes. You and Jason will be awesome parents, far more stable than Mom pre-Carl."

There was a loud beep on the line, and my sister said, "We can talk more later, I've got to go. I'm not supposed to be using this *particular* phone, and I'm getting dirty looks from some suit."

We said our good-byes, and after I hung up, there was a static pressure in the air from the million questions piling up: Had Meghan gotten pregnant on purpose? They were so young. Too young. And how was it that my younger sister was constantly further ahead in life than I was? We were in that phase. Marriages and babies everywhere. After the chaos of my younger life, I was convinced I wanted neither. Rob still held out hope I'd change my mind once we were properly settled. And then that got me spinning even further because I might be twenty-eight, but I was nowhere near ready for so-called real life.

I said out loud, "Stop."

Someone behind me asked, "Stop what?"

Wheeling around in my chair, I saw Beth standing there.

"What do you need to stop?"

"My stomach," I said, recovering nicely. "I'm so hungover."

"Me too. I'm going to run down and get something to line the inside of my guts in case I start throwing up."

"You didn't drink that much last night," I said.

"Oh, I so did. And I regret every single moment of it. Want anything from the cafeteria?"

"No, I'm fine, I stopped at the coffee place around the corner from my house for my first cup, and have a good coffee from Garrett's floor for my second."

Beth was my closest female friend at work. We'd both started as publicity assistants. Charged with scheduling for our higher-ups and photocopying, we'd taken solace in the fact that turnover was so high in our department that we'd be promoted to publicists sooner rather than later, and we were. Beth loved working in publicity and totally looked the part—her long, straight, black hair, and her calm, dark eyes put even the most restless personality at ease. She had such a talent with people. Her favorite way to describe her job was "creating the limelight while staying to the left of it." She worked on better brands than I did: the high-profile film channels and the networks that carried our original series. Her job often entailed *actual* star wrangling. But I couldn't resent her for it—she loved the work. It was her passion. And she understood it wasn't mine.

"I'm going to get a greasy chocolate chip muffin and drown my sorrows," she said.

"Enjoy yourself, Ms. Chan."

"Oh, I will."

My phone rang again. This time the display showed a name I'd have recognized in a heartbeat: the trading firm where Rob worked.

"Hey."

"Hello, boozehound. You made it to work?"

"Barely. I was a little late."

"You're always late." Rob laughed. "Plus, I bet everyone was late. Judging from the time you landed at home, I'm guessing the party was fun?"

"Did I wake you up?"

"You were singing 'Crazy in Love' at top volume before you passed out on the couch."

"You're making that up." I laughed.

"Nope. I at least managed to get you properly in bed so you could have a couple hours of sleep before my alarm went off."

"I'm rough today."

"Can you pick up some stuff for me on the way home for dinner if I email you a list?"

"Yes."

"Thanks, babe."

"You're welcome. See you after work. I'm—"

Click.

It made me crazy when Rob hung up the phone before I was finished talking. There was no malice—his whole job was talking on the phone, to clients, to other traders, to various government bodies. He'd developed this superfast, superefficient way of getting through a call. A bit of banter, bro code for we can always get a beer together if we need to, down to business, and then on to the next. Still, there were days when I wanted our relationship to be the exception to the phone rule.

We had been together for ages. And that familiarity bred an easiness that I didn't expect. The quick kiss good-bye, the perfunctory shopping lists, the open bathroom door. We had merged into one, which is what my sister always said a long-term relationship was like, but I missed the heady days when we first got together. Drunken sex and kissing until your mouth hurt. Resisting my urge to let my mind spin about Rob, my sister, my never-ending quest to change my life, I settled down to do some work.

The next hour passed by uneventfully. I called my mother to talk about Meghan, but there was no answer. My mother's bright, cheery voice binged on the answering machine, and I waited for the moment that my stepdad yelled *Linda, who are you talking to?*

My inbox pinged, and I opened an email from Beth outlining the huge event we were working on for New Year's Eve. My cursor blinked, begging me to make the next move, reply with a "Looks great," but I couldn't seem to do *anything*. My sister was thirteen months younger but had the annoying habit of doing everything first. She met and married her high-school sweetheart, had a job exactly where she wanted to work, and was happily moving on to the next stage of her life: parenthood. And here I was standing so still I could barely move my mouse.

"Kelly?"

Siobhan was leaning against the edge of my cube. She rested her head on her arm, and the freefall of clacking vintage Bakelite bracelets followed her movements.

"Are you as tragically hungover as the rest of us?" she asked.

I nodded. "Absolutely."

She yawned. "Killer evening."

"Indeed."

"Anyway—" She paused for dramatic effect. Siobhan was the *master* of dramatic effect. It was almost as if she purposefully put the ellipses in when she was speaking. "Checking in to make sure that you're still the number two for the film channel launch on New Year's Eve?"

"I am."

"I've seen all the plans, and it's going to be a great night, but I'm a bit worried from a staffing resource POV."

Siobhan was always undermining the actual project manager by talking to the "second in command." She often pitted Beth and me against each other for no other reason than needing something to do. As if she was trying to plant seeds of doubt in our heads about the one part of the party, launch, or stunt that might go wrong or where we might eventually fail, so that she could swoop in at the last moment and tell the higher-ups how she saved the day. Office politics are the absolute worst.

"We're good. Beth has enlisted some former interns to help—we have at least a dozen confirmed—and I've got a rough draft of the event schedule in front of me. The whole party is in great shape."

"Glad I can always count on you two. What would I do without you?" Siobhan clacked away, leaving a mist of trendy celebrity perfume behind.

In typical Siobhan fashion, she had taken a half-baked brainstorm idea—to launch our new film channel on New Year's with an exclusive gold invitation-only party—and turned it into a giant project that should have been run at her director level. But because she was very good at ideas but not so much at execution, all the heavy lifting for this marquee event landed on Beth's shoulders.

I rolled my head to stretch out the back of my neck; everything ached, and it wasn't even lunchtime.

A cabinet opened and shut next door to me. And I knew it was the most dreaded, most irritating moment of my workday: my co-worker Marianne's break to do aerobics *in her cubicle*. Starting off with some simple jumping jacks, she then did a routine of kicks, squats, and burpees before finally cooling down with some low-key running on the spot. It was loud and highly annoying. Her oddly pitched grunts and quasi groans made it impossible to concentrate on whatever you might be doing. The sound of her workout even bled over if you were on the phone. Both Beth and I tried to surreptitiously complain to Siobhan, but Marianne was also good at her job, and our director's advice was to take a break and let her be.

Still, Marianne's healthy outlook and sunny disposition were enraging. I could appreciate her intentions, but it was obnoxious of her to subject her co-workers to fifteen minutes of puffing and moaning "Come on, you can do it!" before emerging, red faced and self-satisfied, to grab a glass of water. If anyone unfamiliar with the routine dared ask what the hell she was doing, she would spout platitudes about oxygenating her brain. Our cubicles had no walls—they were just metal frames with hideous, gray-patterned fabric stretched across, so there was no way for me not to hear her, and she knew it. Deep down, I think she did it to annoy me. Whenever she opened her drawer to grab her sneakers, that was my cue to put my phone on Do Not Disturb and escape to the dingy office kitchen on our floor for a cup of the disastrous coffee. In my world, "healthy" equaled skipping the second or third spoonful of sugar.

I shouldn't drink so much coffee, but listen, if Marianne piped up once more with the refrain, "Oh, Kels, you should really switch to a cup or two of green tea—so much healthier, but with the same bite! Who doesn't need a little hit of antioxidant midmorning?" then I might try kickboxing to give my day that little jump-start. If Marianne was addicted to exercise, then I was equally addicted to caffeine; no compromise would have brought either of us to the other side of the line. And I hated being called Kels. In fact, I hate all nicknames. Kelly is a nice, plain name; there's no need to shorten it.

The day already felt like that long stretch of the 401 between Toronto and Kingston, the part right at the end of the drive where you're about to turn off and have to hang on to your eyeballs so that you don't fall asleep before you get there. I was saving my other work-avoidance tactics for later in the day: the bathroom break where I rested my head against the stall and closed my eyes, even if only for a moment; the cleaning out of my inbox, which took very little brain power; the visit to all my co-workers on the floor to see if they needed anything.

Whenever my workday slowed down, like this one had, I felt like the character from the other truly great Hugh Grant movie, *About a Boy*. That whole monologue where he explains how he breaks up his day into half-hour blocks—his islands, he calls them. A half hour for bad television. A half hour for shopping. A half hour for lunch. I'm constantly doing that to my days. A half hour for email. A half hour for returning some phone calls. A half hour for writing a media release. But today it was impossible to concentrate on anything for even a half hour. The slow, sluggish air made it hard to stay awake. It was as if our entire office was already signed off for the break.

The company holiday party had been predictably ridiculous. No expense was spared; we were on top of the world right then in terms of healthy revenue, so the idea was "Let's spend some of that movie money by getting down with amazingly bad but refreshingly hip '80s dance music and an open bar!" Judging from how chipper Marianne sounded, she had barely touched a drop of the free booze. And I sort of remembered her saying good night to me a full five hours before I stumbled home myself. Marianne was counting down her squats instead of counting up. *Fifteen, fourteen, thirteen, you got this girl.* Instead of screaming "What are you trying to prove," I pulled myself out of my insanely comfortable office chair and stomped over to the kitchenette.

Beth, who sat on the other side of Marianne, was already there. "Every freaking day without fail," she said. "Like we're back in grade eight gym class. You remember that time of year when they'd make you climb up the rope, do sit-ups, and then run around the track or something. What was that called?"

"Canada Fitness. What kind of person doesn't drink coffee or eat sugar, and then bounces around every day to perk up?"

"She's bonkers." Beth yawned. "Every year I came *this* close to failing that thing. The one year I managed a bronze badge, my father was dumfounded when I brought it home. Even my parents—and you know my parents—understood my physical limitations."

I stretched across the filthy counter next to the coffee machine to rest my head. It smelled faintly of old bleach and mold. "I loved that test. What happened to me? Now I find a set of stairs challenging. I loved doing sit-ups. I could do hundreds and not even break a sweat. Multiple cups of coffee can't even keep me upright today. How am I going to manage until six?"

"You need to soak up the alcohol in your system like I did with that muffin. I splurged and went to the breakfast place in the underground instead of the cafeteria. The 'muffins' where they must be deep-fried—the ones that are totally crunchy on top and raw in the middle. If you thought your stomach was upset before—"

"Oh, stop, stop! I'll hurl, I will."

The high-tech machine with the mediocre brew was bubbling black liquid into my mug. Having a dry, pasty mouth was never a good sign. When Rob had helped me crawl into bed at half-past four this morning, the events of the evening had tumbled back into my memory. Had we actually ended up at a strip club? Was that even possible?

"Oh, my *god*, Kelly, I don't know why they don't give us the day off."

"Seriously."

"It's not like we're going to get anything done." Beth sighed. "It's all Christmas specials and weak news."

"And no one even reads *TV Guide* anymore, anyway. How is it still in business?"

Beth picked her cup up, peeled herself off the counter on the other side of the coffee machine, and leaned into my shoulder. "You think I could sleep under my desk without Siobhan noticing?"

"She came by earlier. You must have been away from your desk. She's looking for the staffing plans for the launch, worried you haven't hired enough temps."

"I showed her the entire plan three times this week. From start to finish, pointing out all the exact places the temp staff I've hired for the night will be working." Beth continued, "She's going to be the death of me."

"The event will be a great," I said. "And I, for one, can't wait to spend New Year's Eve at work."

Beth laughed. "We're earning our bonuses."

"You're earning your promotion."

"I wish."

"You so are. I bet Siobhan will announce it when we get back in the new year, and soon you'll be running the department, and I'll be able to say, 'We were colleagues once. Way back when, I attempted to do the same job as Beth Chan, and it became so painfully clear that she was much better at it than I was that I gave up and went to work at Tim's.'"

Beth snorted. "I'm going to march over to her office now and take her through the launch plans. *Again.* And I guess I'll work on the summer design mag pitches. They plan so far in advance. Maybe I can catch a bored junior editor who's stuck in the office."

"I wasn't joking about the promotion. You are a far superior publicist to me. You actually *like* this job."

There was no doubt that Beth had a whole lineup of media pitches in her outbox ready to go—she's that organized. I was always that little bit behind, relying too much on my personal relationships to get things done in a pinch. Calling in favors, looking for an in—that's how I survived. It was a miracle I still had a job.

Beth left me to the gurgling coffee machine and headed off to find Siobhan. I dumped a whack of sugar into my mug and made my way back to my desk. Our floor was cubicle after cubicle, with a large quartet of open-concept desks where the assistants and interns worked. Floors above us had actual offices, like Garrett's. But on these floors, where the publicists were, privacy was impossible. Everyone was used to ignoring the more personal conversations that went on from row to row around the edge of the building, where the lucky ones like me had windows. I sat back down and stared out, squinting at stormy Lake Ontario. I loved to look out my tiny sliver of a window at the beautiful cityscape. I wondered what people were getting up to in the offices and condos all around me as I gazed at rows of window dressings and patio furniture being pummeled by the weather. I wanted to take a camera and a mic pack around and interview them about their days. Cut it all together into some slice of life doc that highlighted how we had crept so far away from humanity in these places.

Marianne was still working out, and I managed to ignore her completely by turning my attention back to the fact that I had to find some way to make a documentary about the history of the sewing machine *sexy*.

Beth pinged: *5, 4, 3, 2, 1 . . . now be sure and breathe . . .*

I shot back a quick *LOL* and then, *Lunch?*

She replied, *Can't. Meeting the BF.*

Everything OK re: SB?

Yup. She's fine.

TTYL.

U2.

We logged off, and I went back at it—and thought of a better angle for the documentary. It was kind of an early feminist series looking at how technology freed up women's time because they didn't have to do all this work by hand. I wrote my tag: "Imagine your hands were freed from a thousand stitches."

With my presser done, I got started on my customer service email. By a stretch, this was the worst part of my job. I could not believe the stuff people complained about: the volume level of the show compared to the commercials (which were always louder); last-minute schedule changes that weren't properly advertised; an incorrect card at the end of a show advertising the wrong thing.

On and on. One of the publicity assistants on my team sent me the more serious problems—those complaints that needed to be dealt with on a more senior level.

> Dear Mrs. Smith, we sincerely apologize for incorrectly representing the graphic nature of the television show that aired on December 1. I understand that your sensibilities were shocked. However, this is network television, and people do have sex. Not sure if you've made it out to the movies in the last, oh, fifty years, but there are a lot of bare breasts in entertainment these days. And the film did come with a warning that it was for adult eyes only . . .

This was the draft I did *not* send. I was desperate for something more stimulating to do, but in the current climate, I was lucky to have this job. Still, I had to ignore the constant churning of unhappiness in my stomach, the regrets that piled up like extra calories. Of all the things that I regretted, the event that hung around my subconscious and stayed almost as long as this hangover was dropping out of my film MFA just before I finished. After Queen's, I had ended up at Ryerson, but I was in all kinds of debt—my penchant for living beyond my means had not yet been curtailed (Rob and I weren't living together yet; he was at Western finishing his MBA). I lived large. I had a great apartment right on College Street, refused to get a roommate, and burned through all my student loans in record time.

When this job as a publicity assistant at an actual television network came up, I had seen it as an opportunity to learn the ropes and get paid. You know, the once you're in, you can move anywhere approach to a career.

Working in television isn't the same as what I was doing in film school. I've got real work experience now, but I had thought I'd start in publicity and move over to programming. In reality, it isn't easy to make the leap. My dream of being on set has not been fulfilled by showing up to photo calls for pampered, grumpy lifestyle hosts.

Beth pinged: *OMG, has she finally stopped?*

I hit Reply. *I was halfway to dumping my coffee on her head.*

What IS it about today?

It's the day after the party, she needs more more more more more oxygen!!!!!

She's not even hungover like the rest of us. I'm. So. Annoyed. Some of us have to concentrate. She makes it IMPOSSIBLE.

What are the odds we can ask Siobhan to switch her desk to the—

A voice behind me said, "Someone was a little crazy last night. I will forever remember that it was your idea to go to *the club*. I'm putting that in the bank and saving it for when I need to blackmail you properly."

Garrett. Leaning against my cube in the exact same spot where Siobhan had been an hour ago. My stomach dropped. It always did.

"Hello, pot?" I laughed. "Have you met my kettle? You were as drunk as I was, maybe more so. We should call you sloppy Joe."

He came into the cube and sat on the edge of my desk, swinging one of his legs ever so nonchalantly. "Man, that dance floor was addicted to my moves. And so . . . I might need a play-by-play of what you remember from The Landing Strip."

"Shhhh," I hushed him. "Please don't remind me. It's so embarrassing. Let's forget that ever happened. Did you just try to tell me that the dance floor was 'addicted' to your 'moves'?"

He approximated a robot. "I'm so fly."

"Flypaper, maybe—stuck in another decade, like the stuff hanging on the wall of my camp cabin circa grade six."

Garrett's blue eyes sparkled. I hated noticing cheesy, romantic details about someone who was a platonic friend. One who could only *ever* be a friend. "So . . ." He slid off the desk to stand beside my chair and whispered, "What did you tell Rob?"

"Nothing." I moved away so Garrett wasn't so near to me. Yet I wanted to move closer, as always. "When I talked to him on the phone this morning, he simply mocked me because of how drunk I was."

"I might leave the strip club portion out when you see him tonight."

"You think?"

"Lunch in a half hour?"

"Sure. Beth's abandoned us. Raj is coming down. I'll meet you in the lobby. I can only walk across the street to the nasty food court."

"Grease in ye old food court it is, milady."

"Tudor documentaries?"

"Henry the Eighth, I am, I am," he said on his way out of my cube. "See you at one."

The butterflies. Flipping and flopping all around my insides. Making me flush, schoolgirl-crush style. That was my every reaction to Garrett. Like I couldn't believe we were friends. Like one day he was either going to wake up and realize that he was madly in love with me and then we would run off together, or that I was a totally uncool fraud and then he'd run screaming into the wind.

I loved his lanky frame and his collection of T-shirts. A set of earbuds hung semipermanently around his neck, and he wore the best kicks. The boys in programming could get away with murder when it came to their definition of "business casual." And when he brushed away his light, floppy, freakishly gorgeous hair from his forehead when he was concentrating, when he smiled . . . I melted.

Like my sister said, he was my work boyfriend, although I'd never admit that to her. Ours was a curious relationship somewhere between pal and crush. Part of my obsession had roots in the fact that he was so different from Rob, who wore suits and worked in the financial district. Deep in the belly of the beast, my real boyfriend moved money around for a living, and he was very good at it. He had that part of our lives tied down so well that I would never have to worry about it—though I did feel guilty about never being able to contribute in the same way. My mother's terrible history with men and with marriages wasn't always her fault, but it did contribute to the feeling of safety my relationship gave me. And Garrett was a safe outlet for my curiosity about what might have been—at least, that's what I told myself.

Garrett's real life girlfriend, Jen, was an enigma. We'd met a couple of times, ever so briefly, but I knew very little about her. They lived together, too, and had been together forever. She worked for a nonprofit, something to do with saving the environment. Garrett and I didn't talk about our significant others, an unwritten rule. The façade of our work boyfriend/girlfriend relationship could only exist in a bubble.

Rob had no idea of the amount of the time I spent with Garrett or the depth of my feelings for him—that I spent entire workdays waiting for him to email me, IM me, or stop by my desk. I fantasized about us booking the Four Seasons and spending an afternoon together, naked, drinking expensive room-service wine. And every night after work I went home and got into bed with my guy, whom I loved. Nothing would ever happen with Garrett. Nothing *could* ever happen with Garrett. But I was forever confused about whether I wanted it to or not.

Rob and I were so different, opposites attracting at the start of our third year at Queen's. He had rescued me from the worst high school relationship, from myself, and he had shown me that love, sex, couples, and relationships could be okay—normal, even. And here we were almost a decade later. Still, I struggled with moments of being unsure about us, about continuing down this path that looked so straight, so narrow. And hanging out with Garrett gave me that little something I needed to make it through my long, tedious days. Perhaps it was selfish. Maybe it was cheating. Yet I would never take a real step in that direction. Never.

Rob has told me repeatedly that he'd support us if I went back to school, that there's no quid pro quo in our partnership. But I'd watched my mother get burned by men when I was younger, and it had damaged me. I wouldn't let Rob pay for my school, and I certainly wouldn't let him support me while I was doing it—that was a line I couldn't cross. So the cycle continued. I saved, but it was never enough. I started spec scripts, but they never got finished. I jotted down ideas in the same notebook where I kept my spending journal. Stepping, never leaping.

My will to change always faded by January 2. It took a lot more effort to dream about running off to Africa to make documentaries when I was being confronted by the limitations of the industry day in and day out. Garrett went through it on a near-daily basis, staring back at his beleaguered budgets and temperamental advertisers, bosses who needed to please executives, executives who needed to please boards, and boards that needed to respond to shareholders.

Sometimes it was easier to sit and respond to the messages in my inbox about someone's boob making its way out of her blouse on prime time. I was okay shilling for the latest hot-stuff decorator for now, at least until I could handle the soul-crushing reality of spending five years developing a story that deserved to be told but would never get sold and would eventually end up on YouTube with five hundred views—or let's get real—five views. Except on days like today, it was painfully clear to everyone, from Siobhan to Marianne, and Garrett in between, that this job and I had a limited lifetime together. Admitting it? Nope, wasn't there yet.

Chapter 3

N THE FREEZING-COLD food court across the street, I wolfed down a cheeseburger while Garrett, a vegetarian, made gagging noises with each bite that went into my mouth. I paused only for air and a fry or two to balance out the grease now lining my stomach. For the first time that day, I didn't feel totally washed out and hungover.

"You were so hammered," Garrett said as he stretched out his legs sideways and rested his head in his arms.

I wiped away some mustard on the side of my mouth. "Yup."

"I saved you from the utter humiliation of ripping your top off during some Beyoncé song."

"Shut up, you did not."

"Have you ever known me to lie to you?"

"I wouldn't know if you'd lied, dumbass, because that's the point of a lie, that the other person never finds out."

"You speak the truth."

"It's a great song. I mean, she's crazy in love," I said. "She shakes and shakes it all out of her system in the video. I was simply doing the same thing."

He laughed. "You are not Beyoncé."

"No one is Beyoncé except Beyoncé."

"If I hadn't already been so wasted"—Garrett yawned—"I would have asked Rodney from my department to take a picture of you and then sent it around on the company intranet—you know, that ridiculous thing your department does after every staff party, posting photos of people like it's a yearbook or something they expect all of us to sign when school's out." He crumpled his bagel wrapper and tossed it into the garbage bin. "Three points."

"I'm not playing today."

"You suck every day."

Putting my burger down, I took a long sip of Coke. "I forgot completely that Siobhan made Rodney take photos. Holy shit, I need to get on the committee that picks the pictures."

"So . . . ?"

"So I can (a) make sure there's at least one embarrassing photo of you up for all the company to see and (b) to ensure that I'm nowhere to be seen."

"Wait—"

"Shhh." I pulled out my BlackBerry. "Always happy to volunteer." I recited as I typed. "To help out with the intranet party photos—forgot to mention when I saw you this a.m. Please let me know what you need."

Garrett kicked my foot under the table. "Kiss-ass."

"I'm not kissing ass; I'm saving my job."

"At the expense of mine."

"Oh please." I kicked him back. "Siobhan doesn't have a clue who you are, and it's better that way. Plus, programming does *not* report to marketing. Like, in any world."

"She knows my boss, though."

"Everyone knows your boss. She's the head of nonfiction programming. And a complete inspiration to budding documentarians everywhere."

"I'm going to steal those photos." Garrett started in on my fries. "Code break my way into the file-sharing folder where the photographer dumps them all, and start a blog."

"A blog."

"Yup."

"You're going to ruin my life for all eternity by posting embarrassing photos of me on the internet?"

"It's all a part of my master plan to make you realize you're wasting your time at that job and you should really apply for the assistant job that's come up in our department."

"Can't do it—the pay cut alone makes it impossible."

"Money will not save your soul, Kelly."

"You sound like Beth," I said. "Plus, you're so mentally weak the only code you could break is an alphabet game on *Sesame Street*."

"Hey! No fair, I'm not the one who needs a hamburger and seventeen cups of coffee to get through the workday—my brain only functions on one hundred percent organic."

"Pshaw."

"Did you just say 'pshaw'?"

"Pshaw," I repeated.

"Okay, granny pants."

"Your pastry this morning was butter layered upon butter layered upon butter," I said, laughing. "You're so selectively vegetarian-slash-vegan it kills me."

"I'm one hundred percent organic, baby, and I plan to stay that way. How else do you think I can keep this rock-hard subsystem known as my abs?"

"Please. I'm eating."

"I almost forgot, about Siobhan—"

Garrett stopped midbreath to stare at the woman who managed the dub department. It was the world's most boring job: making copies of tapes and commercials and anything else that people might need. Erica was stunning, of course. One of life's worst ironies: gorgeous girl, boring as the tape that she watched roll and roll. He whispered, "Man, her ass looks awesome in those jeans."

"Food still going into my mouth."

"It's perfect. I have a mad, illogical crush on her."

"You and half the company," I muttered.

"What?"

"Nothing." Finishing my cheeseburger, I crunched up the wrapper and picked up my tray. "I'm heading back upstairs. You can sit here and drool or you can come with me, your choice."

Every time he said something like that about Erica, the butterflies took a nosedive into my colon. Why did it bother me? *He was not my boyfriend.* And comments like that had cemented our friendship. Garrett talked to me like a guy—at least, that was how I imagined he talked to other men, all about asses and tight jeans and grossly unfair beauty. He had a crush, and he was talking about it with a friend. *It's what you do.* Except I wanted him to be as smitten with me as I was with him, wanted him to look at *my* ass, wanted him to raise his eyebrows knowingly when *I* walked in the room.

Garrett got up and stood by me, watching Erica while I tossed my stuff. "How much do you think she works out?"

I hip checked him back into the conversation as we made our way out of the food court. "What were you saying about Siobhan?"

"Dude! I can't believe you didn't notice your boss completely making out with Andre, the head of marketing."

"You're making that up."

"I'm not."

"Maybe I was drunker than I thought."

"Considering it was your idea to go to the strip club in the first place, I'd say that's probably the case."

As we stepped outside into the cold, December air, I wished that I had grabbed my coat. Trying to suck it up and run across the road had been a mistake. Bloor Street had gotten sloppy in the half hour since we'd been underground. And the cars weren't adjusting their driving, whizzing through the snow as if it was July and not the middle of winter. Garrett tucked me under his arm and raced us back to the south side, horns blaring. Collegial, friendly, but my heart paused on the gesture—the warmth of his arm around me, how close he held me. It was dangerous, to like it this much.

"Are you prepared for dinner next week?" Garrett asked while we waited for the elevator. "I know cooking is not your strong suit. Jen's excited by the way, she's dying to get a chance to talk to you, you know, properly."

"Prepared? What's to prepare? We're going to order curry from up the street."

"Sounds good and totally veg, thanks for that."

"Sure. Rob's excited too. He wants to get to know you both so he can hang out if I end up going to one of the all-night dance parties my friends from high school have taken to organizing. They have this crazy listserv that I'm stuck on for some reason. I keep threatening to make him go."

"Awful."

The elevator dinged, and we stepped inside. I was moments away from getting the shoulder pat: two quick taps that said *See ya later* and *Thanks for lunch*. I hated the shoulder pat. On days like this, when I was hungover, exhausted, and mentally unprepared for another four hours of work, it felt impossible not to touch Garrett properly. To not wrap my arms around his sturdy shoulders and tug him toward me as hard as I could.

The dinner—my worlds were about to collide. I had almost forgotten that a couple of weeks ago Garrett had been visibly upset and complained about how he and Jen weren't heading home for the holidays. They couldn't afford to fly back to the West Coast, what with their whole house-buying plan looming on the horizon. The two of them were staying put in Toronto, lonely and trapped in the snow-laden city while everyone else gathered with their families to read Charles Dickens (his dad read *A Christmas Carol* out loud every year, which was sickeningly amazing) and eat turkey (or Tofurkey, in Garrett's case).

So I had stupidly offered to have a mini Christmas for them at our condo, thinking it would be a good excuse to see Garrett outside of work, because the thought of going almost two weeks without being in his periphery made me feel kind of sick. It was all set. He and Jen were coming over the day after Boxing Day, and Rob was thrilled. Like I said, Rob had never really seen eye to eye with many of my friends, so he was excited to start afresh. His exact words: he could "start afresh" with these new friends. Friends who would not turn up their noses at his preppy collar, his high-flying trader job, the fact that his parents lived in Bedford Park, or that his father headed up one of the biggest law firms in the country.

The doors opened to my floor. And there it was, the pat. "Hope you make it through the rest of the day. Drink some water. You look way pale. No more coffee. If I catch you on the way to Starbucks this afternoon, I'll going to confiscate your card."

A witty comeback was nowhere to be found in my brain, so I stuck out my tongue and blew a raspberry at him. A *raspberry*. Like I was five and he was seven and had just pulled my hair.

The work boyfriend: a constant source of humiliation of mammoth proportions. Lucky for me, Garrett had a good sense of humor, and my juvenile response set him off laughing. The doors closed and he was gone, elevating back to his office to watch more documentaries about interesting and important topics like the impressive performance of our Canadian troops during the First World War. To make some calls. To produce something. I closed my eyes, leaned back against the wall, and shook my head.

Arriving at the glass doors that marked the entrance to our offices, I reached into my purse to grab my card key only to realize that I'd left it on my desk. That meant having to call someone to come and get me. Beth was out for lunch with Raj, and I didn't want to embarrass myself any further with Siobhan before she discovered any photos of me if I couldn't get assigned to that intranet task. That meant the only viable option was Marianne. Chances were she'd jog over. And regale me with perkiness on the long, cruel walk back to our desks. I called from the phone beside the doors.

"Hel-lo, Marianne speaking. How can I be of assistance today?"

"Marianne, it's me, Kelly. I'm outside the gates. Forgot my card key on my desk. Can you come and let me in?"

"You are always forgetting that card, aren't you? You need to get one of those clips that attaches it to your clothes."

"I sure do."

"Be right there."

The awkward conversation on the way back to my desk was not worth the thanks and praise I had to give her for the favor, nay, the blessing, of letting me back onto the floor. To top it all off, as we landed back at our cubicles, she said, "So, like, you and Garrett are *such* good friends. He's ridiculously cute. And such a *nice* guy. I totally went to high school with his girlfriend, we hung out all the time. They've been in love for, like, ever. Totally the couple to make it, you know?"

I had eaten lunch with Garrett every day for the last three years, and we'd talked about how awful our friends were in high school so many times. Like I said, mine were still organizing all-night raves fifteen years after a rave was even a thing. The majority of them were deep into experimenting with many, many illegal substances. A few had real jobs like Rob's. We had a dozen conversations about my bad drinking habit senior year, mainly the result of a terrible boyfriend and a will-they, won't-they relationship that was beyond messed up. Garrett knew about it all—about how my prom date, someone I begged to go so I wouldn't have to face my ex alone, spent the entire time chasing, photographing, and then dancing with another girl, and how much that hurt. How once Meghan had found Jason, we'd become this odd threesome. And he'd told me about how his friends were burning out on the slopes at Whistler, having migrated from Banff.

All this time, he hadn't, not once, explained that he knew either Marianne or Jen from that period in his life. All he'd ever said was that he was kind of the odd guy out at his high school because he didn't want to smoke weed whenever he and his friends were skateboarding. And he only joined the ski team because there were, literally, no other sports. The class was too small, plus his gym teacher could keep them on the hills for half the day once a week. He, too, was a ski bum.

He never stopped by Marianne's cube, never talked to her as he passed by. And he'd surely never told me that he'd been with Jen since *high school*. That was years and years and years—more than a decade by this point in our lives, since Garrett and I were the same age, twenty-eight. That meant they had weathered prom, summer jobs, entire semesters away at university, and traveling after graduation, which I know Garrett did extensively, and now, moving all the way across the country to work in Toronto.

"Have you met Jen yet?" Marianne asked. The tone in her voice edged into an octave that felt disingenuous, and even a little disapproving.

"That's why Rob and I are having dinner with them over the holidays. We figured it would be fun. The four of us have never gotten together before."

"I would totally crash that party."

My mind was so lost on the shock at the length and depth of Garrett's relationship that I wasn't really listening to Marianne. I sort of mumbled, "Sure, sounds great," or something as we walked back to our cubicles.

"Awesome! Send me the details, and Cash and I'll be there for sure."

"Aren't you going home for the break? Weren't you talking to your mom the other day."

"We thought about it, but Cash's sister is about to pop, and he wants to be around for the baby." Marianne continued telling me about her sister-in-law's pregnancy. Damn, I hated how much this adulting thing was going around.

Cash, how ironic, seeing as he'd been a starving artist without a real job for about fifteen years. He was finding himself, living off the bread crumbs of the odd freelance writing gig and a royalty check here and there from a band he was in during university that had cut one amazing record that was still selling. He somehow always had enough money to support himself. I was insanely envious of his lifestyle. Who wouldn't want to sit back and find themselves if they had the financial capacity to do it? He had opted out of the real "job job" ages ago and never looked back.

Sometimes, on days like today when my mind is adrift in the space of what-ifs and never-beens, I feel like I'm having a midlife crisis twenty-five years too early. Logically, I'm still at the beginning of my adult life, still trying to sort out what is to come and what I want. Many of my university friends had gone to law school, med school, grad school, even ended up with well-paying starter jobs, career-in-the-making kinds of opportunities. The grapevine informs me they're as unhappy as I am—and many found any excuse to throw their good luck away, like sleeping with the boss and getting fired (check), getting downsized and moving back into their parents' place (check), getting married in a giant ceremony that screamed "We'll be divorced in six years" to avoid being alone (check). Now two of my friends were going back to school, one to become an over-educated pastry chef and the other to take an entry-level position as an intern at a publishing house. At least they can say they fol-lowed their dreams, and it's good to get all this finding yourself out of the way before life got real and you had kids, double mortgages on vacation properties, and extramarital affairs. But what if all the hard work ends up with even more debt, more unhappiness, and a listless life like Cash's, where his art was so amorphous no one was even sure it existed.

"We'd love to have you, of course we would," I said. "It's great that we have the almost two whole weeks off."

"Exactly! That's another reason Cash and I didn't want to fly back home. We've never been tourists here. We've got a whole list of activities we're going to try. Skating at Nathan Philips Square, visiting Casa Loma, we're even going to take the TTC out to the Science Centre."

We were still standing outside our cubicles. This was the longest that I had talked to Marianne in ages outside of a meeting or in an official work capacity. I couldn't stop myself from asking, "Are your parents still there, in Banff?"

Marianne nodded. "When I was a little kid we lived in Ontario, both my parents grew up in Don Mills. We moved out west when I was in grade two. My dad bought a hotel in Banff."

I hoped my face would not betray the shock that registered in my mind. I was still reeling. Garrett had told me he spent grade nine in Banff, but then the rest of the time in Vancouver. Or maybe I'd just assumed he'd gone to high school there because he was always flying back there to see his parents. Garrett knew so much about my life growing up—all the bonkers time with my mother's various boyfriends after my dad bailed, my absolutely dumpster heap of a relationship throughout high school with someone who used me and my acceptance of it as "better than nothing," and how Rob was the first decent, kind, and loyal person I'd been with—we'd spent hours archeologically digging through my past. And I'm only now realizing how one-sided our friendship must be. Surface level. He let me drone on because I was good company and could pass the painful hours we spent earning a paycheck. My eyes threatened to water. He didn't trust me with the truth. He was passing time.

"I'll email you the details—I'd better get back to work," I said quickly.

Marianne squeezed my shoulder. "Let me know what I can bring. I've got an amazing recipe for sugar-free apple crumble. And local, organic apples I've been saving for the right occasion. Delicious."

Two extra people in my tiny condo for dinner. One extra person who had a leg up on knowing Garrett. They had history, he and Marianne. The kind of history that meanders around dinner parties when drunk people reminisce about high school and their common experiences and all the fun they had together growing up. And as I emailed her my address and other important details, thinking about Marianne having that with Garrett made me want to throw up.

To distract myself, I turned my attention to sending out feelers for the sewing machine documentary. Pitching was second nature to me, and a few of the local newspapers always reviewed the more esoteric docs, so it was easy to ascertain their interest and line up some early coverage. I called to order the dubs from Erica and tidied up my media release, but still minutes felt like days, seconds like hours. The clock on the bottom corner of my screen blinked and blinked. I put my head on my desk, desperately wanting the day to be over.

Chapter 4

WHEN I GOT home with the items from Rob's shopping list—plus potato chips and beer, the only cure for a hangover that I knew—my lovely boyfriend had dinner going. The apartment smelled delicious. I'd called my sister on the streetcar ride home, possibly annoying most, if not all, of the other riders. But I wanted to let her know that deep down I was happy for her and Jason. That I couldn't wait to be an aunt. Me being unable to grow up wasn't her problem, and she shouldn't have to feel bad about the happiest moments in her life or have me ruin everything. I had to fake it until I could make it.

Our little condo was in an up-and-coming neighborhood of Toronto, right beside Trinity Bellwoods Park and within walking distance of so many elements I loved about the city. Amazing boutiques with clothes I could afford. Great restaurants and a juice bar that I hit up far more than I should on Sunday mornings.

As much as I had resisted the idea of buying a place, I was glad Rob had had the foresight to insist. Owning real estate felt so adult. And it wasn't a part of my world growing up. But when I came home to our own thousand square feet of a few sparsely but tastefully decorated rooms, I was happy. The series of slightly run-down apartments Rob and I shared after graduating from Queen's had been appalling: a grungy basement that leaked, the second floor of a house that had zero insulation and was entirely painted pink, and a very, very (I can't say that enough) loud place over a bar on College Street, where neither of us slept during the six months we lived there, waiting for the construction on our condo to be completed enough for us to move in. That whole time Rob had been trying to convince me that we had made the right choice and that the place would appreciate like crazy.

We fought so much in those months about how we were going to pay for everything, from the down payment to the condo fees. The refrain: I wasn't great with money. It slipped through my fingers and caused shiny bits and bobs to appear in my purse or shoes to hide under my desk. With the condo, we needed to live carefully—and within our means—but that wasn't the cause of our fighting. That subject was the fact that his parents wanted to buy the condo for us. Entirely. In cash and in full.

After the millionth time I said there was absolutely no way, under no circumstances, that that was going to happen, Rob said, "They want to give us the right start in life."

"No," I said. "You might feel comfortable with your parents handing over that kind of money so you can live mortgage-free, but I'm not. This is our place. Ours. We need to pay for it ourselves. I can't feel like I'm beholden. What happens if we split up? They won't let you put the condo in both of our names—it'll just be in yours. I'll be living in your house. Under your parents' terms."

"What if they loaned us the money and we paid them back?"

"No."

"You'd rather support the bank than let my parents help us?"

"It has nothing to do with big banks or any of that crap—it has to do with me and wanting to pay for it myself. If you're forcing me into home ownership, I need to *own* it."

But the underlying emotions were something I never tell Rob outright. No, I wasn't great with money, but I had always paid all my bills and never skipped a month's rent, even if it meant eating beans on toast for a straight week. Far too many times, when Meghan and I were small, my mother had been completely broke and broken when whatever relationship she was in—pre my stepfather Carl—fell apart. We'd end up in a hotel for a few weeks until my mother could sort out where we'd live. She'd beg, borrow, pinch, and save until we had our own place again, until the next guy, and the next. I never felt safe unless I had my own place with my own name on the lease and with me paying the rent. I promised myself I'd never let a man kick me out of an apartment or have only his name on the lease promising *baby, baby it'll be fine* because for a straight decade when we were in primary school, it was never okay.

We argued about it about a dozen times, once with Rob calling me a stupid idiot for kicking a gift horse in the mouth, but finally he let me do it my way. We saved for the down payment. We paid the condo fees. We had only second-hand furniture for the first year, until we could afford new things. But my name was on that mortgage.

"Hi!" I shouted as I opened the door. "Chicken wings?"

"Yup."

"Comfort food, come to me. Oh, how I need you tonight."

Rob laughed. "I knew you'd need something good but still kind of greasy. I could smell the booze emanating from your pores this morning when I got up."

"Gross. You must really love me to put up with such stink."

"Christmas parties are always out of control. Remember the size of the steak at ours last year? Bananas."

Pulling off my giant winter coat and boots, I stashed them both in the closet and came through to the kitchen. Rob's dark hair was messy, and he was wearing an apron over his at-home outfit of old khakis and a polo shirt from high school that still fit him.

"What time did you get home?" I asked.

"Around quarter after six."

"Early night for you."

"Things are slowing down for the holidays. Only one day to go."

"I can't believe they're making you work until end of day on Christmas Eve."

"Comes with the territory. You want rice or frozen fries?"

"Frozen fries. Why are you even asking? I had a burger and fries for lunch. But make them the sweet potato ones. Here, I picked them up on the way home."

"Aren't those chips in your hand? That's a lot of starch for one day."

"Look at my face. You do not understand the severity of this hangover."

Rob shook his head and took the other grocery bag from me. He put the beer in the fridge after taking one for himself. "Dinner will be ready in a half hour."

"I'm going to take a quick shower."

"Good idea. I can't believe you were at work stinking that bad. I'm surprised no one noticed and tried to spray you down with air freshener."

After punching him gently on the shoulder as I passed, I made my way into our bedroom. Collapsing onto the bed, I finally pulled off my tights, which were almost cutting off the circulation to my midriff. My mind wandered like it did at the end of every workday. Did I delete all of Garrett's goofy messages from my BlackBerry? How was I going to tell Rob that my sister was pregnant without bringing up the dreaded what do you want from our future, Kelly, conversation. On top of that I had to explain that Marianne and Cash were also coming for dinner. The one thing I couldn't tell him was that finding out that Garrett didn't think about me nearly as much as I did about him broke my heart this afternoon.

"I don't hear the shower!" Rob shouted.

"I'm going!"

But our bed was just too comfortable. What felt like moments later, Rob squished the backs of my legs to wake me up. "Come and eat, you drunken fool. We need to talk about Christmas. My mother will have a coronary if we don't come over for dinner tomorrow night. She spent the last twenty minutes on the phone telling me so."

* * *

With dinner out of the way, Rob and I spent a blissful evening watching bad holiday television, my legs in his lap, his hands resting on my knees. Moments like this were tailor-made for guilt because I was home and comfortable, and I loved him. We fit together perfectly on our couch, and I adored that his clothes always smelled a bit like the bleach he used on his undershirts. Part of me wanted to tell Rob everything about the holiday party, from start to finish. How close I danced with Garrett. How close we came to stepping over the line at the strip club (from what I can remember). Because I couldn't admit the part about ending up at The Landing Strip with Garrett, I decided to spin some other gossip instead.

"Apparently Siobhan made out with the head of marketing at the holiday party," I said.

Rob paused the television show. "I thought she was married."

"I'm confused on that point," I said. "She's still got her ring on but I'm not sure if they've separated."

"She's a piece of work."

"Yes." I laughed. "Yes, she is."

But I was a piece of work too. Especially awful, and playing, rewinding, playing again in my mind was the part when I sat on Garrett's lap as a half-naked, barely legal, somewhat gnarly looking girl gyrated in front of us. Garrett had taken it all in stride. He had giggled in that high-pitched, superintense way he had throughout the whole thing. And wasn't that crossing the line? Wasn't it cheating to see a naked woman with anyone other than my long-term boyfriend? I didn't know. I really didn't.

The phone rang at about nine-thirty, and Rob said, "That'll be my mother again. I told her we'd talk about tomorrow night."

"It's fine, we should go. My mother will understand. We can split up the day, spend Christmas Eve and then morning with your family and have dinner over in Etobicoke with mine."

Rob brushed my legs off his lap and jumped up to answer the phone on the very last ring before the machine picked up. "Hey, Mom."

"Oh, by the way," I whispered, "our dinner party next week got a whole lot more crowded."

The fact that he couldn't hear me was the point; I would break that news to him later. It wasn't like Rob would care either way about Marianne and Cash coming to dinner. He'd listened to me complain about her, but he was kind and only judged people after meeting them, not based on my (sometimes) baseless opinions. Having Marianne around was pressure for me, not him. I would have to work immensely hard to keep it together in front of her because Marianne didn't know what not to say. It wasn't like I was hiding my friendship with Garrett. And yet there was no way to know what Rob might think if he had a thorough, complete picture of our day-to-day interactions.

Was it possible to be completely in love with two different people at once? Because I felt that way. Rob was home; he was comfortable, safe, secure, all the things that I wasn't. His future was organized, and he already knew exactly what he wanted to do with it. Mine was not so clear. Deep down, I knew enough to admit I was miserable, my stomach a pit as deep as a coal mine. The job wasn't going anywhere and the direction it did go wasn't for me. The only times I felt better were when I was halfway through a bottle of white wine, crawling through the pubs with my work friends after five o'clock, hanging off Garrett and waiting for him to realize that he was kind of in love with me too.

Rob. Garrett. Rob. Garrett.

The whole point of a work boyfriend was supposed to be fun and frivolous. Separate from your spouse at the door, and you never invite them to a party. Now, in five days, my worlds were going to collapse into one. Marianne could naïvely spill the beans about the endless lunches, the countless conversations in his office, my cube, and she would do it in that way of hers. "Oh, Rob, you didn't know? They're so, like, totally besties at work!" And he would be taken off guard and hurt because the two of us had always put each other first.

Sure, he had female friends and ex-girlfriends, of course he did, but this was different. We always had said that if actual feelings got involved in a work friendship we would step back. Because it had happened once with a woman at Rob's firm. He wasn't perfect, and a young woman, Lily, the daughter of one of the senior account managers, grew attached to him. The way he explained it, he had thought she was looking for a mentor. But I think she liked him from the start and didn't care that he had a girlfriend. It was okay; I'd been that girl. I knew how it went. I made a vow a long time ago not to blame other women when things went wrong. To take the high ground. We didn't need to hate each other—feelings were complicated. People were complicated.

When he first started as a full trader on the floor, he used to go out almost every night after work. It's a stressful job, and competitive, with drinking, drugs, and late nights. And when Lily showed up to a party, fresh, excited, smart, and blond, the tone changed. She knew who he was, who his parents were, where they lived in the city. She instinctively understood what the combination of all that information could mean for her, and she unleashed a not-so-secret campaign to break us up, culminating in one really awful night when they made out in the back of a cab hurtling back to her place on Eglinton Avenue. Rob showed up at home, woke me up, and confessed. Things weren't good between us for months. So we made a pact to be together. To tell each other honestly if it wasn't working. And to confess if any friendship with the opposite sex slipped into something more serious.

Now, with Garrett, actual feelings were involved, and it was a mess. I wasn't brave like Rob; I couldn't confess.

Maybe I was cutting it close to the edge, but I'd never technically cheated on Rob. Aside from sitting on Garrett's lap at the strip club, I had never so much as drunkenly slobbered over another man the entire time we'd been together. Not even in the last two years at university when it would have been easy, forgivable even, for us to cheat on each other. Not even when we were living in different cities for the six months between when he left Kingston and when I did. It was a relief to be with him, to feel loved, and to love in return. It felt right to come home after a night out with my co-workers and climb into bed with him, day after day.

But now, all I thought about was kissing Garrett, having sex with him, smelling his skin, brushing my hands through his hair, sleeping in his T-shirts—and it was unfair.

Rob wandered back into the living room with the cordless phone. "Sounds good. Yes, we're really looking forward to it too. Yes, I promise, I'll drag Kelly kicking and screaming to make sure she's on time."

Rob hung up. "You know, there's no way we can be late. My mother will never survive the affront."

"She does not even remotely get me."

"No, she gets you perfectly. She doesn't believe in being late. She thinks it's rude and disrespectful of people's time."

"I am not *always* late."

"You *are* always late."

"Things get in my way."

"You let things get in your way."

"Stop."

"Realize this: if we are late on Christmas for any reason, even if a snowstorm, a crazy Quebec-like ice storm or something as bizarre and totally implausible as a freak sandstorm threatens the entire city, we will still need to be on time for dinner."

"Understood." I yawned and stood up. "I'm going to bed. If you can pause the lecture for the night, please kiss me good night."

Rob leaned over the back of the couch and did just that.

* * *

As I lay in bed with my book, having finally had a proper shower, removed all the makeup from the last few days, and put on my insanely comfortable pajamas, dread filled me like a helium balloon. Part of me wanted to be late, simply to spite Rob's mother. It had been years since I stopped trying to make her like me. We hadn't gotten off on the right foot. I hadn't gone to private school, and my choice of career (or lack thereof) had always been a bone of contention. Over dinner, my position would be referred to as my "little job," or it was backhandedly implied that when Rob and I got married (which was simply not happening), I would have to quit work to adequately set up hearth and home for my ever-brave man who had to set out into the mean world of corporate finance every day. Oh, and babies—don't even get me started on babies. Not wanting them was out of the question. And there was no way I was telling Rob about my sister before this dinner, for him to blurt out the news over Christmas cake and for his mother to say something snarky like "Isn't she your *younger* sister?" Or "That should set your biological clock straight, Kelly. There's nothing like a little competition between siblings." And I'd want to reach over the hors d'oeuvres and strangle her.

At Rob's family occasions, I kept quiet, kept my head down, sipping whatever glass of expensive wine his father poured for me. I would not have an opinion. And *that* wasn't easy. I'm naturally outspoken, and in my family, if you didn't speak your mind (or end up yelling at each other by dessert), it wasn't considered a successful holiday gathering. At my mom's house we had roaring arguments about politics, entertainment, books, our lives, our decisions, and between the three of us women, my stepfather and two stepbrothers often didn't know what hit them. Deep down I thought that our differences were the reason Rob and I had ended up together. Beyond the buzz and pitfalls of finding each other while we were so young, he loved my mother and had an infinite amount of patience where she was concerned. He'd always been that way with my family; he doled out advice to Josh and Daniel in a way that didn't make them feel like idiots. He'd helped Meghan out with her finances more times than I could count on my fingers and toes. And since my stepfather was an accountant, there were always long conversations between the two of them about the markets and a whole bunch of other stuff that the rest of us ignored—but it always woke Carl up, and that, too, made my mother happy.

After terrible high school boyfriends and watching my mother's brutal decisions about men, I had been ready for Rob. Ready for someone to love me properly. To call me his girlfriend, to hold my hand, and to make sure I was okay. In my cobbled-together family, I was proud to have chosen him, to have found him. The struggles to fit in with his family? His older brother who was already a sports and entertainment lawyer and his wife who was equally qualified to love him (she has an MBA from Western and does "consulting," whatever that is) are nice people, but we have nothing in common. "Oh, Stephen and I don't watch TV," she said to me once when I tried to talk about *The Sopranos* or *Sex and the City*. Who doesn't watch TV? Apparently, they sit in bed swapping copies of *The Economist* and listening to opera.

To each his own, and I'm sure the pair of them work such long hours that anything other than a quick dinner at the end of the day is impossible. But I'm such a sore thumb in those situations, and Rob tries so hard to ignore it, to make me feel comfortable, that it only ends up making me feel worse. Inadequate. They're always trying to hoist a career change on me, to convince me to go into marketing, to "parlay" my skillset, to update my resume, to talk to a friend of a friend of a friend in the never-ending network that is their social circle. Hard pass. They're good people. They're just not *my* people.

* * *

I had met Rob through my friend Tanya, who was his cousin, at the university pub one drunken St. Patrick's Day. He kept buying me green beer and trying to convince me that because I had a Gaelic-sounding name I must have Irish blood somewhere down the line. I laughed and kept insisting that my name was my dad's and I had no idea if there was anything in my family history that suggested I needed to be out celebrating on March 17.

After the end of classes, just before exams, the three of us went to a rock show downtown, and he ended up back at my awful apartment north of Princess Street. We had one of those typical nights when you end up with a near but not total stranger (read: when you're falling-over drunk), and physical attraction propels the whole mess until it bleeds over into the wee hours of the morning. Tanya had hated the band and had headed home hours earlier, but Rob spent the night sitting at my kitchen table. My roommates came home and joined us, brought more beer, and we played a rollicking

game of Never Would I Ever. It was so late it was about to be morning, the kind of night that paused because the dark was so dark and
the air so cold. We kept the heat down, and Rob said it was freezing,
how could I stand it—*Poverty*, I explained. He laughed, set the beer
bottle down on the counter, and said, *Let me keep you warm.*

In those days, that was all it took for me—someone showing a
little kindness—and I'd open my bed and mistake it for my heart.

* * *

Six weeks later, both of my roommates had packed up, leaving
dust bunnies in their wake after their parents had picked them up
and piled their stuff piecemeal into family cars. Best friends since
grade school, they were co-au pairs for a very wealthy newspaper
baron, and they were jetting off to Europe with the family in a week.
I envied their job prospects. I still hadn't made up my mind whether
I was going home for the summer or couch surfing with my sister
at her new basement apartment downtown until I found some sort
of serving job. Rob had practically been living at our place, until I
kicked him out so I could study. *I'll see you*, I said. *After exams.*

Rob was a straitlaced, totally preppy commerce student who
wore his Queen's jacket without an ounce of irony; he tossed it on
over every piece of clothing, in every season. I spent much of my
time in a pair of old combat boots that my stepfather had given
me the summer before school. Most of my clothes were old band
T-shirts and leftover vintage pieces plucked from my mother's closet.
I wore them unironically. I had exactly two pairs of jeans. I could fit
all my laundry, sheets included, into one load at the laundromat on
Clergy Street. My winter jacket was an old peacoat of Carl's—and
when he saw me in his old boots from his time as a cadet and his old
jacket, he offered me an allowance for school. *No*, I said. *Thank you.*
I didn't want to owe him anything if their marriage imploded. Carl

wasn't my dad; he was kind and thoughtful, but I couldn't take his money. I scrimped and saved and paid for school myself with heavy loans and a food budget that would make my mother weep for its lack of actual nutrients. Every time Rob came over in those heady first few weeks of us sleeping together, he brought snacks—healthy ones like apples, and not-so healthy ones like his favorite salt and vinegar chips.

You don't have to feed me, I said. *I like to,* he replied. *Plus, have you seen your cupboards? I don't think they've had actual food in them for months.*

Rob didn't have to spell it out. He balked at the fact that I had a part-time job working in a small flower shop downtown throughout most of the year, leading up to exams. He made the mistake of saying that I was like a real townie once while I was studying for my philosophy final, and I remember asking him what was wrong with being from Kingston. He was taken aback, like he'd never thought about being from anywhere other than Toronto.

His family was exactly what I expected. They cottaged. They took expensive summer vacations to places like Paris and London. My family members piled off and on like Lego bricks: mother, absent father, sister, various miscellaneous men and their children, now a stepfather and his two boys. We did not cottage. We came home, argued, left, came home again, argued some more, and shared holiday dinners that were nothing short of epic in terms of who might be mad at whom, who wasn't speaking, and who simply refused to show up. Sometimes my stepfather would even invite his ex-wife into the mix. Any number of my cousins, stepcousins, or various other relatives might arrive on my mother's doorstep, and they'd be fed too.

I was part of the earnest Queen's contingent—the kids who had good grades and didn't understand the hierarchy of the place before landing there for Frosh Week: the tendrils of contacts that spanned generations and the network of legacies from a world I naïvely didn't even know existed. I was smart. I wanted a good education. I needed to get as far away from Toronto as I could without leaving the province and doubling my tuition.

Tanya was your typical Queen's student. She was prelaw, had gone to private school like Rob, and she knew all the same people he did. They had gone to camp together and dated in each other's circles like nobody's business. I admired how Rob's life had constancy. How he knew what was expected of him and didn't mind stepping forward and filling in the blanks. Respectable career that grew out of his education (check). Responsible use of his capital in terms of its growth and setting him up for later in life (check). The only dangling outlier: a girlfriend with the same background and values. Uncheck? I liked Tanya—we had a couple of history classes together, but we were convenience friends, tossed together because we were both in the same place at the same time. It's a throughline for this part of my life, hanging around with people I didn't have much in common with but who were nice, friendly, and solid.

When the school year ended, and we all went our separate ways, I didn't see Rob again, and it was pre-BlackBerry. I didn't have his number at home, and I hadn't given him mine. Anyway, I'd cut off my phone in Kingston once my roommates left because I didn't want to pay the bill, and we weren't coming back to this apartment. Carl came to get me in his brother's pickup, and he carted my worn-down furniture home to the basement to store it for the summer.

Rob drifted away, and I was fine with it—a fling, nothing serious; we were too different anyway. Meghan had just moved out, too, and she let me crash in her bachelor apartment at Yonge and Eglinton. We worked at a bar across the street, and I doubled up by doing extra weekend shifts at the old movie theater on Yonge. I loved that job, and watched so many great films that summer.

My mother begged us both to come back and stay with her and Carl, but it wasn't ever really home. Neither my sister nor I wanted to return. Meghan needed her freedom, and I didn't want to be parented. No matter how hard it got between me and Meg, we never boomeranged after leaving. My mother was happy and settled, but that didn't mean that we were too. The city was big enough that I didn't run into anyone from high school, even though I could have if I wanted to. And I could have called Tanya or even some other friends from Queen's, but I didn't—I kept my circle tight to me and Meghan, the two against the world perspective we'd always had. My high school years had been rough, and the last thing I needed was to do what I had done last summer, which was fall back into an awful, toxic relationship with my ex and then feel bruised before starting my third year of university like I did my second. Bad relationships were my north star. The worse my ex treated me, the more I went back, the more worthless I felt, the more I decided that was love. And cocooning myself with my sister was the only way I knew to break the habit.

* * *

At the end of that summer, back in Kingston, I ran into Rob at a massive house party Tanya dragged me to. The living room of the house on Alfred Street was packed, the air in short supply. When he smiled at me from across the room—half a head taller than anyone else, tanned from spending the summer sailing, handsome, and so inviting—I melted in an embarrassingly typical girly way. The way he leaned in close, half talked, and half whispered, nuzzling deep into my neck before pulling me tighter and tighter—it wasn't like anything I'd ever felt with anyone. I felt sexy. I didn't feel angry, or used up, or desperate for his attention.

It still felt like July, even though it was early September when I pulled Rob out of the party. "You disappeared," he said. "I came to see you after my last final and poof you were gone, like you never were there at all."

"Sorry," I said. "Do you want me to make it up to you?"

"Yes," Rob said. "I do."

As we made out back at my new, sparsely furnished apartment (my roommates were still missing), I was surprised I was still so attracted to him. He was long, broad, and naturally strong. I loved the sight of his arms when he was on top of me, and the fine hair on his chest. "I like you so much, Kelly," he said. "Try not to disappear again."

We lay in bed, and he told me how he had started off at Queen's taking history so he could go to law school, like his dad, but he had hated every minute of the humanities. After he switched to commerce he found out how happy he was being embroiled in numbers. Up, down, back, and forth—the market, in all its unpredictability, was exciting for Rob. He could play in the stock market. He had that freedom. I told him that I didn't even know what a stock was and had no idea how they worked besides watching Gordon Gekko in *Wall Street*.

He laughed at my film reference, and I took off his shirt again so I could run my hands up and down his smooth stomach muscles. The next time the sex was urgent, over almost too quickly, and then he confessed. "I kind of have a girlfriend."

"Why are you here if you have a girlfriend? I've been there and done that, and I'm not up for it again."

"It's been off and on for a long time. She goes to school in Montreal. I haven't even seen her since the beginning of the summer. It's something we do, break up and get back together, you know? Don't you have someone like that?"

I wasn't ready for a confession, not a full one, anyway. "I did," I replied. "And then I grew up."

"Harsh!" He laughed. "Ouch! You're burning me up with your maturity. I'll call her tomorrow. I promise."

We'd been together ever since.

* * *

Rob came back into the bedroom and flopped onto the bed. "God, my mother drives me crazy when she's not happy with something. Are you sure you don't mind staying the night?"

"If it'll make her stop calling six times a day until we do what she wants, yes," I said. "And I'm so sorry, but Marianne from work and her ridiculously named boyfriend Cash are coming to dinner on the twenty-seventh along with Garrett and Jen. Don't worry—I've already promised Garrett that I'm not cooking. We'll order Indian food. He's a vegetarian."

He started to object, but before he could say anything, I squished down to face him and cut in. "I apologize. Sincerely. She invited herself. I forgot my card key today after lunch and called her so she could let me in. I was all preoccupied and Marianne asked about our holiday plans, said something about knowing Garrett since high school, and all of a sudden, she's baking dessert."

He threw his arms around me, squeezed my ass, and pulled me tight to him. "We'll make it work. But you can pay me back for the inconvenience of feeling like the odd man out with your work friends. Right now." He kissed my neck.

"Thank you for not making me feel like a total shit."

"You are a total shit. But I still love you."

We kissed for a while with our clothes on, like teenagers. Then he changed into the sweats he always wore to sleep and turned on the TV to watch the news. I grabbed the remote and switched over to the channel that was always playing *Law & Order*. I yawned as Rob pressed himself back up into a seated position. "Where are those chips? Seriously. I need the whole bag."

He shook his head. "You are going to end up a potato. It's not good to eat so much crap. And you can't in bed. Go"—he pushed me out of bed—"watch TV in the living room, I've seen this episode of *Law & Order* sixteen times."

"Look." I flashed him. "I'm still young. It hasn't caught up with me yet. I can eat all the chips that I want."

"Out!" he said. "New Year's resolution for the household: no more chips, no more all-nighters, and no more burgers for lunch," he said.

"Fine. But it's not the new year yet, so I'm eating those chips."

After falling asleep on the couch and getting a decent night's sleep, the next morning I could face the last day of work before the holidays. As usual, Rob was long gone before I even gained consciousness. He'd left me a note printed neatly in all caps: PLEASE PICK UP A BOTTLE OF NICE WINE FROM THE LIQUOR STORE IN THE UNDERGROUND BY YOUR OFFICE. I WON'T HAVE TIME. LOVE YOU. Tucking it into my purse, I left the condo, late as usual. If I made all my transit connections, I might get to work by nine-thirty, which wasn't too bad for me.

We usually finished work at six. I could muster the strength of mind it took to happily work until the sky was completely dark, and we should all be enjoying predinner cocktails. That said, they never made us work the whole day on Christmas Eve. Siobhan would start sending people home after lunch and shut the phones down with a message that we'd all be returning after the New Year. But because Beth and I had the huge party on New Year's, I guessed we'd be the last to be let go.

There were three messages from Garrett in my inbox by the time I'd gotten my coffee and settled in. One about a crazy documentary he'd watched called *Darwin's Nightmare*, another about how his girlfriend had made some intense vegetarian pot pie for dinner and he'd spent the night in the bathroom, and the last wondering if I wanted to get a holiday drink whenever I was freed from my phones.

Couldn't you have compiled all this into one message? I typed. *Making me open three emails is a huge workout for a lazy day such as today. Give me the dub of the doc, hope your stomach's healed, and yes, drinks are necessary.*

Beth popped her head into my cubicle. "How different do I look?" Her long, pin-straight hair was the same and her brown eyes were perfectly made up as usual. "New sweater?" I guessed.

She sat down on the chair in front of my desk, crossed her legs, and placed her hand on top of her knee. "Guess again."

"Cute new necklace?"

"Let's try this again." Beth waved her hands in front of my face. "I can't believe I'm going to have to *tell* you."

I turned my attention back to my computer. "Tell me what?"

Her left hand knocked on my monitor, and that's when I saw it. "Oh my god. It's a ring. You're *engaged*?" I whisper-shouted.

Beth grinned. "I am!"

"When did this happen and why didn't you call me?"

"Yesterday at lunch. Raj pulled the ring out of his coat pocket and said, 'How about it?'"

"That was the proposal? 'How about it?' Wait, I was in the office after lunch yesterday, and you didn't say a word!"

Beth's cheeks were aflame. "It was charming. Raj is so low-key. I had the ring on my finger right after he proposed but then I was so worried about losing it or it dropping off my finger that I put it in my purse until after work."

"You said yes, of course."

"I did," Beth said. "I'm so excited! I couldn't sleep at all, and we were on the phone until almost two in the morning making plans to tell our families."

"It's so strange you don't live together."

"Our parents would have disowned us both. Hard enough for my parents to accept that he's not Chinese. Plus, it's going to be a hard-enough sell that we're getting married. I think his parents would collapse if we lived together. Buried and done with."

"The plans, spill."

"We're thinking we'll get married in the summer in Haliburton.

And then we'll have the Indian portion of the wedding the weekend after."

"Can you handle that, two weddings?"

"Yup. I've been thinking about it a lot lately, the merging of our cultures, you know?"

"Also," I added, "double the presents. Let me see that ring again. I'm so happy for you."

Siobhan wandered into the cube while I still had Beth's hand in mine. "Oh"—her bracelets clacked, up, down, up, down, like a nervous tick—"I'm so glad I found the two of you together." She paused. Clack. Clack. "I've been looking at the list of RSVPs, and I was wondering if I could send you a list of people I want you both to personally follow up with."

"Sure," I said, jumping in before Beth. "I can do it today. I've got a quiet morning."

It's not like we could say no to her request. But I wasn't surprised a number of her invites hadn't confirmed. New Year's Eve was a hot ticket in the city, but there were bound to be people in the industry—and out—who had other plans that would be actual fun.

"We can add them to the front of the line VIP access," Beth added. "That should sweeten the deal. And comp their champagne?"

Siobhan's face approximated a half smile. This was the closest she came to happy. "Perfect, I knew I could count on you two."

And then she wandered out of my cube. I was about to complain when Beth shook her head. "I am going to do everything in my power to make sure this party is not a disaster. My reputation is on the line, you know?" Beth said.

With no hint of irony in her voice, she continued, "It's going to be the best night ever. I have to believe it's going to be *the. Best. Night. Ever.*"

"Don't you stop believing."

Beth held out her hand and said, "I will hold on to *this* feeling."

"Hey," I said. "Congratulations. I'm so happy for you. You and Raj will have a long, happy marriage, I know you will."

"Does the sight of the ring bring up any twinges?" Beth asked.

"For me?" I laughed, maybe a little uncomfortably. "Oh no. I'm not the marrying kind."

Clack. Clack. Clack. Siobhan was back *again*.

"Beth, I have another idea about the film channel launch. Walk with me to my office."

"Sure." Beth jumped up. "What's up?"

The two of them wandered off down the hall to Siobhan's glassed-in office on the other side of the building. Doubtless, Siobhan was discussing some change in the catering, an update to the menu, and I could imagine the pressure building in Beth's brain as a result. How was it that management never had any limits on their expectations?

Shaking my head, I turned back to my computer and checked most of my listings to make sure they were correct. Marriage. No, that was definitely not for me.

Watching as my mother was crushed when my father left and then seeing the succession of heartbreaks masquerading as relationships that she went through in the years B.C. (Before Carl) had soured the idea of marriage completely. I didn't see the necessity of it, and I couldn't comprehend why anyone would want to legally entangle themselves in something that had such a poor success rate. Rob's markets did better than most of the marriages in my life. Apart from Rob's parents, I could not think of a single couple in my extended family who were still together. Who hadn't completely ruined each other in the process of proclaiming their unhappiness and battling it out in the courts.

I appreciated Beth's excitement—she hadn't been chasing a ring like it was the "ever after" from her own personal fairy tale. She genuinely loved Raj, and the fierceness of that affection drove her through the complexities of dealing with both of their family's expectations. They would make it work, have beautiful babies, and end up taking amazing retirement tours to places like Egypt and the Arctic. I had faith in my friend. I *didn't* have faith in the institution of marriage.

Before I remembered I was upset with him, I picked up the phone and dialed Garrett's extension. He answered with the usual "Buddy, what's up?"

"When you've finished breaking the waves and checking me later, call Beth and convince her to come out for a drink tonight."

"Kelly, her desk is, like, two feet from yours."

"Trust me, there's something she wants to tell you in person—you need to ask her. Be casual, but firm."

"All right, so we'll meet at the pub at three or so?"

"Yeah, but I've got to go right at five because I've got dinner at Rob's mom's tonight."

"Ah, family."

I sighed. "Happy fucking Christmas, right?"

After hanging up, I hunkered down and did some work. Reviewed Siobhan's list and sent the follow-up notes. Revised a press release, helped the assistants with some press release language, and surfed the internet to see if I could find bloggers interested in reviewing some of our shows. Easy work. Mindless work. At around two, Siobhan sent out a department-wide email telling us to switch on the holiday messages on our phones and to head out. She would take one for the team and stay until five.

Garrett sent me a quick note: *We got the okay to leave, you?*

Yup, I answered. *Getting my coat, I'll meet you downstairs in five minutes.*

Within thirty seconds of Siobhan's note, the entire atmosphere of the office changed; laughing and talking replaced the click-clacking of keyboards; and everyone was up on their feet making the Merry

Christmas! And Happy holidays! Rounds. Rescuing my coat from the overflowing cupboard, I hugged my co-workers on my way out the door.

I reached Beth's cube. "Ready?"

She replied, still typing, "I'll meet you over there. I need to get the final New Year's schedule for the celebs off to their unit publicist."

"Do you want me to stay and help?"

"No, go get a drink. I'll be right there, I promise." Beth typed as she talked. "Plus, Siobhan approved a loaner laptop for me so at least I can do the rest of my planning from home. Nothing says holiday like all the extra hours spent on a giant media bash for preternaturally juvenile television stars."

"And on that note, I'll see you in a bit."

"Uh-huh."

As I stepped inside the elevator, somehow, it didn't feel like the holidays. The usual elation I felt at knowing that I didn't have to deal with anything home- or garden-related for a full ten days was missing. It meant ten days away from Garrett. It meant ten days of real life. It meant ten days of coming to terms with my sister being pregnant and Beth getting married. Ten days of deeply intense conversations with Rob about our future. Ten days of avoiding any kind of emotions. It's the most wonderful time of the year.

The elevator barely passed two floors before the doors opened and a group of ad men piled on. They ran the in-house creative and were loud, obnoxious, and not remotely as funny as they thought. One of them held the door to stop it from closing, not once, not twice, but three times before the errant member of the group stepped on board. He was tall, well dressed, and wore specs that reminded me of Marty McFly's father. They were laughing, and the one who had held the door kept teasing the slow guy about holding me up, inconveniencing me, keeping me from my holidays. Before we all stepped out of the doors, Mr. Specs said to me, "You work in publicity, right? Are you heading over to the pub?"

I nodded. "I'm meeting some friends, yes."

Mr. Specs said, "Good. I'll buy you a drink for putting up with us on that ride. Want to walk over with us?"

"Thanks, I'm okay. I'll wait for my friends."

Backing out of the elevator, he smiled in the way good-looking men do, knowing they're flirting, expecting your knees to grow weak, and waiting for the fawning to begin. Hard pass.

I sat down on one of the comfy leather chairs in the lobby to wait for Garrett and checked my BlackBerry. Mr. Specs and his friends left the building, and I breathed a sigh of relief. Garrett smacked the back of my head softly as he came up behind me. He pulled me off the chair by my arm and tucked it into his as we left the building to walk over to the pub in the almost dark of the December afternoon. My body reacted to him almost immediately. It always did, and then the guilt settled and I remembered myself—pulled away and kept a respectable distance between us. Garrett immediately launched into a list of movies he was going to send me to watch over the break so we could talk about them when we got back, a tradition we started years ago when we first discovered our mutual love of film.

"We're doing sci-fi this year," he said. "I've decided."

Last year we did unsung classics, and I made him watch *Badlands*, which was my favorite movie of all time.

"But I'll be able to rent them easily?" I asked. "Nothing obscure, right?"

Garrett closed the space between us and tossed his arm over my shoulders again. "Yes, it's the one genre where you're seriously lacking in your knowledge. I have a feeling you actively avoid it."

"It's not my favorite, I'll admit. Outside of *Star Wars*. Harrison Ford can do no wrong."

His hand had slipped into my hair, and he squeezed my neck.

And I flushed, happy we were in the cold for a moment, and my immediate moth-to-flame reaction to his touch was hidden. *You're mad at him, Kelly. He's kept important shit from you, Kelly. You're a good ego boost for him, Kelly.*

I pulled away again and purposefully ignored Garrett's confused look. *You're in big trouble, Kelly.*

* * *

The pub around the corner from our office was filled to the brim with company people. Mr. Specs and his friends were already huddled around the lone pool table with a pitcher of beer. The dub department and its beautiful matron, Erica, were laughing in front of the fake fireplace. And all the various assistants, who banded together, had a giant group in the middle of the restaurant section. There were no tables left, so Garrett and I sat down on a couple of stools at the end of the bar, closest to the front door. I rested my back against the wall and sat facing him. He ordered us drinks—beer for him, cider for me—and I let him drone on about the planned home film festival as I quickly downed the pint. He was deep into an analysis of *2001: A Space Odyssey* when the little voice in my head said, *Don't do it, Kelly. Don't make it a big deal.* But she was already tipsy and my mouth completely ignored the advice.

"You know, my shit week next week is all your fault," I said, trying to make my voice light, jokey.

"With my sci-fi recommendations?" he said. "It's not going to be that bad. Honestly, I think you—"

"Marianne."

"Huh? What's out of the ordinary about you being irritated by Marianne?"

"You've been holding out on me. You all went to high school together. Add to that the fact that you and Jen have been together since then, which is like *forever*, and it feels like I don't know you at all."

"Kel, give me a break."

The bartender turned his attention to us, and Garrett ordered two more drinks. He looked honestly upset. "We grew up together, and she and Jen were friends, but it's not like we're inseparable or anything. Jen still talks to her, but beyond seeing Marianne in the halls or when I'm coming to see you, I never talk to her. It's not like we're friend-friends. It's not like us."

"You always said you lived in Vancouver. And isn't Banff, like, the smallest town in the history of all towns? The kind of place where everyone knows everyone? And you always told me that high school was something you couldn't wait to escape from."

Garrett sighed. "You *know* me. Marianne got me my job here, or, well, she referred me and got paid. That was the last we were ever really in touch outside of work. She knew I wanted to get into television, and she was already here with Cash. That's it. You know everything." He paused. "My parents moved to Vancouver after my dad got a job at the art gallery there—he used to run the Banff Centre. That's why I went to university out there. Jen too."

"You have listened to me complain horribly about Marianne for months, and you never said a thing." The bartender delivered our second round of drinks and Garrett paid, again, and shifted his stool closer. He pressed his leg against mine and let me vent, but I could tell he was upset. "I'm *awful* to her behind her back. But she's Jen's best friend or something from grade school and they've known each other forever."

He didn't say anything else for a moment. "She's not my favorite person in the world. I tolerate her because she has proximity to my life."

"You're going to have to tolerate her a lot more in a few days," I said. "She's coming for dinner too. Oh, and she's making dessert. Something totally healthy, but that tastes fabulous, and won't we be so excited to finally eat the local apples she's been saving for just such an occasion."

I slipped my arms back into my coat and pulled my bag off the hook under the bar. "Have a great holiday. There's Beth. I'm going to let her give you her good news. I've got to go."

"Kelly." He grabbed my arm. "Come on, why is this bothering you so much? Don't go like this. We're not going to see each other again until after the holidays. I'm going to miss you."

He's going to miss me.

I couldn't tell if the current running between us was fueled by my anger or if it was amped-up natural attraction. Whatever it was, I couldn't slow down my emotions. I was so mad, I needed to not be at the bar anymore. "I've got to go. Merry Christmas."

Stopping Beth on her way to meet Garrett at the bar, I made up something about needing to get some last-minute presents for Rob's family.

"Come on, it's only a few minutes," Beth said. "I wanted you to be there when I told Garrett."

"Rob texted that he's desperate for me to get home. We've got dinner at his mom's tonight. I can't be late."

"Stressful."

"I'll see you at the party on the thirty-first. Have a terrific holiday. I'm so happy for you, honestly."

We hugged, and Beth almost squeezed the life out of me. "I'm so going to make you a member of the wedding party."

Good, kind Beth. She deserved every bit of happiness that was handed to her, and I didn't want to be that selfish friend who met good news with unapologetic misery.

I didn't look back at Garrett on my way out, but I could feel his eyes on me, like they were always going to find me in a room, and for the first time in our work boyfriend relationship, I didn't want them there, making me feel like a fool.

Chapter 5

THE COLD AIR did me good as I walked along Bloor Street in the general direction of my apartment before turning south at Philosopher's Walk. I stopped in at a pub on Harbord where I knew no one from work would be, as I couldn't face just going home. Drowning my sorrows took longer than expected, and though at least two of the pints were free from generous revelers who appreciated flirting on my terms, I spent all my mad money for the week. I stumbled the rest of the way home, the cold air sobering me up ever so slightly. The elevator up to our floor took forever, and by the time I opened the front door, Rob was already standing there, coat on, bags packed, and a stern look on his handsome face.

"You're drunk?"

"Tipsy," I said. "Not drunk."

"My mother's going to kill you."

"How's she going to be able to tell?"

"Are you kidding me? You can barely stand up and you're doing that whole goofy smiling thing you do when you've had too much to drink."

"Three pints."

A little white lie. I wasn't in the mood for Christmas. I wasn't in the mood for any of it, not the presents, not the food, not any of it. I was lying. My sister was pregnant. Beth was engaged. Garrett was a liar. My head hurt. My heart hurt.

"Two too many."

"Are you being serious? I'm not slurring my words. I don't smell like beer. We were celebrating."

"What are you talking about?"

"Beth got engaged."

No response. Not even "Hey, that's nice, that'll be a fun wedding for you."

"Pull yourself together, you've got eyeliner smudged halfway down your face and if we don't leave now, we're going to be late," he said. "You'd better change too. I'm going to get the car. I'll pick you up in front of the building in five minutes. If you're not there, I'm leaving without you."

"Fine."

Rob pushed past me and then turned back. "Did you remember to buy a bottle of wine?"

Fuck.

"No," I said quietly. I started babbling nervously like I did whenever I really screwed something up. "I got all swept up in leaving the office, and I headed right to the pub, and then I took the streetcar home instead of the subway, and I didn't pass the LCBO, and—"

"Dammit, Kelly, you had one thing on your to-do list, get a bottle of wine for my parents, and you couldn't even manage that. I've been madly rushing around for an hour organizing the presents, packing your overnight bag—and you can't even do one simple task. How do you survive in the wild? How?"

"There's a bottle of white in the fridge. We can take that. It's not like your mother won't have any wine. It's your mother we're talking about."

"She hates cheap wine."

"She expects nothing better from me." I was rationalizing.

Rob laughed, which thankfully broke the tension. "You're right. Downstairs, five minutes. Let's go."

It took at least seven minutes to race around, pull off my work clothes, and find something equally presentable to wear. I wanted sweats, a T-shirt, and some slippers, but instead I decided on a sleek black Calvin Klein wrap dress that fit me nicely. I had gotten it the last time I was in New York for a conference we all attended about television, publicity, and the new internet age. I'd spent most of my time shopping, I'm not going to lie. I powdered my face and brushed my teeth as fast as I could before swiping my lips with gloss. Grabbing the wine from the fridge, I was outside and in the car in ten minutes flat. It was a miracle.

Do you know why I'm late? I confronted Garrett about him keeping important facts about his life from me. About the fact that I tell him everything, some stuff I don't even tell you, and he's my closest friend in the world.

Instead, Rob and I didn't talk much on the drive to the north end of the city where his parents lived. I rested my head against the cold glass of the car window and closed my eyes. He placed his hand on my knee, and I entwined my fingers in his for a brief moment, the fight over as soon as it had begun. Such was our way. The radio was playing holiday music, David Bowie and Bing Crosby, the Pogues, and the occasional Elvis tune. Soft snow was falling, predictably causing a traffic mess, and Rob had now resigned himself to the fates. We were late. There wasn't much to be done about it. The car revved as he shifted up and down with the pace of the traffic. There was nothing to say. I was dreading the anxious night I'd spend at Rob's parents' place, and I longed to be at my mother's, because at least I feel welcome there. And I could finally talk to my sister about everything. About my mixed-up feelings for Garrett. About how it was messing with what I knew to be true about loving Rob. About how unhappy work was making me. The bad decisions I'd been making lately. About falling back into fucked-up Kelly from high school.

Last Christmas, my mother had had a full house. It was one of those wonderful times when the stars aligned, so it wasn't just us, but a whole crowd of extended family, and Annie, Carl's ex-wife and one of my favorite people in the world, was there too. In all the years that Carl had been married to my mother, I'd been consistently surprised by the fact that Annie was open, honest, and unconcerned with convention.

This year, Annie wouldn't be coming; she was off somewhere exotic. Bali, I thought. My stepbrothers were both in university, which meant my mom would be in full-on family mode, huge dinner, doing all the laundry, mothering them in a way she never quite managed with me and Meghan. Last year, Annie joked that at least Josh and Daniel would always have their own rooms at my mom and Carl's—she was done picking up after them. All their stuff was boxed up, sorted, and donated. With her wicked grin, she'd said, "I'm heading around the world, boys. Don't get lost in my wake."

Last year Annie had given me some ridiculously expensive hair product, which made sense because she was a hairdresser at the time. In her off hours she was a part-time actress-slash–drama teacher–slash–whatever took her fancy. She was free and didn't give two hoots—her words, not mine—about what anyone thought. I couldn't help admiring her.

My mother had been terrified the first time Annie showed up to drop off the boys after we moved in with Carl. It's never pleasant to deal with ex-spouses, and when Carl and my mother had met (she was his secretary), he had still been married to Annie. Still, my mother didn't cower from anyone. I'll never know exactly what was going through her mind, but when she opened the front door to Annie, whose hair was so red it almost glowed and whose lipstick was even brighter, and the two boys standing there, all three of them giggling, she sighed in relief.

"Annie," my mother said, "it's nice to see you."

Annie half picked up, half kicked the boys into the house. "Here!" she laughed. "These are yours for the weekend. Thank goodness, I couldn't take another minute."

The boys, who had been ten and twelve, tumbled into the house and Carl's open arms. And that was the start of a ridiculously healthy relationship between all of them. Every Christmas, if she wasn't spending it with us, Annie would drop the boys off on the day after Boxing Day, her arms full of presents, telling jokes and repeating the same story of how she and Carl never should have gotten hitched (her words), but because "everything happens for a reason," he gave her the only good thing to come out of her life: her boys. She'd once said she'd danced a jig when Carl told her about my mother, and then she'd make some crack about how glad she was when she learned he was *finally* taking off with his secretary. "I'd been praying for that for years! I needed an escape but I didn't want to be the bad guy."

Last Christmas Annie had said, "We're the same. I see it in your eyes. You've got big dreams, girlie. You're going places. And in order to go, you've got to leave. You maybe even have to leave him, as gorgeous as he is."

She had laughed as Rob took a mock bullet to the chest and pretended to fall into his mashed potatoes. Annie grabbed my hand under the table. "I'm serious, you need to go. It's not enough to be safe. I gave my life away being safe. I love my kids, and I'm so thankful they're in the world. But we're the same, you and me. You can make a different choice, Kelly."

Later that night, when we were clearing the dishes, Annie forced my mother off her feet and into the living room and then said something that echoes through my mind often. "I know you love him, that much is clear, but what I don't get is why you want to live with him."

"It's just what we do. It makes sense, to be together, to live together."

"It'll be that much harder when you leave him."

"I'm not going to leave him," I said.

"Yes, my darling girl, you *are* going to leave him. Have the good sense to do it before he gets hurt. Thank goodness your mother came along when she did. Carl deserves to be loved by her. And she was always the one for him. He simply had to go through me to find her."

"But Rob—"

"Kelly," Annie pulled my arms out of the soapy water and turned me to face her. "We're not related. And yet we're alike, so, so alike, and I love you like the daughter I never had, or really wanted, *ha*! Listen to one piece of advice: leave now before you get married, before you have kids. Real estate can be sold, but when little bodies are involved, you'll waste so much time hurting him, and he'll hurt you, maybe even punish you. I don't want that for you."

"I'm not you, though, and I do love him. And we're good together."

Maybe those were my famous last words. And maybe it was good Annie wasn't going to be there this year because she'd see right through me.

* * *

As we drove toward Rob's parents' place, every house along Avenue Road was decorated distinctly but with good taste. No garish Canadian Tire plastic Santas sat atop any roofs. Instead, the holiday lights were almost exclusively white, huge wreaths adorned doors, and giant trees could be seen in almost every living room. By the time we pulled into the Morrises' driveway, we were almost forty-five minutes late. The lights on Rob's house were lit up bright and beautiful, and decorative globes hung on the hundred-year-old tree in the front yard. The paint on the exterior of the house was perfect, and snow capped the roof, creating an impossibly perfect Christmas card scene.

Before we even knocked, Camille, Rob's mother, opened the door. "Was there traffic, Robert? I'm afraid we're all already seated. Hurry, hurry, get your coats and boots off, come, come."

Rob pulled off his scarf and passed his mother his coat, and then he held mine as I wiggled out of it. "I'm sorry," he said. "I should have called before we left. Things were backed up almost from the moment we left the house. Lawrence was insane."

"You're here now."

With both of our coats in hand, she kissed Rob on the cheek before opening the antique wardrobe by the door and stowing them away. She swept us into the hallway. As always, I was amazed at how Camille, with her perfectly upswept hair and pristine Chanel suit, could manage to look so relaxed while being so controlling.

Camille pulled me into an awkward hug. "Kelly, hello, dear. You look lovely, as always."

"Thank you, Camille," I said. "As do you. Those pearls are stunning. Happy Christmas."

"Robert, take those overnight things up to the guest room. You and Kelly can sleep in there. Then come down and join us at the table. Kelly, you'll be seated next to Audrey, beside Arthur. Go on through while I put this bottle of wine in the fridge."

Rob headed up the massive staircase two steps at a time while I walked through the hallway and into the dining room. Arthur, Rob's father, stood up and said hello. Rob's brother and sister-in-law nodded as I took my appointed seat.

The table was impressively set with a giant poinsettia arrangement blessing its center. The room smelled amazing: expensive candles mixed with the gourmet meal that Camille had catered—we'd be having turkey. In fact, we *always* had turkey for Christmas and Thanksgiving at Rob's mother's house. I would have loved for her to switch things up, but Camille had very specific ideas about holiday entertaining. We didn't have opinions; we had praise, and it needed to be enthusiastic. Such a heavy, intense Christmas dinner at Camille's made for a rough couple of days of nonstop eating between our two families.

Over in Etobicoke, my mother made turkey, too, but she did it herself; she brined the bird for a day, sometimes two, made her own stuffing and cranberry sauce, whipped the potatoes within an inch of their life, melted marshmallows on top of the sweet potatoes until they were soft and gooey, and served corn she had cut off the cob in the summer and frozen so it would still taste fresh in December. We ate the leftovers for days, made turkey stock, made sandwiches.

Once she and Carl had started living together, my mother had taken the idea of family seriously. Gone were days of frozen meals cobbled together with the three of us huddled around a cheap kitchen table with squishy seats and less-than-comfortable metal backs. Gone were the days of my mother handing us some cash on Christmas Eve, saying, "You know yourselves so well, get what you want." Gone were the days of feeling disappointed and sad when no call from our father came—it was no longer expected. Even if he had called, I doubt my mother would have let us talk to him anyway. "Quite simply," she would say, "assume he's written himself out of your story. You're strong, independent girls. You'll be fine without him."

On Christmas mornings, Meghan, Josh, Daniel, and I would spend an awkward few hours together opening presents while Carl and my mother smiled expectantly at us. The presents were opened slowly, with each person getting a turn, and they were clearly marked as being from my mother, from Carl, or from both. She signed her presents for the boys Love, your stepmother, Linda. And Carl signed his presents for us Love, your stepfather, Carl. The lines were clear, but we were also now wholly connected. The boys were a decade younger than me and Meghan but they were insanely fun to be around—they loved video games, loved board games, loved to do family things around the holidays, and got a kick out of us coming to their hockey games. And it all worked, as patched together as it was, especially when you added Annie to the mix.

As busy as my mother was rushing around cooking, cleaning, and generally panicking about everything from the state of her floors to the fact that the Christmas tree might be drying out, the day was always genial and relaxed. Before and after we ate, we'd cycle through various holiday movies old, new, and simply inappropriate (*Bad Santa* had been Daniel's choice last year, and I would not recommend watching it with your middle-aged stepfather), drink warm eggnog or hot chocolate, and lazily admire all our presents.

My mother was trying to make up for the rough years between my father's leaving and her finding Carl, the love of her life. Now she was obsessed with tradition, imprinting good memories to lay over the shallow grave of the bad. Her hyperfocus on stability now that we were adults and didn't need it wasn't lost on her, I didn't think, but it hadn't stopped her holiday furor in any measure.

At Camille's dining table, excessively polite chitchat continued until Rob came down and everyone was seated. Halfway through the first course—thick, heavy soup with rustic undertones, as Camille's caterers *loved* root vegetables—Stephen picked up his wine glass and announced he had something to say. I closed my eyes and slowly cracked my neck. Tried to focus.

"Audrey and I are having a baby!"

And that makes two.

There was no way I couldn't tell Rob about my sister now. Plus, I'd now be spending the next year with baby craziness on both sides. No escape. It made sense for Rob's brother and his wife. They were on the Camille timeline. After all, they were one whole year into their marriage. Camille cooed and stood up, hugged her firstborn, and embraced Audrey. I stood up, said a congratulations that I tried very hard to make sincere, and hugged her tight. Rob cleared his throat and said, "It's going to be quite the night for announcements, Mom."

As he stood up, he took a small box out of his pocket. Immediately, I set down my wine glass and eyed him suspiciously.

"We haven't talked about the subject in a while," he continued, addressing me, "and I know that you're not one hundred percent convinced about marriage, but I have to ask. Kelly, please, will you at least take the ring and promise to think about it?"

Inside the box was a gorgeous antique art deco ring. I think I actually gasped. Camille said, "It was my grandmother's ring. We had it resized."

"Kelly?" Rob said.

"Yes," I said, loving him enough to know I wouldn't embarrass him in front of his entire family. I nodded. "Yes, I'll think about it."

Rob had a smile that cracked open his face in ways I found irresistible. It was what had first drawn me in. When he stepped around the table to put that ring, which obviously meant so much to him and to his mother, on my finger, my stomach bottomed out. "I know how you feel, and we could also be engaged forever." He kissed me and said, "That's all I'm asking right now."

Instantly, I felt guilty for the strip club, for being completely pre-occupied with my "other relationship," and generally being an awful girlfriend the last few days. My internal life didn't meet my external one at all, and I hadn't the slightest idea how to fix it. And I was lying. All the time. Little half truths were scattered all over the floor of our relationship, waiting for Rob to pick them up and realize I was a coward. This is what you did when you loved someone. You married them. You had babies. And then you lived together in semihappiness, never hating each other at the same time, until someone died.

"We all know you're *unconventional*, Kelly," Camille said.

"I've never before said *almost* when marriage has come up," I joked.

Luckily Rob's family laughed, and the merry mood continued with Camille excited about the event planning she would be doing, and both Rob and Stephen telling her to slow down. Audrey expressed her gratitude for all Camille's expert help, saying that she'd need her input about everything, especially the nursery. The wine never tasted so delicious. Tears threatened, but I held it together.

Ever since we'd bought the condo and properly started living together, Camille had insisted on asking Rob and me when we were getting married every time we got together. "Never," I would always say. And Camille's response was always, "Never say never, dear."

Arthur laughed now. "Time for a toast. To my ever-growing family."

Glasses clinked around me, and all I could think about was how I was going to tell Garrett that I had managed to up and get engaged. The words weren't there. We had had maybe a half-dozen joking conversations about me getting knocked up and becoming a lady who lunched. Garrett was convinced that Rob would impregnate me with his seed and lock me away like Rapunzel, "only with less hair." He'd crack himself up and then rub my stomach, talk to it like there was a baby in there, and I'd haul off and punch him in the shoulder. It wasn't like I was making a choice not to get married or have a baby—it was simply not what I wanted at this stage of my life. Or maybe ever.

"Don't marry that guy," Garrett had said about six months ago. We were sitting at the good food court under the bank building eating mulligatawny soup. Garrett had looked exhausted, and he wasn't sleeping. I was talking about how Rob and I were spending my two weeks off at his cottage, which was more like a compound, complete with a grounds staff, and joked about doing a Muskoka celebrity crawl.

"Wait, what?"

"Don't marry that guy."

"You know me, I have no plans to get married, like, ever," I said. "You know all about my mother's history."

"I'm not talking about your mom, and that's why there are therapists, you can work all that shit out. You. Don't you marry that guy."

And when I pressed him, asked why on earth not, he clammed up. Made some excuse about being joking. But the hum of something else had fallen over us for a moment, and it wasn't something easily forgotten.

* * *

"The ring looks beautiful on your hand, Kelly," Camille said.

"Thank you," I said. "I wish I'd had time for a better manicure." More laughs. Rob looked so happy.

Camille chattered on about obstetricians, family names, and engagement parties. Arthur even cracked a joke about Camille ordering the catering for all the upcoming parties the moment this dinner was over. I added, "Why wait until then, let's look at some menus now."

That tickled the entire table. *See,* I told myself, *I can do this.*

After dinner, I lay alone in the huge guest room bed while Rob caught up with his father and brother over scotch. I held my hand up in front of my face. The ring *was* spectacular. It glistened in the soft light of the bedroom and made my hand look elegant. Slipping it off, I put it back in the velvet-lined box and placed it on the bedside table. Turning onto my other side, I decided I'd leave the ring in the box. How had I ended up with all the things in life I'd promised myself I would never choose now standing before me? I was now the proud owner of a gorgeous ring from an equally gorgeous fellow. I was lucky enough to have a sort of well-paying job adjacent (in a way) to an industry I wanted to be a part of, and even if I hated the work, I got up every day like I was supposed to and worked hard. And now I had the opportunity to become a full-fledged member of the Morris family.

Of all the days to halfway propose, Rob had chosen Christmas Eve, forever making an anniversary of the holiday a story for all the ages of our relationship. I could have killed him. Turning back the other way, I stared at the blinking clock—it was one o'clock. Rob must be two or three scotches deep with his father and brother by now, all of them likely raiding Camille's meticulously organized and labeled leftovers.

For a crazy moment I wondered if Garrett had gone back to the office. He worked all kinds of odd hours, often screening during the holidays because it was quiet, and he liked the solitude and *The Shining*-like nature of the building when the lights were turned off and no one else was there. I could call him and break every work-boyfriend rule, the most important being that what happened at work stayed at work, and what happened at home belonged at home. But he wouldn't be there this late on Christmas Eve, even if he and Jen hadn't flown back to the West Coast this year.

I grabbed my BlackBerry and sent Garrett a quick note. *You will never believe what happened at dinner. Turns out I'm that kind of girl. We're engaged.*

I clicked off my phone and concentrated hard on the ceiling. All this drama in my head, and I *still* had to make it through Christmas and Boxing Day, and then my worlds would spectacularly collide. I'd get to see Garrett in person, show him the ring, work up to asking him what he thought about it all, while begging my heart to keep it light and innocent. Right now, though, right now, I had to stop thinking of him as an escape hatch for my life.

The door slid open over the plush carpet and Rob came into the room. He brushed his teeth, washed his face, and then climbed into the bed beside me.

He lay back with his arms above his head and quietly said, "I know you don't want to get married. And that whole holiday-dinner spectacle has probably enraged you, but it meant so much to my mother. She's had it all planned for weeks, the double announcement celebration. That's why it was so important for us to get here on time tonight." He continued, "She's controlling, and you hate that, and I promise, no pressure, but I do want you to have that ring. I want you to know that I love you and want to be with you for the long haul."

I opened my mouth, but he kept going. "We've made it this far, and it's terrific. I didn't know I could love someone for this long and want to love them for even longer. I know we're long haulers, but I don't want to call you my girlfriend when we're forty."

"I hear you," I said. "I will say this, I'll think about it. Seriously and consciously, and with an open mind."

"You're wicked awesome."

"Did you watch *Good Will Hunting* with your dad and brother?"

"Hmmmm." Rob tugged me over by the waist to the middle of the bed, slipped his hand into the bottoms of my pajamas, and rested it on my thigh. "Yes, yes, I did."

As I lay there nestled into his familiar body, I understood there were good and bad times for arguments, and that this was not the former. My mind rolled over the thought of a big wedding with so many details out of my control. Camille and my mother coming into contact with one another. Annie's opinions. My own reservations about the finality of it all. Again, like with Garrett, the words were out before I could put my tongue on pause. "I hate it all: the white dress, the flowers, the aisle, the bridal showers. Ugh, a reception line."

"You aren't a fortune teller," Rob said. "You don't know how our wedding or our marriage could turn out. Not every husband is like your dad. Look at your mom and Carl, they've made it work. We've been together for so long, Kelly. I can't wait another decade for you to get over whatever it is holding you back. What if you get sick or I get sick, or something happens? I want us to be a family and face it all together."

"Not every marriage is like *your* parents' either." I hated whisper-shouting. I hated that I was whisper-shouting on Christmas Eve about a massive diamond ring that was likely worth more than my whole post-secondary education. "Who cares what we call each other? It's what we mean to each other that matters. I don't need a piece of paper for me to think our relationship is serious. And I certainly don't need that ring."

"They want to buy us a house."

"*What?* Didn't we go through this with the condo? Your parents are not buying us a house."

"My father's selling off some of his other real estate—the triplex and three of the condos. They're using the money to buy us a house because that's what they gave Audrey and Stephen when they got married. You know my parents: everything needs to be fair. Every time we talk she asks if I've managed to convince you about 'the marriage question.' She thought seeing the ring might do the trick. And it's an estate situation. My dad needs to divest some of the money in a way that helps his taxes."

"We don't *need* a house. We have the condo. What on earth would we do with a house? And where would we buy one? I'm certainly not living up here. I don't want to move out of our neighborhood."

"Translation," Rob said, "you don't want to move away from Max and your coffee shop."

"That's part of it. I *like* our life. I don't need your parents to buy me a house. They don't understand how I need to do these things myself."

"Okay, okay, we don't need to fight about it now—my mother thought it would be a perfect wedding present."

"For a wedding I haven't even agreed to have yet."

"I got the ring on your finger once, that's the first step in my long-term plan to finally win you over, and you did promise to think about it with an open mind. That's all I'm asking." He nuzzled my neck. "I'll bring you over to my side before you know it. A house in Lawrence Park. Two kids. A cottage. You won't know what hit you."

I pushed him away gently. "Don't even joke about it."

Rob yawned, pulled his hand from my bottoms, and squeezed my waist. As if talking about his parents buying us an entire house, mortgage-free, was not a big deal at all. Like it was expected. Like the ring. Like the horrible Christmas meals in semiformal attire using the good silver. He fell asleep quickly from the scotch, his arm growing heavier on top of me.

What was my next step? Resign myself to a life that I had never dreamed of leading—and not in the kind of oh my god, this man has walked into my life, and now I've got a ring and maybe a house, and I'm set for life romantic plots that enrage me. Was there a way out of this without leaving the only person who had ever stuck by me, no questions asked, behind?

I slipped out of bed to use the bathroom and turned my phone back on. I didn't know why I expected Garrett to ping me back. I just wanted him to hear me call through the internet ether. Instead, there was a message from my sister. *Hope you're having a nice Xmas eve w/ the in-laws. See you tomorrow at the mother's. I'll be the one throwing up. Morning sickness is no joke.*

I held my phone tightly as my hands started to shake. My heart felt light, like it was floating outside of my chest. I quickly typed back, *Babies seem to be the thing this holiday season. Getting knocked up is going around like hand, foot, and mouth disease at a daycare. Story to come tomorrow.*

My BlackBerry flashed red. Garrett? No, my mother.

Kelly, this is the one who gave birth to you. I finally have the turkey under control (the poor bird was too cold outside so I made Carl lug the tub into the kitchen and leave the window open. He's already complaining about the cost of heating). Anyway, it's late. My hands are tired from chopping. The boys got home okay from school. I think exams might have done Daniel in—he's not loving Western. You'll be happy to know that Annie left a package for you (and one for Meghan). Looking forward to seeing you and your gorgeous Rob tomorrow. Love, your mother, who can't get to sleep and it's well after 1 a.m.

I typed back, *Mom, you don't have to tell me it's you—your name comes attached to the email. Can't wait for turkey. There better be lots of potatoes. We'll see you midday, maybe earlier. Go to sleep! Love you too.*

She replied again: *Cheeky cheeky. Says YOUR MOTHER. You go to sleep.*

It was hard, sometimes, to know if my mother really didn't understand email or if she was willfully being obtuse. But she was right, I should have been in bed. Rob was deep asleep now; the house, this room, deathly silent. He barely moved or made any noise while he was sleeping. It was uncanny and sometimes a little unnerving. My legs were growing stiff and sore, all crunched up against the side of the tub.

I wrote to my sister again: *I'm sure Mom will have soda crackers and ginger ale for you, like when we were kids. Maybe cinnamon toast?*

* * *

We had been living with my mother's boyfriend, Anatoly "Toly" Ivanovich. He was religious in a way that made both Meghan and me deeply uncomfortable, but my mother had convinced herself that the Catholic school was probably better than our old one across town, so she enrolled us. I think we managed a good three-week stint before Meghan refused entirely to attend religion class and skipped it regularly. As I was a year ahead of her, I wasn't scheduled to have religion that semester, so I was free of that particular torture. But we were both subjected to the daily prayers strumming through the morning announcements, and that was enough for me. Our grades were suffering. And Toly was insufferable. Meals made by my mother needed to be on time and on the table. We were at the whim of his moods, his inability to give any of us space, and the fact that the apartment was so small that we were all on top of each other all the time. The run-down place backed onto the lake, which was the only blessing.

Meghan and I spent a lot of time in the shoddy old playground to the side of the building, swinging away for hours to avoid spending the dead hours after school in the apartment before dinner, and when Toly left for his night shift. Did I mention if we did come home right after school we absolutely couldn't make any noise because he worked nights as a security guard for the huge grocery distribution center on the Queensway? Toly wasn't bad or mean, but he was old school, and we were miserable. My mom put constant pressure on us to just get along with him for her sake until Meghan screamed, "Why? I'm the kid. You get along with him." And stomped out of the house.

My mother's relationship with Toly lasted for about six months. It unraveled as quickly as she stitched it together. She had gotten the job as a receptionist-slash-secretary-slash-personal assistant at Carl's accounting firm, a small family-owned business he had inherited from his father. Toly tailed off into my stepfather. We moved right from his apartment to Carl's family home.

I met Carl twice before we all moved in together that August. Once at an awkward family-welcome office party and the second time at a terrifically awkward dinner when my mother explained he was her long-lost life partner, and we'd be moving in a week. She had laughed a lot during that dinner. Meghan and I had given each other knowing looks. It was the uncomfortable, forced laugh that we knew meant she needed us to help her make sure this worked out. It wasn't like we had any other choice. We'd have to trust her.

Our father was so far out of the frame he couldn't even define the picture. At that time, I wasn't even sure where he was—in England somewhere, maybe. We weren't the type to run away from home. We weren't abused or even mistreated. Our mother was flighty. She'd describe herself as ever searching, and depending on my mood, I could be more or less critical of her self-description. But she loved us, and everything she did in her life was to try to make our lives better. She had made mistakes, but each time she tried again, getting her own heart crushed from another poor, hasty decision, but she did it for us. For the idea of family, which meant more to her than anything.

A year later, my mother and Carl were married. All of her tossing us from place to place as she changed jobs and updated boyfriends had stopped the moment she and Carl said I do at City Hall. Up until then, my mother had kept us on the straight and narrow with little money but a lot of ingenuity. Still, we were lost in the sea of her emotions, in her clinging to the idea that once we made a complete family with a male member at its head, everything would be better. I know now that wasn't necessary. Our unit had been complete with the three of us, but my mother had never thought so. She had felt inadequate and ashamed that her marriage hadn't worked out, and she had played hard at happy families until she couldn't anymore. Then Carl became the anchor for her boat, and once she found him—as messy as it was in the beginning—she never stepped into open water again.

The end of August that year fooled everyone in the city into thinking fall might start on time. Instead, early September was stifling, and the morning Meghan and I started at our new school, the day started off murky and humid. There was only one way to conquer a new school: face it head on and with attitude. We wore matching black twenty-four-hole Doc Martens tightly knotted up to our midcalves. Our backpacks were riddled with band buttons, and my sister had just shaved half of the hair on her head. Besides our boots, we were dressed in our black tights and kilts from the Catholic school—it was our first-day uniform. We were a team, Meghan and I—we were so close in age that it was easy to be friends, but always being a year apart in school meant we didn't have to fight over boys or other ridiculous things. And we'd cycled through so many schools until we moved to Etobicoke to live with Carl that it was just easier to be the two of us. Meghan met Jason the first week there, and they became inseparable. We became a threesome. And it worked; it always worked. Sure, my sister drove me crazy and I'm sure I made her batty, but there was always an us against the world mentality. And I felt selfish for a moment thinking that her baby was going to change all that, but it would. It was another signal that we weren't all carrying on like we had for years.

* * *

My BlackBerry blinked. Meghan. *I can hear you spiraling over there in preppy land. What's up? I haven't had the baby yet. I can still be relied upon for advice.*

I wrote back: *The same old arguments. Rob gave me a ring. And I might have real feelings for Garrett. You are literally the only person I can admit that to.*

A RING? AND WORK BOYFRIEND DRAMA. I told u so.

Tell you tomorrow. SRSLY huge diamond tho.

ARE YOU GOING TO MARRY HIM?

Undecided. Talk tomorrow.

K, love you.

You too.

I deleted the message thread, turned my phone off, took a deep breath, splashed some warm water on my face, and went back to bed. The bed, expensive and luxuriant, was one of the most uncomfortable in which I'd ever slept.

Chapter 6

MY HEAD WAS pounding the next morning when I woke up—too much wine, too little sleep. Rob lay still, the bedclothes barely disturbed, as I kicked my feet out, trying not to bother him. The tip of my nose was freezing, and I shivered as I reached across to the bedside table for a tissue. The ring was still there.

I sat up to open the box and look more closely at it now that I was sober. It was platinum, with a pear-shaped diamond in the middle and three rows of smaller stones coming up to meet in the middle and encircle the main rock. If you were *that* kind of girl—no, if you were any kind of *girl*—it would take your breath away.

As I slipped it on my finger, it felt heavy and uncomfortable. Every part of me wanted to be with Rob. But no part of me wanted this ring. I was still seething that he'd put me in the position of choosing between him and exactly what he knew I didn't want. The logic of his argument settled in my mind—maybe it would be nice to be what connected our families. Maybe it would be hilarious to see what Camille would do when faced with Annie.

At Queen's, school had been important to me. I had loved every minute of the learning part of university. The social bits? Well, I wasn't as good at those. Knowing whose father did what or what kind of family business was funding cab rides and train tickets home versus taking the bus (city or Greyhound) was never something I paid attention to. I had found Rob without knowing where he came from or what his father did, and I was completely naïve. Foolishly, I had thought that if you were a nice person, if you were open, honest, and kind, you could get along with anyone. Rob's mother had proven to be the exception to this rule. And just like I was in first year all over again, here I was surrounded by people who had a common language, whether it was about their social graces or their prep school, and my choice was to either give in completely or to lose the one person who had loved me unconditionally for the last eight years. Where was the choice in that?

Asleep, Rob looked young and peaceful, and the desperate tenderness I felt for him threatened to overtake my senses. Would it be all that wrong to get married? People grew up and out of their hard-won opinions all the time. Was I just afraid of the commitment? Surely, if I did say yes, Rob could prevent Camille from bullying us into having an elaborate ceremony and expensive celebration. Maybe if I could do it my own way, quick and dirty, on a beach somewhere with just us, my family, and his family, that would be tolerable. There was nothing I liked more than a vacation. The South of France? Getting married in a vintage Chanel suit carrying another vintage, Louis, on my arm sounded perfect. It also sounded unreal, impractical, and unmanageable. The fact remained that I didn't want to be married. It had nothing to do with a wedding. I didn't want the band of gold and all it represented weighing down my finger.

I slipped farther under the covers and curled up tight into Rob, hoping he didn't wake up, feeling secure with the weight of his body next to mine. Our relationship worked because our falling (and staying) asleep together worked. I slept better beside him than I ever had growing up and with a bed to myself. Even with his legs sprawled all over my side of the bed, I could drop off the minute I laid my head on the pillow, as long as he was there. Rob felt comfortable in his skin, comfortable in his life, in the love he felt for me. And I did my best to hold tight to him however and whenever I could, no matter how restless my legs were. Sleep came at last, thankfully.

When we woke up about an hour later, Rob squeezed me tight. "Merry Christmas. Man, I hope my mother has cinnamon buns."

"Doesn't she always?" I yawned. The late night, the wine, the weight of it all had caught up with me. I was up but didn't want to get out of bed or engage in any form of active communication. "If your house wasn't so huge, I bet you could smell them."

"Our house isn't that big."

"Yes, it is."

"Do you want your present now?"

I sat up quickly and shouted, "You didn't! We said no presents this year! We're saving for our trip to Germany this summer—you promised!"

"It's not a big deal, I promise." Rob got up and pulled his duffel bag off the chair beside the bed. He handed me a small, square package, neatly wrapped. I had nothing for him. Not even a card. I had taken our no-presents rule seriously. We were planning an amazing trip for the summer. I was saving my measly two weeks' vacation and we were going to the Alps. I'd always wanted to go, and Rob's parents had so many frequent flyer points that they'd offered to cover as much of the airfare as we could claim with the program.

"Trust me," he said, "it's second hand, and I bought it before we decided about Germany, so you can't be mad."

It was too large to be another sparkly surprise, which calmed me down. Carefully pulling at the edges of the paper revealed an old box. It took me a minute to figure out what it was. The pictures on the front were of a happy-looking family, like the kind you'd see in an old '60s-era school primer with boys in red sweaters and short pants and mothers dressed like June Cleaver. I opened the box to find an old handheld 16-mm camera. It was a complete vintage kit with undeveloped film and everything.

"Where did you find this?" I ran my hands along the smooth casing. The camera looked brand new, and it was surprisingly light in my hands.

"Last summer, at one of those strange garage sales out by my parents' cottage. You remember, the September long weekend that you had to work? I spent the afternoon rambling around the back roads. It's boring as hell up there with them, without you." Rob laughed to himself. "They're drunk by two and fighting over Yahtzee, or who last washed out the dog's bowl, or anything else they can think of." He yawned. "Anyway, I thought it might be fun for you to shoot stuff around the city."

"Look at you, using the lingo. 'Shoot stuff around the city.'" I laughed. "Thank you. I feel terrible that I have nothing for you. Nothing."

"I don't need anything. I never do. Plus, you know I'm stoked about our trip. I'm planning to use some of our savings to buy *totally rad* skis that will cost me an arm and a leg to fly home." He stretched, revealing the tender part of his stomach that I adored. "Oh, your hands are cold," he said, shivering.

"It's not my fault. Your parents' house is bloody freezing. It's too big for the heat to circulate."

Rob pulled the duvet tight around us as we lay back down, the camera and its box stowed on the night table beside the bed. His hands felt familiar, their touch comfortable, and we fell into our pattern, not careful or cautious, but easygoing and relaxed—exactly what you would expect after years of having sex together. Did I long for something more passionate? I didn't know—I was still so attracted to him, the way he managed to make me feel attractive, sexy even, despite the extra cushion around my middle and my often unshaved legs. None of it mattered. He told me he loved me all the time, and I knew he even found my toes sexy, even if my pedicure was three weeks past its expiry date.

There was a slow, easy spirit to the sex we had—it was that kind of a morning. Neither of us had to be at work, and it was Christmas. The guest bedroom was far away from Rob's parents' room, so there was no fear they'd overhear us. But as comfortable, as nice as it was—Rob on top, me holding him tight, both of us relaxed—I couldn't quite settle.

"Did you finish?" Rob asked quietly, collapsed on top of me.

"No," I said. "But that's okay. I'm a bit out of it. I'm going to pee."

When I came back into the room from the en suite, I was wearing one of the luxurious white robes his mother always kept in the closet. "I'm going to grab a shower. I don't want to smell like sex at the breakfast table. It might negate the delicious scent of the cinnamon buns."

"You'll take forever. Let me go before you. I'll be two minutes in the shower and then I'm downstairs and out of your way."

He leaped out of bed and muscled his way past me into the bathroom. I went in behind him and sat on the toilet. The two of us chitchatted through the hiss and steam, and two minutes later he was out of the tub (Rob was nothing if not true to his word) and getting dressed. "I'll see you downstairs. Don't take too long or my mother will come up to get you. And please wear the ring. For me. It doesn't have to mean anything. Okay?"

The shower was hot and had amazing water pressure. I stood there for a while in that exquisite enamel bathtub, leaning against the wall and letting the heat relax me, feeling guilty for wasting so much energy. I could only procrastinate for so long, only stretch out this bit of time to myself before the hectic nature of the holiday descended. I didn't want to go downstairs. I didn't want to be a part of Rob's family's happy rituals. The longer I stayed with Rob, though, the more his family would become my family. I'd have to live with the formality of Camille for the rest of my life. Not to mention the fact that if I hadn't won her over by now, there was little chance I ever would. All these years in and I still had a feeling she thought I was just Rob's passing fancy. A penultimate stop before he arrived at his Grand Central Station in the map of marriage.

Up until the last couple of years or so, I'd managed to skillfully avoid integrating my life with Rob's in any formal manner. I hadn't come to his parents' for Christmas but kicked around my mother's house instead, always inviting him to join us. Boxing Day I'd stay by myself in our condo and spend a rare quiet day watching the movies I wanted to watch, eating junk food, and ordering salty Chinese takeout from the grungy restaurant down the street. That time was good for me. I'd make notes about movies I'd like to make one day and wake up early to spend some holiday money in Yorkville before Rob got home.

Then he'd arrive at the door, his arms laden with presents from his family to me, and spend an hour making me feel guilty for not coming with him. "My mother would love to have you!" was what he said every year. Eventually there came a point when it was impossible for me to seek refuge at my mother's. About four years ago, we were at my mom's house for her quasi-annual New Year's Day brunch. We ate waffles, eggs, bacon, and any still-edible leftovers; it was an excuse for my mother to gather everyone together. Rob always came, and that year he and my mother ended up talking about my feelings about Christmas.

"Oh, it's not the holiday for Kelly, ever since she figured out there was no Santa Claus. Meghan still believed up to that point. My eldest must have been six, maybe seven. We were at some out of the way mall in Barrie. God, it was so grungy. And there was a Santa Claus there. The girls had had their Santa pictures done two weeks before at a photo studio in Sears—a much classier setup. Anyway, the two Santas looked nothing alike. Ever focused on continuity, my Kelly said to him, 'You're not Santa.'

"He tried to backtrack and make up some story about how he was sitting in for Santa, because, you know, the real Santa was so busy. But she was having none of it." By this point my mother was already laughing. "She stood up in front of the entire line of people, screaming kids and terrified babies, and told them all to go home because it was a hoax and *none of it was real.*

"After that there were no more photo ops, and every time December rolled around Kelly would huff and puff through the month talking about the hoax that was Santa and wouldn't it be better if we gave up the ghost about it all and got down to the turkey?

"It's no wonder Kelly avoids your house, Rob. I bet your mother goes full out and you and Stephen still believe in Santa, waking up on the twenty-fifth with full stockings, the whole gambit."

My mother told that story a lot, so I was surprised that Rob had never heard it.

After my father left, throughout the circus of my mother's love life, there were lean years, no-present years, and no-fairy tale years, and I believed that I was all the better for it. I had no expectations of a magical holiday season. I liked where my family was now. But Rob didn't understand that I wasn't a *holiday* person. There was no magical childhood behind the scenes to prop up the façade into adulthood. And I didn't want kids, so why did I need to even bother?

Over the years, the arguments about Christmas had all centered around how I didn't open myself up to the idea of even liking his family. How I'd convinced myself that they didn't like me and that was why it was uncomfortable. The worst thing he ever said to me was "You can't blame your father leaving your mother for your emotional shortcomings, Kelly. At some point you need to put it in the past and leave it there. I'm here. I'm the one who stuck around. I love you and you're being selfish."

He was convinced that I'd be swayed by the family setting and
how nice it was at Camille's, but really, he wanted me to be more
a part of his life. And so we integrated. And I had to give up my
Boxing Day, my big bag of chips, and my bargain shopping. After
that I went to see Rob's family for holidays. Easter dinner, birthday
dinners, Robbie Burns Day—you name it, they celebrated it, and
now I was always there to witness it. Maybe I had been selfish, only
thinking about how I felt about it all, and promised myself I'd keep
an open mind. I'd try.

And then Camille pulls something like this—the ring, the house,
the *expectations*.

Leaving the steamy bathroom, I checked my phone. There was
no message from Garrett. I didn't know what I was expecting. I had
been terrible to him the day before. Deep down, I needed to hear
what he thought about me now that I was engaged. In a cheap and
petty way, I wanted to keep on hurting his feelings like I had yesterday. I wanted him to know all about my happy life and my perfect
boyfriend and my amazing ring. The right course of action stretched
out in front of me like a yellow brick road: right guy, right ring, set
for life, happy families, house in the 'burbs. Why wasn't I gratefully
throwing my arms up in celebration?

Chapter 7

THE AMOUNT OF breakfast food laid out on Camille's dining-room table could have fed Rob and me for a week. There were three different kinds of eggs, pancakes, French toast, expensive pastries, Rob's beloved cinnamon buns, fruit salad, six different kinds of toast, trays of jams, jellies and spreads, and cereal in case we didn't want something hot. It felt like coming downstairs to an elaborate hotel buffet.

"Come! Come!" Camille shouted. Impeccably dressed already, she refused to even entertain the idea of opening presents until everyone had a full stomach and something warm to drink. As predicted, there were mimosas: a giant crystal jug full of freshly squeezed orange juice and actual champagne. I took the chair closest to it. The conversation was happy and polite, and Camille kept things that way. If my underwhelming response to Rob's proposal had caught her off guard, she was too polite to say anything. She was determined to have a good holiday, and nothing would stand in the way of that.

I downed three glasses of champagne and OJ in quick succession, pushed the eggs around on my plate, and waited for that warm, half-drunk feeling to take over. Talk about babies permeated most of the conversation. Camille was asking Audrey if she was having morning sickness, which started the two of them off on a pregnancy conversation that I prayed they'd exclude me from.

"Kelly," Camille said, "you'll have to help me plan the baby shower. You have such a gift for parties."

"My sister's having a baby too. Maybe we can do a two for one." Their expressions were horrified. "I'm joking. Yes, I'd be happy to help with the party planning."

"Meghan's pregnant?"

Rob looked heartbroken. Damn my mouth.

"She told me yesterday," I explained. The champagne had been stronger than expected. "She wanted to tell you herself, today. I can't believe I ruined her surprise."

Liar. My whole body shrank.

He recovered quickly. "I'll act like I don't know. I promise."

We didn't keep things from each other. And we certainly didn't lie to each other to cover up a mistake. The destructive part of myself was rearing its ugly head.

Camille asked, "What time are you expected at your mother's house?"

"As long as we get there before the turkey's done and not after it gets cold, my mother's happy," I replied.

"There's time, then, for presents before the two of you jet off to your next engagement?"

"Rob wouldn't let us leave before he has a chance to open his presents," I said, keeping my tone purposefully light. "Dinner won't start until at least three."

"Wonderful," Camille said. "To the living room, then! Bring your drinks with you but leave the plates. We'll tidy up later."

I was the last to leave the dining room. Rob didn't even glance in my direction as he got up. No one else would notice, but the cold shoulder had descended. And I wasn't sure if it would last all day or not.

No one could fault Camille for her attention to design. The décor of the living room was modern enough in its aesthetic, meaning that everything was a soft white with accents of blue, but it still managed to feel comfortable, even homey. The rug was silk and had an intricate pattern that wove blues and purples in and out of the main beige background. It looked expensive because it was expensive—imported from India, where old saris were reworked and then woven into the patterns. Camille and Audrey had spoken for a good hour about the rug at Easter last year, right after the decorator had finished the room. The tree was in an alcove, tucked into their giant front windows. It glittered with silver and gold accents, all the decorations matching in a way that made me think Camille had hired her decorator to come in and make the place festive. There were absolutely no personal touches to any of it. The room could have found its way onto the pages of any design magazine in Canada, it was that well put together. Even her presents were professionally wrapped with beautiful paper and massive bows. The few that Rob and I had contributed, hastily dressed by me and even more generic in thought, stood out like awkward second cousins at a family reunion.

"Rob," Camille said, laying her hand on his shoulder, "you do the honors. It's your year to be Santa. Oh, I almost forgot, the stockings. They were too heavy to hang from the fireplace proper. Let me get them, we'll start with those first."

Rob left with his mother to help her carry the stockings, and his dad was busy with the fireplace. The room descended into that uncomfortable silence that defined these family occasions. Stephen and Audrey were speaking in hushed, happy tones to one another, and I sat watching my foot bounce up and down, trying to figure out how to tell my sister that she had to make a big deal of her pregnancy announcement to make up for me treating Rob so poorly. When I looked up, Arthur was standing beside the long couch, looking at the fire, which was perfect. He had such a kind smile, and he looked so content. Perhaps I was too hard on all of them. I set the champagne flute down on a coaster, half finished.

"There's the perfect amount of snow this year," he said. "Good for skiing but not so much it halts the entire city."

"Have you been out to Collingwood much? I'm sorry, I have no idea if ski season has started."

"Technically it started at the beginning of December. But we're not much of a ski family until the real cold sets in after the holidays. Camille and I are going to spend three weeks at the condo in January. I've taken something commonly known as a *holiday*."

"To be honest," he continued, his eyes sparkling a little, "I've been contemplating retiring. I want to travel less for work and more for pleasure. I've only got so many more years to live."

"Dad," Stephen interjected, "you'd be bored in an instant if you retired now. I mean, the Halsberg case alone."

"Halsberg is something for us to sink our teeth into. I wish we could be more forthcoming about the details, but still, I'm ready."

I wondered if I could spend my entire adult life being this polite. Why couldn't Arthur spill the juicy details about the Halsberg case? It had been all over the news—a high profile stockbroker-turned-CEO had been taken down for insider trading and inappropriate corporate behavior, and every time we turned the television to the local news, Arthur was on the screen.

Quiet descended upon the room again. Where were these stockings? In the deepest, darkest, most remote part of the house? How heavy could they possibly be?

"When I was growing up in New Brunswick," Arthur said, "there was this storm on Christmas Eve. My father worked as a logger, and we were afraid the weather would trap him at camp. My mother, she was a worrier, paced up and down for days, bouncing my youngest brother—I was one of nine, did you know that?" He looked at me and I shook my head. "My father got home just as the weather turned for the worst. Two days later, after we'd had dinner, after we had settled down from the excitement of the holiday, my grandfather opened the door to try to dig us out and the snow stood well over his head. That was one of the happiest Christmases of my life. We were inside, all of us together. My grandmother was still alive—she only made it to the next February. And we had precious little, nothing like what Camille organized for my two spoiled boys growing up."

"Hey!" Stephen protested. "We're grateful, not spoiled."

If we'd had to wait this long to open presents at my mother's house, there would have been a complete uproar. Presents were the first order of the day on Christmas morning. We had no civilized breakfast; there was coffee, tea, and the crush of everyone scrambling to be the first under the tree to get at their goods.

Arthur continued, "My mother, barely five feet tall, cooked a giant batch of pancakes smothered in apple butter. I had no idea that Christmases like the ones Camille puts together were even something that happened."

"Dad, what was your crazy uncle's name, you know, the one who snowshoed from one end of the town to the other during that storm to make sure the mail got delivered?" Stephen asked. "The one who eventually died in a snowbank, years later?"

"Richie."

"Right." Stephen laughed. "He was a batty old drunk. He'd show up to our Boxing Day lunch already plastered and Mom would pitch a fit."

Audrey giggled, a little tweet. She deferred completely to Stephen. Until recently, I had been disdainful of Audrey, of her completely backward approach to modern feminism—getting the man, keeping the man, the ring, the whole unbearably archaic aspect of her personality. These days it was plain to see that she was desperately in love and would have done anything to keep her relationship moving forward. As much as I would have liked to, I couldn't fault her for that. She had a will that I admired and respected, especially because

the idea of throwing yourself headlong into marriage and mother-
hood before thirty-five terrified me.

Audrey, however, seemed happy. No, she didn't *seem* happy, she
was happy, to her core, in that aching, finally belonging sense so many
girls my age demonstrated at their weddings or their baby showers.
There wasn't something wrong with them, but maybe there was
something wrong with me. Or maybe we were all simply different
and that was okay too. I made a promise to myself to be kinder to
both Stephen and Audrey, if only in my mind.

Like Beth with Raj, Audrey made a good partner for Stephen.
She was a Camille in training, open to the idea of giving up her
consulting job, raising her kids, perhaps starting a mat-leave business that would be all the rage, and never questioning her next
steps. All her steps had been taken. Maybe there would be a couple
more babies, maybe her business would fail, maybe Stephen would
have an affair—who could know what the future would hold? But
I was willing to bet that she would be the one standing at the finish
line.

Arthur had begun another story about his mother, about how
she had come over from England with his father to escape a life in
the Birmingham factories. "They wanted wide-open space. Never
understood why I left New Brunswick to come to school in Toronto.
They never liked the city."

The ring felt heavy on my finger, reminding me that what Rob
offered was a partnership, but the gnawing nature of its permanence
weighed upon me. I wanted to fit in. I wanted to feel like a part of
this, to become as natural in this environment as Audrey was. Still,
a nagging thought echoed in my mind: What on earth would I talk
to Rob about for the next forty years? We loved each other, there was
that, but we had precious little in common. He saw that as a positive, said it gave us each room to be ourselves without any pressure
to be the kind of couple that did everything together.

"I'd hate that," he'd said one afternoon when we were walking around downtown. We'd run into a co-worker of his who was married to an assistant in their department. They spent every lunch hour together, traveled to and from work together, and had never spent a night apart since they had first gotten together after a drunken mess of a cruise around Toronto Harbour that one of their biggest clients had paid for as a thank you for making him an obnoxious pile of money. "To be smothered by someone you see every day in every aspect of your life? I love that you're so different from me. We'll be able to complement each other our entire lives."

In my life, Garrett stuck out like an endangered species, the very last leatherback sea turtle. He was the person with whom I could talk naturally and intensely about the things that mattered to me: making films and documentaries, and how much I wanted to do that with the rest of my life. Garrett would often start sentences with, "When you're an award-winning filmmaker, Kelly," or "When you leave us all after selling your treatment to someone in Hollywood for millions . . ." And even though I knew he was bolstering my confidence, he knew what I wanted out of life: to become an outlet for people to tell their stories.

As much as Rob wanted to be there for me, and as much as I believed that he was, there was a giant, gaping hole in our relationship. Rob didn't read books or even really like movies beyond their ability to inform him about the markets or entertain him on a rainy afternoon. He never read in bed and skipped right past the arts section to move on to the *Financial Times*. I was constantly bringing home dubs of great documentaries and trying to get him to come with me to Hot Docs when I had tickets from work, but he always begged off. "You'll have more fun if you take Meghan or Beth. Or call Tanya, she'd love to go."

I didn't know if the pure act of being together could sustain us in a lifetime of being forever tied to one another by metal bands around our left-hand ring fingers.

Audrey rested her head on Stephen's shoulder and closed her eyes. Rob and Camille returned with their arms filled with expensive-looking stockings that were stuffed so full it was a wonder their contents didn't spill out onto the floor. We spent the next forty-five minutes cooing appropriately over one another's gifts. The opulence of the packages and what was inside them was not lost on me—big, luxurious packages expertly wrapped by the elves at Holt Renfrew, boxes that contained far too much tissue paper and were filled with exquisite objects made out of cashmere. When I said thank you, it was genuine. Camille's kindness and inclusion were not lost on me. I knew it was hard for her too.

As I sat quietly on the couch, the room started to spin ever so slightly. I tried not to glance at my watch or fiddle too much with the ring, and I avoided my BlackBerry entirely. The minutes stretched out around me, and I felt like I was stuck between stops on a crowded subway. *Deep breath*. I closed my eyes. *Deep breath*.

"We should probably think about going," Rob said. "You've got to prepare for your next meal."

How Camille found magical elves to work for her during the holidays, and how we never saw a whisper of them dropping food off or setting it up, made me wonder how much money was involved. Her side of the family was expected this afternoon.

"I'm sorry we'll be missing everyone this time around," Rob continued.

Camille squeezed her son's face, and pulled him closer to her on the couch. "Not to worry. We'll relay your good news!"

Learning my lesson from earlier, I kept quiet. There was no need to correct Camille. Officially, I hadn't said *yes* yet. For a second, I thought about pulling the ring off and handing it back to her with a quick, "No thanks, not for me." But it was Christmas. These were people Rob loved. These were people who loved Rob.

Audrey stood up and stretched, her teeny baby bump only slightly noticeable. "I need a nap!" she exclaimed. "Let's go lie down for a bit, Stephen."

"You don't have to ask me twice," Stephen said. "Mom, thanks for everything. Maybe wake us up, if it's not too much of a hassle, a bit before dinner?"

"Of course, go lie down, you two. If you can't laze around on Christmas, when can you?" she replied.

I couldn't recall ever having seen Camille laze around, not even at the cottage on the Sunday afternoon of a long weekend. Even then, she would be buzzing about in her garden or making drinks or canoeing across the bay their cottage faced to pay a visit to one of the other mansions-slash-cottages in their vicinity.

After Audrey and Stephen had left, I said to Rob, "We'd better get moving."

I stood up, happy to be headed in some direction besides drunker and deeper in the plushy goodness of Camille's ridiculously expensive couch. "My mother will start calling soon. She'll have convinced herself that we've crashed the car or slipped into a ditch if we're too, too late."

"I'm sure she's not expecting *you* to be on time, Kelly." Camille laughed. "She must know you at least a little bit. I'm not sure you're ever on time."

"There's a first time for everything," I said. "Maybe it'll be a New Year's resolution come early: Kelly Haggerty will be absolutely, to the second, on time."

"I have exactly the thing to help with that," Camille said. "I was going to save it for your engagement party, but knowing you, there won't be an engagement party, so I hope you like it."

Camille opened one of the baroque-style side tables in the living room, retrieved another small box, and handed it to me. At this point, I was dreading the moment—small boxes seemed to contain terrifying pieces of jewelry. But there was no need for me to be afraid: inside was an exquisite vintage Cartier watch.

"This was the first piece that I bought with my own money," she said. "It's not my style any longer, but I thought you'd like it. It will match your ring perfectly. They're both from the same period, early 1910s art deco."

"Camille," I said, honestly breathless, "it's beautiful. I love it."

"Good," she said. "It keeps very good time. No excuse now for you to be late."

"New Year's resolution, here I come," I said, securing the watch around my wrist.

It was delicate with a simple black onyx face, and it was gorgeous.

"I'll get the haul down here into the car if you can get us sorted upstairs," Rob said. "Don't forget my toothbrush."

"I won't forget your toothbrush, I promise." Turning to Arthur, I said, "Thank you both for a lovely Christmas. Dinner and breakfast were delicious, and you are so generous, I almost don't know what to say."

"Thank you works," Arthur said as he wrapped his arms around me in an embrace that was stronger than I had expected. "Lovely to have you as always, my dear."

My eyes welled a little as I retreated upstairs. Teamwork and trust. That was what Rob believed we had together. He thought of us as equal partners working together to build something. And a life with Rob would be a good one, better than I deserved.

I had betrayed him and everything he thought we were with the growing pit in my stomach. There is a moment when you are traveling, in the instant before you realize you are hopelessly and truly lost, when you lose all sense of the right direction. That feeling was pervading my relationship and my life these days. I couldn't seem to escape feeling like I'd taken two wrong turns, and there was no hope of finding my way back. But the question was, back to what?

Back to living by myself in some shitty basement apartment? That seemed awful, lonely. Forward to Garrett? That was a fantasy, and it should stay that way. But today made it very apparent that I wasn't just betraying myself, but Rob too—I was the square peg in the round hole, not him. Not his family. Me. And it wasn't fair to either of us. I was finally admitting it: we didn't want the same things. Love conquers all, that's what women are always told. But does it? Can it?

After packing our bags, I tidied the guest room as best I could. There was no way I could make the bed as neatly as it had been when we arrived. Concentrating on pulling the corners tight, I didn't hear Camille come into the room. When I looked up, she was there in the doorway, watching me blow my bangs out of my face, huffing as I plumped the last pillow.

"There's no need, Kelly," she said. "The maid will strip the bed next week. You could have just left it."

"Camille, I didn't hear you come in."

"My father didn't approve of Arthur when I first introduced them. At the time, he had no idea of how successful my husband would become. His reaction, based on his wanting the best for me, made me feel ashamed to love Arthur. I was ashamed of how much I wanted to build a life for him, make a family with him. Almost from the moment I met my husband, I knew my life would not be complete without him. He's worked hard professionally to give me the kind of life my father expected. I respect him for that, but I've always regretted the fact that us choosing each other forced him into that position. I have never in my life wanted to diminish my husband. I always knew that wherever he led us, we would make it work. Money or no money.

"If Robert isn't what you want—if this family isn't something you can wholly become a part of—please, love him enough to make that decision now and not later, when it will hurt forever. You're both young enough to let each other go without permanent damage."

Too stunned to move or even to respond properly, I felt scolded. But *seen*. "I love Rob," I said.

Camille came fully into the room to stand in front of me and put both of her hands on my arms. "It's not a question of loving him. It's a question of knowing what you want from love. And I don't think you know the answer to that. I do like you, Kelly, I always have. I only wish you knew yourself as well as you pretend to think you do."

She squeezed my arms, held me tight for a moment, and then turned to leave the room. I sank down on the bed, our overnight bags piled around my ankles, and burst into tears.

Chapter 8

THE COLD WAS a blessing. The December air masked the mess I'd made of my face. My cheeks felt blotchy, my eyes were puffy, and I hoped that Rob wouldn't notice. Camille insisted on saying her good-byes outside, and then she waited until the last possible moment to step back into the house. Despite everything she had said, despite the beautiful gifts and the kind advice, I found her last "Merry Christmas" bittersweet. I fought hard to control my emotions, to stay in the present, to hug her tightly, and to make sure I never betrayed what had happened between us upstairs in the guest bedroom.

"That was nice," Rob said quietly. "I can't believe your sister's going to have a baby. And I promise, I'll be surprised when she tells me. I know it's hard for you to keep a secret that huge."

"Meghan herself said that Mom told her not to tell anyone. Something about it being too early."

"I get it," he said. "It's zipped away, and I've already forgotten that I know. Still, exciting. We'll be that childless aunt and uncle who spoil the kids, get them all hopped up on candy, and then send them home. I can't wait."

Rob started the car and backed out of the driveway. We drove through his neighborhood, where he had grown up, gone to private school, and stayed during summer breaks from university. Rob fit in here, with these houses with all the space around them. I could see him and his friends driving their parents' expensive cars. Dating girls from the adjoining private school and smoking a bit too much weed in their basements. Never spending a summer in the city, but barefoot at cottages or sailing camps, returning in September to start the whole cycle again.

"My mother is happy," he said. "Thanks for that."

"It was lovely," I said. "The watch—I was stunned."

The guilt. The regret.

"It's not that hard to let them in, Kelly." Rob put his hand on my knee and squeezed. I grabbed his fingers and held tight.

"How did your parents meet?" I asked. "Your dad was telling stories about the East Coast, and I gathered that was well before he was married."

"They met at law school. My mother went for a semester before she met my father. My grandfather was a judge, and he had only girls. She wanted to please him by at least trying it. She hated school, hated all of it. All she ever wanted was to be a mom."

"They seem happy."

Rob laughed. "They're drinking too much, rambling around that huge house by themselves. But, overall, yeah. It wasn't a bad place to grow up. I'm very lucky. The couples in about half of the houses on this block have split up, and those divorces were *acrimonious*. Too much money floating around turning everyone into a devil looking for a new dress."

"You can't *only* blame the wives."

"I'm kidding," he said. "That sounded terrible, didn't it?"

"It sounded sexist."

"Hey!" He protested. "I'm a feminist."

There was next to no traffic in the city, which was unheard of as Rob headed west. "You would have liked my dad's parents," he said. "You think my mother doesn't like you? You should have seen what it was like for her. When they went back east my dad would become a different person, pick up a strange accent, speak French, and disappear for hours with his brothers, tying one on. He was the only one who left home. Whenever he went back, every minute he was there was some sort of a reunion tour."

We eased onto the highway finally, and Rob continued. "My mother hated it out there. She tried too hard, dressed too well, and you know how she can be. She's incapable of adjusting unless it's under her terms."

"Why did your father leave, if he was so happy in New Brunswick?"

"If I had to guess, probably because his brother died—his name was Stephen. My brother's named after him. My uncle Stephen left home at thirteen to go work in the logging camps too. There was an accident. That's all I know. My dad never talks about it."

We never talked about Rob's extended family. And then it hit me all over again, marriage was me becoming a permanent part of the clan. Or, like my sister, starting a new unit—just the three of them. I didn't know how to feel about all of it, any of it.

Snow was falling on the gray city. Toronto was a ghost town during the holidays. It always amazed me how easy it was to drive from one end of the city to the other at any time other than rush hour—how quickly you could go from one side to the other when there was no traffic. I loved those times where the city felt emptied out, even lonely, as we bumped along the Gardiner. Toronto was beautiful even when it was murky and sloppy like it was today. The endless construction, all the towers going up everywhere, and this drive, from Rob's neighborhood out to my parents' was one of my favorites. Down Avenue Road all the way, across Bloor, south on Lansdowne to Queen, then through Parkdale to the highway. Each neighborhood was so different, and I loved to look at them all, imagine the stories the people who lived in them would tell, from the man asking for change at the on ramp to the elderly man with a shovel two doors down from Rob's house who shoveled for everyone. I wanted all their stories; that's what I wanted in my stocking—their lives.

"I never see them," Rob continued. "Now that we're not little anymore, we never go out there. My grandparents died when I was small, and my aunts and uncles have all married and divorced and married and divorced. I have, like, dozens of cousins."

"You have dozens of cousins? How come I've only ever met Tanya?"

"She's my mom's niece. She's my only cousin from that side. You know, if we got married, it could be a kind of family event. We could fill an entire hall full of New Brunswickers—all rowdy and rambunctious. Now that would make my mother lose it. She's likely already planned a good portion of our wedding in her mind, whatever it might become—if and when you say yes, that is." Rob glanced over at me, recognizing the expression on my face. "I'm sorry. I'll stop talking about it, give you some space. You look overwhelmed."

"Honestly, I'm fine. Starting to get a little hungover from the champagne and OJ and too little food, but that'll be fixed with rum and eggnog at my mother's."

One end of the city gradually became the other. We exited the highway and drove along the Lake Shore, passing run-down corner shops, the neat-looking corners of a college, and retrofit storefronts slowly transforming from questionable to cool as the neighborhood remade itself yet again.

The whole trip from Rob's parents to my stepfather's house took about forty minutes. The area was full of bungalows with large lots that were disappearing as property developers bought them up and replaced them with giant suburban houses. They had always looked out of place to me, sweeping staircases and giant pillars next to one-story houses built just after the war. Because it was still affordable, the area was becoming popular for a lot of young couples looking to own a house but still be able to get downtown via the streetcar line.

Even though Meghan and I had spent the last couple of years of high school here, it had never felt like *our* home. Despite all the order that Camille insisted upon, Rob didn't think twice about walking into his mother's house, dumping his bag at the door, crashing onto the nearest couch, and promptly turning on the television as if he was fourteen and just home from school. He never rang the doorbell. I always did.

My mother answered the door wearing a gigantic sweater over knitted leggings and holding a giant cup of eggnog.

"Kelly-kins! My darling girl, I was about to send out a rescue party." Her hair was gray-platinum and her lipstick bright red. "Come in, come in! We've been waiting to open presents. Rob, you handsome devil, get that butt in here so I can squish it!"

My mother pulled us into the hallway to help us with our coats. "Kelly, Annie's here. Her flight got delayed, so she's joining us after all. Rip-roaring as ever."

The tone of my mother's voice was all caps and exclamation points. Rob found it hilarious that she was so quirky. She embraced him fully once we were out of our coats, spilling half of her drink in the process.

"Merry Christmas, Mom," I said. Her perfume enveloped me as we hugged, bergamot and rose, delicate and dainty, the exact opposite of my mother. "The house smells incredible. Please tell me you made creamed corn this year."

"All your favorite foods. All Meghan's favorites. All Carl's. We'll be eating for weeks, but it's worth it. I've got mussels on the go now for an appy. I'm just hoping they won't poison everyone, and we'll be all shits and giggles before the main course is on the table."

My mother found everything funny. It was a charming attribute. Conversation was never dull. Her laugh could fill a whole room and then some, it was so plentiful. Humor was how she had survived my father, Toly, and all her other failed relationships. I'm sure it was the only thing that had gotten her through parenting us as teenagers too. And Carl always laughed along with her—they were jolly together.

"Your stepfather's parked in front of the television. He and Annie and the boys are watching *A Christmas Carol*, the deliciously old one. I've made popcorn. Go snuggle."

And just as I was about to pull away, my mother had grabbed *that* hand. "What on *earth*!" she shrieked. "Carl, Carl, *Carl*! Annie! Carl and Annie, *get over here*! Meghan, you'd better come running!"

My mother pulled me toward the family room off the kitchen where everyone was folded into the various bits of haphazard furniture. Pullout couches and giant cushions all faced a truly massive television that Carl had bought with his bonus two years ago. Annie and Meghan stood up to see what the commotion was all about, and Carl paused the movie.

"Kelly is *engaged*. Look at this ring! Kelly is engaged! Rob, oh, congratulations to you both! How wonderful, a wedding, a big, juicy wedding is coming my way and I cannot wait. Oh, you could have a holiday wedding, we could have holly and wreaths on all the tables, serve turkey for dinner . . ."

I looked at Rob and half smiled. I had already ruined Camille's Christmas. I couldn't ruin my mother's too. "Mom, you're getting ahead of yourself. Really. Rob just asked me yesterday. I haven't even had time to process what it all means."

Annie whooped. Meghan screamed, "Finally, let me see this ring!" and in a matter of seconds, Rob and I were swept up in the massive embraces of my family members. Even my teenaged stepbrothers stood up and gave us both a hug. Everyone was so happy, and when Carl shook Rob's hand, he said, "You're in for it now, my boy. I've been married to a Haggerty woman for well over a decade now, and I still haven't fully recovered. Champagne, woman, we need champagne!"

"I'll get the glasses, Linda, if you get the bubbly," Annie said.

"Carl," my mother shouted from the kitchen, "it's a good thing you bought a good bottle for New Year's. We'll need to replenish before the countdown. But you're right, we need a family toast!"

My sister held tight to my hand and whispered, "After dinner I want the whole story."

"Yes. Also, you have to make a big deal about telling Rob that you're pregnant." She looked at me funny. "I didn't tell him yesterday for many reasons, which I'll tell you later, and when I said something today, I needed a cover story."

"Sneaky, sneaky."

"Come on." I laughed. "Help me out here."

"As if I wouldn't."

"Thank you."

"Oh please," she said. "I like being married."

"I know you do," I said. "You were born to be married to Jason. It works for you. I'm not sure if it'll work for me. How is baby?"

"It's the size of a pea, now. And doing a number on my whole being. I'll never forgive Jason for this."

"You never forgive him for anything," I said. Meghan glared a little until I hip checked her. "Joking."

My mother came back into the room carrying the champagne, followed by Annie holding a tray of flutes. Carl popped the cork, and they toasted our happiness. My mother grew teary. "A grandmother and a mother-in-law in the same year, how am I going to survive it?"

Annie said, "Good thing you're not the one giving birth *or* getting married."

"Mom!" Meghan said. "You were the one who told me not to tell anyone because I wasn't far enough along. By the way, I'm up the duff, in case you didn't get that from my mother's grandmother comment."

The whole family attacked the pair of us on the couch. My stepbrothers dove for us, followed by Carl and Annie—and Rob tumbled on top toward the end before I shouted, "Be careful, Meg's got a baby in there. Save the Twister for after dinner!"

There was more genuine laughter, and there was nothing to do now but settle back into the warmth of a solid champagne-centered glow. Watching Rob, and seeing how comfortable he was with my family, I could tell how fond he was of them. Of how laid back they were. The cacophony when we were all together, the different conversations mingling, everyone talking over each other and shouting to be heard. He appreciated how we bought joke presents alongside the ones that were more thoughtful. He entertained every single question Daniel had about the markets—my stepbrother had just returned home from his second semester at Western. Josh was at McMaster. They were both doing business degrees, their brains mimicking Carl's in every possible way.

"You didn't even bring me any sparkling water," Meghan complained. "Being pregnant sucks." When Jason went to grab a glass of champagne, she said, "Don't you dare. I'm dry. You're dry. You won't let me touch a drop so you're going to suffer alongside me for the remaining seven and a half months."

"Meghan," Jason said, "you're going to kill me. I don't think I'll make it. Who can stay sober for almost eight months when you're such a stress case?"

"Jason, better watch what you say—she's about to blow." I laughed. "I'd be the one to fetch that Perrier if I were you. And maybe, just maybe, my mother's got some gin in the freezer. Slip it into yours before you come back in!"

The room erupted in laughter. Meghan let go of my hand. "I'm coming with you. No gin. *No gin.*"

As she passed by, Jason slapped her on the butt. "Maybe just a touch of gin? When you've got your back turned? When you're not looking?"

"And these two are going to raise a child together?" Rob said. "I hope it's twins, Meggie, just so that they'll end up fighting more than you and Jay."

More laughter. I envied his ability to fit in anywhere with anyone, and for his easygoing nature. Rob's kind of confidence had been bred into him—the confidence of men who were born to wear a suit, who could hit a ball as easily as they wrote an essay or aced an exam. He wasn't concerned with being cool. No, that was the wrong way to put it. Rob had never gone through that awkward stage in high school. He played sports. He had the same group of friends he'd had since kindergarten. Books, movies, music, places, people—they didn't define Rob the same way they did someone like me, or Garrett.

Annie handed me a glass. "I hope you can drink this."

"Good grief," I said to her as she sat down on the couch beside me. "I'm not pregnant too. I'm no Meghan. And I have no plans to be—like, none. I haven't even really said yes yet, I've only accepted the ring and promised to think about it."

"I'm surprised, my girl, at that ring," Annie said. "I always thought we were two halves of an unmarriable whole. I didn't think the whole ring around the finger gambit was for you."

I made sure Rob was out of earshot and said, "Between you and me, I'm not—I'm not even sure I'll keep it. But it's Christmas, and I couldn't disappoint him. You should have seen his mother's face—she was so happy and excited. I didn't want to ruin it. I meant to take the damn thing off before we got into the house, slip it into my pocket."

"Don't drag this one out, Kelly, it's not going to end well."

We were interrupted by mother shouting, "*Presents!* We've got two hours before the turkey. Jason! Jason, get back in here! Hurry, hurry, you're handing everything out."

"It'll be fine, Annie," I said, laying my head on her shoulder. "Thank you for caring. But I love Rob. If not him, then who?"

Annie smoothed the hair on my head. I felt like I was an eight-year-old who had just had her feelings hurt by a bully on the playground. She said, "Maybe there doesn't need to be a who? Maybe there can just be a you."

Across the room, Carl smiled at me in his soft, generous way. He looked like he was about to say something, but then he changed his mind. And then, in an instant, we were buried in wrapping paper, ribbons, and bows. My mother set up her "appy" station on the giant coffee table—steaming hot mussels, expensive cheese, brittle, delicious crackers, and a whole fruit tray. It was a meal before a meal.

My mother was truly in her element. The rest of us sat back and let it happen. Of course, Annie helped, and so did Carl, and we all offered to do more, but my mother mostly refused. There was no stopping her as she flitted from task to task. After the last of the presents were opened, she disappeared back into the kitchen to start on the vegetables.

I didn't begrudge my mother's happiness. When she had decided on Carl, he never stood a chance. In a sense, he had been passed by one powerful woman to the next, and he never wanted it any other way. My mother had never been alone. Her life was littered with dates and dances and summer romances in a way that mine never had been.

The summer she had met my father, she had returned from a year of teacher's college. She had barely gotten in after high school, and she was struggling to prove to my grandfather that she could do it. In a fit of rebellion she went off one night with a boy she met at a dance—my father—and went too far, too fast. Pregnant with me, she married him in a dingy church basement in Alliston, where she grew up. She jokingly called Meghan and me her Irish twins because we were barely thirteen months apart.

Maybe the pressure of having two kids under the age of three got to him. Maybe he realized he had made a massive mistake and didn't know how to fix it. Maybe he didn't have the language to express himself. He left. He didn't look back. Without paying what the court ordered, he left the country. Meghan and I got the odd postcard, but he always mixed up our birthdays. Couldn't keep us straight, who was older, who was younger, and kept sending us pictures of his new family. Telling us over and over again to come over so we could meet our new sisters.

Divorced, angry, and alone, my mother had skipped from relationship to relationship, always hoping one would stick. The paramedic from Bolton. The factory manager from Newmarket. Toly. One night she came home to his overheated, barely furnished two-bedroom apartment and declared, "I need an accountant. Someone with a quiet life who can balance out all my energy. There are nice men at the office where I'm working now."

"No!" Meghan shouted. "Don't get any ideas. I can't start another new school. Even though I fucking hate this one."

"Stop swearing."

"Stop it with the men!" my sister screamed.

And we'd never shouted so much at each other as we did that night. This, this blended family, this bonus happiness, it's really good.

"Kelly!" my mother called from the kitchen, "come and help me with the potatoes."

Annie yelled back, "We're all on the way. Come on, women, it's time gender divided this party."

My sister was wearing a years-old Humber College sweatshirt with fraying cuffs and massive jogging pants. "Are you going to change for dinner?" I asked. "I know you're up the duff but you could have at least put on a real pair of pants."

"Suck it," she said. "I'm bloated, angry, and hormonal. Pants are not an option. Plus, no one cares what I look like these days, so why should I?"

The three of us entered my mother's kitchen.

"Linda," Annie said, "what would you like us to do?"

"Meghan, make sure the dining room's all set up. Annie, can you stir the gravy while Kelly does the potatoes? I've got to get the Christmas crackers and the cookies from the basement. We're T-minus ten minutes to dinner."

Before opening the basement door, she added, "Girls, I'm going to say this a lot this year: it's milestones in the making. Marriage, your first baby—all calls for celebration. Good news all around. Good food, family—I've never been so bloody happy in my goddamn life."

When she came back upstairs, she peppered me with questions. What kind of a wedding did I want? Where did I think we would we have the reception? Honeymoon or house? How much would we get for the condo?

"Whoa," Annie said. She was stirring, fat, flour, water, fat, flour, water into the pot. "They're barely engaged, Linda. Kelly hasn't even had time to consider the fact that she's now a *fancy fiancé.*"

My head pounded. I didn't know whether I to scream at everyone or to start bawling.

"Let's focus on Meghan's news, please. Babies are way more exciting than rings." I continued, "Let me decide if I'm even going to keep the ring before we plan a giant wedding that I can't afford or move into a house that I don't want. But the minute I'm ready to talk details, I've got your number."

"Okay," my mom said. "I'll put a moratorium on marriage questions for the rest of Christmas. I'm going to say one more thing, and even Annie can't disagree with this: that rock is spectacular."

"Isn't it?" I waved my hand in the air. "I'm so fancy and fabulous now, you won't recognize me in a few months."

"Let's not get carried away," Meghan yelled from the dining room. "It's like the minute you buy an expensive purse you'll burst a pen in it or something and ruin it forever. Careful the ring doesn't slip off your finger and into the potatoes."

"Two minutes to dinner, you mongrels," my mother called to the others. "Get up off your lazy asses and get into your assigned seats. Please note that your names are on the pine cones. *No trading spots.* I have everything organized down to the last fork and I'll *know* if someone moves anything."

The kitchen smelled delicious, and the four of us worked together, all hustle and bustle, to get the food on the table. This meal meant the world to my mother. I wasn't about to spoil it by confessing my indiscretions—that I didn't want to marry Rob mainly because maybe I was falling in love with my unavailable work boyfriend, who actively admired other girls in front of me and had his own decades-long relationship. What a mess.

* * *

The room was warm, and dinner was delicious. My family. All talking over one another, mouths full, and prone to outbursts, more shouting than listening. Thankfully, there were no more questions or conversations about anything wedding or marriage related for the moment. Instead, Carl was teasing Daniel about finally flunking out of school and showing us all how it was done (Daniel was a straight-A student), my mother was asking Jay and Meghan if they were going to stay in their apartment once the baby arrived, and Rob was asking Annie about her upcoming trip. I sat there, quietly watching everyone, not feeling the need to join in, content to be on the fringe. And we ate, and ate, and ate. My mother pulled out a tray of Christmas cookies for dessert, and the entire evening slowed down. Rob sat at the other end of the table and for a moment I saw his father in him, their shared ability to make themselves at home with anyone, anywhere.

Once dinner was finished, my mother released us from our seating arrangement. I sat down beside Meghan and slipped into a comfortable sibling silence. She reached across and pulled my hand toward her belly. I didn't fight it. I had to get over feeling brutalized by what was good news.

"Feel how hard my stomach is—none of my pants fit," she said.

"You did eat a massive Christmas dinner."

"It's not that, it's like there's a shell around the baby, like I'm a turtle."

"Raphael or Donatello?"

"Oh, no, Michelangelo, for sure."

"If the baby comes out glowing green with mad ninja skills, we'll know why," I said. "But your stomach is freakishly hard."

"The wonders of birth."

Meghan tucked her head on my shoulder, like we used to do as kids. "It'll all be okay. You'll figure it out. You always do."

"Remember Tanta," I said. "Wasn't she awful?"

"The worst," Meghan replied. "I'm certainly not naming my firstborn after her or Toly."

* * *

We had been at Toly's mother's house, forced to call her Tanta, even though it felt completely awkward. We had eaten a meal of strange food—I could still remember the borscht, its deep, rich color and intense smell. Tanta had given both Meghan and me nesting dolls. They were beautiful and thoughtful, and she was kind, but it wasn't real. It felt pieced together, and we were sullen, horrible teenagers. I don't think we were rude, exactly, but we didn't make it easy. But if Tanta had been disappointed in Toly for his relationship with my mother and her girls, she had never let it show. He was furious, though, in the car ride home, spewing all over my mother about how horrible we were, how we needed more discipline.

And when we got home, though, that was the end for me. I picked the fight for all ages with my mother. We were barely in the door before I refused to take off my coat and boots. I shouted that I was going for a walk, and that I'd rather live on the streets than spend another night under the same roof with them. My mother told me to get inside. I refused. And then everything came out: The misery of being at yet another stranger's house. The frustration of having to be on my best behavior all the time lest another one of my mother's relationships fail because Meghan and I weren't putting in enough effort. That I was sure it was all her fault my real father had left and that Toly was here today and gone tomorrow, and on and on.

Meghan tried to calm me down, but I pushed her away, hard. Toly grabbed me then, held my arms so tight they were bruised for days, and said I was nothing but a useless, spoiled kid who didn't know how good I had it. The angrier I became, the quieter my mother grew. Meghan slumped down against the wall and cried—but Toly and I screamed and shouted at one another. I had all the fury of a teenage girl on my side, but he held up to my hurricane like no one before or since. My temper was cruel and exacting until he slapped me across the face for calling my mother a coward for latching onto a man who'd rather pick a fight with a girl than a woman.

We left the next morning and stayed for a week in a freezing hotel on the Lake Shore that had seen better days and was filled with Johns and Joes before my mother dragged us back to him for another miserable few months until Carl arrived. To this day, all parquet flooring reminds me of that apartment, its scuffed white walls with black rubber trim, its ancient windows so scratched that no amount of cleaning could spiff them up.

We tried to put the Toly Incident, as it came to be known, behind us, and we celebrated New Year's Eve a week late with a lasagna dinner when he was working—my mother made sure we wrote down our resolutions, and number one on her list was "Appreciate my kids."

Things weren't great after that, but they didn't get worse.

My mother interrupted my train of thought. "Who wants coffee? Or some tea?"

"I could murder a cup of tea," Annie said. Carl said he'd also love a cup of tea, if my mother could find the teapot.

"I know exactly where the teapot is, my darling husband. I do not have senior moments about the teapot. I always put it in the same place. *You*, my lovely man, always put the teapot back in the wrong place, which is why *you* can never find it."

Carl laughed. "Good thing I have you around to always find my teapot."

"Gagging over here, enough about your teapot," I said. "Coffee for me. Please."

"This late at night?"

"Yes, mother, this late at night," I replied. "But I'll settle for decaf if you're not willing to make me real coffee."

"Decaf for anyone else?"

Rob nodded, and Jason said that he'd have tea. With everyone's orders straight, my mother left the room. My stepbrothers took the opportunity to meander down to the basement where there was a second TV. Soon, the sounds of *The Godfather* echoed up the stairs.

Coffee carafe in one hand, teapot in the other, my mother returned. "Meghan, the mugs are on the kitchen table. Can you grab them? It's not good for you to sit for so long."

Meghan rolled her eyes, but stood up as asked. "I'll help," I offered, but my sister told me to sit back down.

"Rob," Carl asked, "are you in the office through the week, or have they shut down?"

"The markets never sleep, and neither do we," Rob joked. "I'm scheduled to be back in bright and early on the twenty-seventh to catch up to what's happened overseas during the time difference. Kelly's got the week off, though. We're having a grown-up dinner party with her work friends."

And Garrett will see the ring. And I will meet Garrett's girlfriend. And Rob will meet them both. And they'll both meet Rob.

Panic spread throughout my body, like I was drowning in discomfort. If I wore the ring, it would be real. It would be more than a quick text meant to hurt Garrett's feelings, meant to show him that Rob was my real life, and that Garrett was someone I hung out with to fill the time at work. But I didn't know how I felt. At all.

My mother's eyes grew wide, and she cocked her head to the side. She passed the teapot to my stepfather to pour tea for himself and Annie, then she poured coffee for us into mugs.

"Calm down, Mother," I said. "We're having people for dinner but I'm not cooking. I've ordered the food already. We're having Indian food from down the street."

"Spare ribs!" she shouted.

Laughter erupted. Annie giggled so hard she almost spilled her tea. My mother loved this story. I had been upset after having a particularly terrible fight with my boyfriend at the time. I'd stormed home, thrown down my backpack, and collapsed in front of the television. Then I remembered that my mother had left me explicit instructions to make the spareribs for dinner—boil them, cover them in some sauce she'd put in the fridge, then throw them in the oven.

I managed step one. Giant pot, lots of boiling water. Then I fell into the never-ending cushion of self-help television, my head spinning about something the boy had said to me, and forgot about the ribs. By the time I noticed, smoke was filling the first floor of the house. I had boiled all the water out of the pot and the bones were smoking the house out. When my mother opened the door, with Carl two steps behind her, she shook her head. It had taken days to get the smell of boiled down to nothing meat and bones out of the kitchen. My extreme inability in the kitchen was a family joke at every gathering.

"Actually, Linda, Kelly's come a long way in the kitchen," Rob said. "She actually makes her own cereal—opens up the box and pours the milk and everything."

"This is why I live in the big, bad city. So I don't have to cook. It's how I stay so svelte."

"You won't be young forever," my mother replied, as ever pointing out the obvious. "Some better habits might be a good idea."

"Merry Christmas!" I said, trying hard not to be snide. "Did I mention that I'm engaged? Let's change the subject. Right, pick on Meghan for a while."

"We're not done with you yet, Kelly-kins. You'll want to eat well before the wedding, drop those last five pounds that have been hanging around since university. I read about this great new diet. Instead of cutting down on foods, you cut out. It's called *cleansing*. I've gotten Carl started on it already. We went into Kensington Market and bought a whole kit! We're all set up for a few days after Christmas."

Carl touched my mother's elbow and leaned in to finish the story. "I'm going along for the ride. I'm not sure either your mother or I can do without our red wine at the end of the day, let alone exist on celery puree for forty-eight hours straight."

"I do not want to be around either of you if you're denied wine," Meghan said. "I'm afraid for my life."

More laughter. Then Annie regaled us with some of the crazy stuff she had cooked for Carl when they first got married.

"I was trying to impress him. I hauled out my mother's impossible *Joy of Cooking* and made this roast and that roast, rabbit stew—ugh, to think about it now, every meal was so heavy. I honestly thought the success of our marriage would be won or lost on whether I could flan."

"I don't think that's a verb."

"Oh, if you've ever tried to flan, you would say it's a verb."

The lightness and warmth in the room was comforting. It was so nice, that real family feeling. The idea that talking led to laughter, which led to more laughter—even when the stories were ones you'd heard a million times. We had all drifted back to the dining room table. The coffee was scalding hot, exactly the way I liked it, and the cookies were delicious. After my sister had her fourth helping, she took some teasing from her husband. "That baby must have one hell of a hollow leg. You're eating like Joey in that episode of *Friends*," Jason said. "You know, the one where he's wearing stretch pants."

My sister punched her husband hard in the thigh, and he mock fell off his chair. "The strength, the superhuman strength that fetus is giving her! We won't survive, it'll eat us both!"

"God, I hated being pregnant," Annie said. "Hated giving birth, it was awful."

Daniel grabbed another cookie before heading back downstairs. "Mom, happy to know how much it pained you to bring us into the world."

"I loved you both when you got here, and you know it." Annie sighed. "But pregnancy . . . I was so bloated with both boys, couldn't get comfortable, and I was so sleep deprived. I don't even remember Josh's conception because I was on a tired high from Danny. What a colicky kid. He'd refuse to settle unless he was on the boob or on my belly. Slept in bed with us until he was at least ten."

"I did not!" Daniel yelled from the stairway.

"Did too," Annie retorted.

"I could have been better then," Carl said.

My mother grabbed his forearm. "You were just fine," Annie said. "Everything has turned out as it should. And I'm sure that Meg will make sure she gets enough rest. Jason works nights sometimes—he'll be well used to the dark hours of the night that haunted me."

"Our problem was having our kids too close together, wasn't it, Annie?" my mother asked.

"Would not disagree with you there. It's all a blur."

"Meghan," my mother said, "wait until the first is out of diapers before you start on the second, please."

"As I have not even birthed the first, believe you me, the second is not even on the horizon."

"Stay away from her!" I said to Jason. "Hands to yourself until your kid is at least three."

"Three? She's pretty sexy," Jay said. "I'm not sure I'll be able to control myself for three years."

Rob joked. "I'll bet if you're in the delivery room during the birth, those images alone might do it."

"Enough," Meghan said. "I can't believe we're talking about my sex life, my birth plan, and my family planning at the Christmas dinner table. Subject change please."

A stillness descended, like how a snowfall quiets a forest. It was a deep, echoing quiet that signaled the end of the evening, except no one moved.

"Oh my god!" my mother suddenly shouted, making us all jump. "Kelly, you absolutely can't schedule your wedding anywhere near Meghan's due date. We can't have her about to pop or to be forced to wear a tent because formal maternity clothes are *hideous*." She counted on her fingers. "So, Meghan's due in July. No one in their right mind would have a wedding in the middle of the summer in Canada—too hot, too hot. Plus, Kelly needs at least a year to plan. That gives you a good six months to get the baby weight off, Meghan. If you're anything like me, it'll just fall off. You'll be run off your feet between feedings and keeping the house up—it's a marathon. My girls, my girls, what a Christmas." She squeezed Carl's hand. "Our family will look so different a year from now. Who knows, maybe by then Kelly and Rob will have similar news."

"*No. Babies,*" I said, pouring myself a fresh glass of wine. "And no wedding. If we get married, I'm going to convince Rob to elope."

"My mother would have a conniption," he said.

"My thoughts exactly." I smiled.

My stepbrothers had drifted back to the living room to play a video game. Electronic beeps and boops floated into the dining room, followed by heavy-duty machine gun noises and lots of shouting. Rob and Jason looked at one another, then at me and Meghan.

"Go, just go," I said to Rob.

"What she said," Meghan added.

"Boys," Carl said, "help yourself to the whiskey if you want. I think it's that point in the evening."

Rob moved to clear his dessert plate but my mother swatted him away. "Nope, not having it. Go enjoy yourself by shooting the enemy or ravaging a city, whatever nonsense those ruffians have started in the other room."

I stood up in Rob's place and started to clear the table. My legs were growing restless, and I wanted something to do to fill up the space in the room that would soon be dominated by more wedding talk, despite my pleas for my mother to cool it. Meghan looked so tired, with deep circles under her eyes, but deeper down, she looked more happy and more serene than I had ever seen her before. Still, she stood up to help me.

"I am still in shock about this whole baby thing. We don't have babies, Meg." I was piling plates into the dishwasher.

"No, Kelly," my sister said. "*You* don't have babies. I have always wanted to have a baby, and we're both really stoked. Don't make your story my story."

"You're right. I'm sorry." After filling the sink with water, I asked, "Lunch next week when I'm off? Maybe the day after my dinner thing."

"Absolutely. I'll ping you tomorrow when we're back home from Jason's folks' place. My mother-in-law is more excited about this kid than our mother. Mom has an online book club with Jason's mother, they're chatting all the bloody time. Mom keeps talking to me about Yahoo groups and the failings of the Bildungsroman. She says that stuff just to make me crazy."

I looked at my sister, face to face, and held her shoulders tightly. "You'll be a great mother."

"I know what not to do, right?" She laughed.

"I heard that!" my mother said. "I did well by you girls."

"Not saying you didn't, Mother," Meghan said. "I would never suggest that you were anything but who you were at any point in our entire lives. That's one thing we could always count on—you being one hundred percent you."

Thankfully, my mother didn't take offense to Meghan's teasing. She and Annie were talking about what it was like to raise to small children so close in age, and Carl was sitting back with a silly, contented grin on his face. Often, my mother's mood carried generosity and good spirits forward, but other times, if she disagreed with you, or worse, if you had refused her advice about something that she turned out to be right about, she'd shut down with an effective, emotionless cold front that refused to lift until you apologized within an inch of your life.

By the time Meghan and I joined everyone in the family room, my mother had forced the video games to be turned off and was asking if we wouldn't rather play a family board game instead. No one was up for it, so instead she agreed that we could turn the TV back on as long as it was a holiday movie. *Christmas Vacation* was playing on a loop on one of the American channels, and we all settled in to watch.

The entire room seemed washed in white—the furniture, the tree, and all the trimmings sparkled and shone with a strong sense that, as my mother felt, this year was special. Maybe she felt happy and settled with Carl in a way that neither Meghan nor I really understood. Maybe she felt like she'd made up for all the shitty holidays past. But as I sat there, holding Rob's one hand, his other arm casually draped around me, I could see the potential of a shared life.

That feeling that you get when you're in the airport limo driving back into the city and you see the skyline—the CN Tower, the condos that litter the Lake Shore, the familiar bumps of the Gardiner Expressway—and then, no matter how much fun you had while you were away combing through the bent and broken avenues of Havana, staring at the *Mona Lisa* amid a hundred camera-laden tourists, or bunking down in a crowded Irish pub after hours, that warmth spreads through you in the back of the car—that was what I imagined being married, living with someone for eternity, felt like.

But I had never felt that way, maybe because we had been shuttled around so much growing up or because home had been fraught with complexities ever since I was young. I didn't know how to settle down and enjoy the idea of having landed somewhere with someone. Rob had had that backbone his entire life, and knew what to expect. But I felt there was a difference between wanting what was expected and then doing what was expected. I felt too far in the latter category. The idea that maybe I was a little too much like Annie, that thought kept roiling around my after-dinner, relaxed mind. What Rob and I had was great for right now. And maybe that's all it was ever meant to be. How would I know? How could I know?

Annie rounded up the boys at around ten and took them home for the night. She said she needed them around her for one last sleep before her vacation. They grumbled but gathered up some overnight stuff and headed out. She whispered to me that I could come and see her any time I needed to talk about my future, and that I should give myself the proper time to consider Rob's proposal. "A night away would do you wonders," she suggested. "You could come home right now with me and the boys."

I shook my head. "It's fine. Plus, I love my bed. I hate spending even a night away from it."

"Remember, I've got that apartment in the basement. It's semi– brand new and still vacant."

"Thanks, Annie. I do adore you."

"You, my girl, are mine, and you'd better never forget it."

I squeezed her so hard that it hurt us both a little, and then they were gone.

* * *

It had been a long day—for everyone. There was little more to be done. Conversation stood still, and there was a holiday pause—that moment of not-quite boredom when all the necessary events had been accomplished, the meal eaten, the leftovers put away, the presents opened and gushed over, and everyone seemed to be sitting still, in a reverie of their own making. "Do you think we've stayed long enough?" Rob whispered.

I looked over at my mother, curled up on the couch beside Carl, looking small and delicate, and I felt ashamed for having always assumed the caricature she presented to the world was anything other than a coping mechanism, a cover-up. "Mom?"

"Hmm," she answered, a happy cross between sleepy and a little drunk.

"Rob and I are going to head out—it's getting late."

"Okay, lovey," she said. "Carl can help you pack up the car."

Gently lifting himself up from the couch, my stepfather stretched a little and yawned. From under his festive sweater, his pale belly showed, blanched and unkempt. "Where are the keys?"

"Sit back down, Carl, we've got it," Rob said.

"If I don't get up now, I'll end up here for the night. My back is shot, and this couch is murder if I'm on it for too long."

My sister said that they'd probably be going, too, and then my mother complained for a minute that we were all leaving too soon. She tried to convince Meg and Jason to stay for more cookies, maybe another cup of tea.

"I'm too tired," Meghan said. "I need a nice long shower and my bed. And my pillow."

"Pillow?" I asked.

"Jason got me this pregnancy pillow for Christmas. It's an amazing giant snake that you wrap yourself around while lying down. I was hesitant at first. But I slept with it last night and it changed my life. I'm not even joking."

Jason laughed. "It's almost as big as our bed. Between how demanding she is about the bloody blankets and now this giant pillow, I'm going to have to move into the spare room soon."

Meghan pointed to her stomach. "Making a human being in here. That trumps your petty beefs. The spare room's all yours, baby."

"It's a good thing that bed is comfortable, or I might already start resenting both you and my unborn child," he said.

"That wouldn't be the first time, or the last."

It was hard to tell if my sister was joking or if she was airing her grievances with Jason. Sometimes I wondered if they even liked each other's company or if the familiar patterns of being together since they were young had simply overtaken their drive to make a change and redefine their lives without one another.

Meghan had always taken comfort in the familiar. She made friends fast and held on to them, even when it might have been better to let go; she hoarded trinkets, letters, cards, any kind of evidence of her life, perhaps just to prove that she had turned out okay despite everything our mother had put us through; and she was loyal, doggedly so.

Happy, unhappy—it didn't matter as long as she was being faithful to the version of herself that she had defined against our upbringing. She needed to be different from our mother. If that meant proving she could get married young and stay married, then she would stay married until the bitter end. My mother had lectured us constantly about how hard it was to have kids. I had listened but Meghan had made up her own mind. What kept her life going was striving for constancy—a consistent address, a phone number that never changed, a steady job—and it was all tied to proving to our mother that Meghan had turned out okay.

And she had thrived—now she was having a baby. She would be a wonderful mother because she was caring in a way that I never was, and that's what helped her survive the emotional wreckage.

As Rob packed up the car, I sat on the stairs and waited, feeling lazy and self-indulgent. My sister sat below me with her head resting on my legs. I checked my phone. No message from Garrett. I looked at my ring.

I asked her quietly, "Do you really like being married?"

Meghan lifted her head. "I do. We've been together so long, I don't know what my life would be like alone. I'm not sure I want to find out."

"Are you happy?"

"I don't think about it that way—honestly, I don't. I think about what I'm building and what I have and where I want to go. Those are more important to me than day-to-day happiness. Jason annoys the crap out of me sometimes, but we're in a great place right now.

We've worked out the kinks." She yawned. "You don't have to get married just to get married, or just because he asked, or, like me, because you like the security of a relationship. You can take a cue from Mom's book and find another way."

"You hated how we grew up."

"I did. But that doesn't mean that you do too. Or that you have to—or need to—resent our mother for, well, being our mother."

"I *am* excited about being an aunt."

"You'll be an awesome aunt. You'll spoil the kid rotten and ruin him or her for me forever. And as long as you babysit whenever I want, no questions asked, you can buy this baby anything you'd like—appropriate, inappropriate, I don't much care."

"Do you feel sick? I mean, all the puking and stuff that's supposed to happen, morning sickness?"

"It's the worst. And taking the subway? It's awful. But mainly I'm fucking tired. I can barely raise my arms to get a glass for water, I'm that tired. Wait, you never told me what happened with Garrett."

"It's not the time. I'll call you later, tomorrow, maybe. I'm overreacting. It's nothing."

"Crushes are okay, you know," Meghan said. "There was a dude who temped at the daycare last year, and man he was smoking hot. He was a trainer part time, all buffed and tattooed—my brain was overworked with him in it for months. He even had a man bun. Imagine having a crush on someone with a man bun."

"You sure that's Jason's baby?"

"Ha." Pause. "Yes. Don't even joke about that."

Laughing, that was how we had survived most of our childhood; with imaginary worlds and inside jokes, but I could see the quiet tension overtaking her—the worry, the anxiety about the baby, about it all. There was always potential in the future, but any path you took had the ability to make life better or worse. Still, deep down I questioned whether a future like Meghan's was for me, whether Rob was *the one*. Garrett's voice echoed through my mind on refrain, "Don't marry that guy."

"There are lots of happily ever afters. Hasn't Harlequin taught you anything?" my sister said.

Except life wasn't books, and books weren't life, and romance lovers hated heroines who cheated—and I came that-close with Garrett at the holiday party. If I decided to marry Rob, that would be the end of our friendship. It would be too dangerous for me to imagine, to let myself feel whatever it was that I was feeling.

People change. Lives move in different directions regardless of how much people love one another. There might be an affair. They might outgrow one another. They might not want the same things; separate goals might make life together untenable. Everything ends.

The front door opened and a shock of cold air hit us both. My stepfather trundled in, stamping the snow off his boots. "Rob's got all your gear in the car. You're all ready to go."

I stood up and shouted, "Mother, I'm going." I slipped my boots on and pulled my coat from the closet. "Rob's outside. Come say good-bye."

My mother yelled, "Too tired to stand. Bye, darlings, talk to you later in the week. We're having a New Year's Day brunch with your stepbrothers. Come around eleven, if you aren't too under the weather."

I walked back through the house to remind my mother that I had the big work party on New Year's Eve, so there was no way I'd be brunch ready by the next morning. I turned to leave, and my mother said, "Wait! Carl's getting you some of the turkey. You don't have to cook tomorrow. We have so much left over."

"No, no, Carl, don't worry about it. It'll just go bad in our fridge, anyway."

"Fine," my mother shouted, "have it your way!" And then, "I love you."

"You too," I said, and pointed at my sister, "And you."

"Right back atcha."

I slipped down the hallway and closed the front door quietly behind me. Snow fell steadily. There was something about the Canadian winter that I adored even though cold feet and fingers were annoying and after five straight months of bad weather you were about ready to burn your hat and boots. The season, with its sobering cold, was unforgiving, but it was also beautiful. Winter allowed the city a moment to hold still for the holidays and let people tuck in nice and warm. The streets were quiet, dampened by the snow. Before the snowplows, before anyone shoveled, before pets had to be walked, the sidewalks were crisp, crunchy even. The air might stop at nothing to freeze your lungs midbreath, but I'd never wanted to live anywhere else.

The car was running and Rob was brushing the last bits of snow from the roof. My phone buzzed. I was reaching into my coat pocket to pull it out when, *wham*! A pile of snow landed squarely on the top of my head, dripped down my neck, and washed my face in its cold.

"What, are you twelve and picking on me in the playground because you really like me?" Rob threw his head back, laughing. "It's so cold, you're such a jerk!"

Dropping my BlackBerry in my pocket, I raced around the car to get my own back. "Come on, this feels like a bad rom-com moment. Do you want to have a snow fight on Christmas?"

"I do," he said. "And it's a fight you'll never win."

He tackled me and we landed on the snowbank of my mother's front yard. He covered my face completely with snow. I struggled but he had me pinned down. Spitting snow out of my mouth and shaking the rest of it off, I said, "Ugh, you suck."

"Oh, poor baby, stuck in the snow. Here, let me make it better."

More snow in my face.

"Merry fucking Christmas to you!" I shouted.

Rob could see my expression change from *Yes, this is flirty fun* to *Get off me now or I'll never have sex with you again*, so he released me.

"Spoilsport," he said as he got up. "That's how I charmed all the girls in grade school, every single one of my grade-school girl-friends. I'd wait for the first snowfall then plow them over—if I wasn't pushing them into a ditch or stealing their books. I was such a charmer."

"Aren't I the lucky one to end up with you. Now help me up."

Rob pulled me to my feet and delicately brushed me off, the leather of his gloves hard and rough on my cheeks. He kissed me deeply before letting go. "I do love you."

"I know," I said. "I know you do. Let's go, I'm freezing. And I need our bed. I think I'm already hungover from too much of my mother's wine."

"Don't give me that face. You've been tipsy since breakfast at my parents'. If I didn't know better, I'd think you can't get through a holiday with me without being plastered."

"Then you'd be right," I snapped.

"Why do you have to be such an asshole? After we've had such a good day?"

"Can we please just get in the car and go? I'm tired of being cold."

"Sure," Rob said. "We can do exactly what you want to do when you want to do it. Why would it be any other way? Amazing way to end the holiday. With you picking a fight and me being pissed off."

* * *

We spoke little in the car on the way home and exchanged even fewer words as we pulled into the parking garage under the condo. It took two trips to take our presents upstairs. As Rob went down for the last load, I finally got a chance to look at my BlackBerry.

Engaged. Garrett had texted. *Congrats.*

His short message conveyed next to nothing. He wasn't disappointed and he hadn't asked any further questions. I locked myself in our en-suite bathroom, turned on the taps to feign drawing a bath, sat down on the edge of the tub, and let the tears come. I was risking everything when I already had so much. When I had built so much, a start to a life, a good life. One I was lucky to have. The water filled the tub and steamed up the bathroom. I dumped some bath salts in and stirred them around.

The last two days had been an emotional whirlwind, as if the holidays weren't stressful enough. Even if Rob was convinced marriage wouldn't change a single aspect of our relationship, I knew it would. The dress and the display and the pomp and circumstance of it all, not to mention Camille . . . marriage was a tremor beneath the earthquake of change.

And I knew it shouldn't matter to me what Garrett thought because I loved Rob, and I only *thought* I loved Garrett. There was a difference. There had to be. Garrett was happy for me, excited, his usual self. We would only ever be work friends. I stepped into the tub, let the water wash over me, and thought about everything I would lose by not being with Rob. One thought—that he wouldn't be there to kiss me good night—and I made up my mind.

Rob was in our room, sitting on the bed when I came out of the bathroom. "I'm sorry," I said. "I didn't mean to snap. It's a lot, everyone having babies, this *ring*. But I love you. I want to get married. I do. Let's start planning for September. That should give us enough time and—"

Rob pulled me toward him between his legs and held me tight. "I love you," he whispered into my ear. It was a tender moment; I felt secure. Rob pushed his hands up under my towel. "Kel, we don't have to decide it all tonight. Thank you, thank you for giving me an answer. It's enough for now. It is."

I leaned into him, soaking his T-shirt with my wet hair. "No, I've made a decision. Please, call your mother and tell her September. I bet they'll book the golf club for the reception. That should make your parents happy and mine somewhat comfortable." I leaned back to pick up the phone and hand it to him. "Call her, it's not too late."

Rob took the phone from my hands, and I stepped out from between his legs. "All right, all right!"

"Mom, hi, hope it's not too late," Rob said into the phone. "Kelly's said yes, we're getting married! I know, it was quick for her." I rolled my eyes at him and shook my head. "Kelly wants to get married this September." Pause. "I'm sure that's enough time to plan a wedding." Pause. "Why don't you try the club—we don't need anything fancy. It's as nice a place as any to get married." Pause. "Sure, we can still look around, but why don't you call after the holidays and see if they can give us some possible dates?"

Rob mumbled into the phone as he walked out of the bedroom to finish his conversation. Light and happy. The fight locked away in the recesses of his mind. I sent a note back to Garrett. *We're going to get married in September. Hope you and Jen are having a nice holiday. See you this week.*

"Honeymoon in Paris," I shouted. "That's my one condition. I want to spend my honeymoon in Paris."

Because as long as I was dreaming this would all work out, I might as well dream big.

Chapter 9

BOXING DAY. What a brilliant idea. All the pressure from Christmas was over, all the family obligations complete. We woke up early, calm, serene, and happy. I wasn't too hungover. Rob made the coffee and let me mix the pancake batter. We piled on frozen blueberries and way too much maple syrup, and feasted on bacon until we were stuffed. I told him he'd better not make me gain any more than five pounds this week or else I wouldn't fit into the dress I had bought for the film channel launch party on New Year's Eve. He laughed and told me that I looked better with a bit of meat on my bones, and that alcohol wasn't a balanced diet. I tried all morning to put the silly text exchange from Garrett out of my mind, convincing myself that being engaged properly meant that I should be in the moment with Rob, not glued to my BlackBerry.

Rob knew me but Garrett understood me. Laughing about the cheesy guy on the streetcar—Garrett. Joking about Siobhan's crazy mood swings—Garrett. Complaining about Camille and her endless looks—Garrett. I talked to Garrett more these days than I talked to Meghan. He knew the ins and outs of my days in a way that Rob couldn't. Rob and I didn't work together. We didn't spend countless lunches together, didn't go to the bar together, didn't spend all day messaging each other. I had an intimacy with Garrett that I didn't share with Rob. The moments added up, and the closeness I felt to

Garrett was making me lose focus on the man in front of me. The man I was actually sharing my life with. The man, for better or worse, I had agreed to marry.

"Are you having buyer's regret?" Rob joked. I was staring off into space. "You just shook your head when I asked if you wanted another cup of coffee. Has being engaged turned you into a completely different person? Who are you?"

"Sorry, I zoned out for a second. Coffee, yes, that'll fix the problem." I smiled; he poured. Piling in the cream and sugar, I said, "Breakfast was delicious. We've had some outstanding meals the last few days. I think all the food crammed into my brain is making it impossible to think."

"Or you're hungover."

"Could be that too." I yawned. "I need some fresh air."

"Oh no, Kelly," he said. "I can feel it coming on, here we go. You are about to explode from family time. The clock is ticking. The bomb needs to be diffused. Get your coat on. Maybe, just maybe, you need to—I'm going to say it out loud, don't hit me, stop! You need to process!"

As much as he was teasing, he was right. With work on hiatus until New Year's Eve, I had no real excuse to get out of the house.

He continued, "The gears are grinding to a halt. She's losing all personality as we sit here. The life is draining out of her limbs. She . . . can't . . . take . . . another . . . breath . . ."

"Enough!" I kicked him gently under the table. "I'm going to take myself outside and go for a walk."

"And there it is, folks. The Kelly I know and love. The one who needs to escape into herself for a couple of hours. Your eyebrows are going to disappear into one another," he said as he rose from the table. I stood up to gather our plates. "Leave them. I'm getting your coat. Go put on a warm sweater. I can't take looking at you all balled up like a porcupine about to be attacked. Go. Now."

I wrapped myself up in my warmest down-filled coat, tied a wool scarf around my neck, and smothered myself in a toque. "Keys?"

"Where did you leave them?"

"I have no idea." He shook his head at me and passed me his keys without another word.

Snow was falling slowly; it was more like dust particles than precipitation. As I crossed Queen, I wished I lived in a massive city like New York or London. There was something so comforting about getting lost in a city that stretched out before you, that you couldn't walk across in day or even two if you tried. In either of those places, you could head out in one direction, walk for hours, for blocks and blocks, and there would still be so much city to see. As brilliant a place as Toronto was to live, it just wasn't the same. I passed through the gates into Trinity Bellwoods and crunched up pathway. The wind swept the cold up and underneath my coat.

Processing.

Processing was a patented Lindaism. Whenever a huge life event happened, she would shutter us away in our rooms or on a long drive—no radios allowed, television forbidden. If handheld devices had been a thing when I was a kid, those would have been outlawed as well.

"Take the time to think," she'd say, her eyes on the road and us going nowhere in particular. When she'd made the decision to marry Carl after they'd lived together for about a year, she had taken us away to a remote cabin in Algonquin Park. To call the three of us camping novices would have been generous. She hadn't even allowed us to bring books.

"Notebooks only. Two pencils each, and don't forget a sharpener, because we'll be processing. Our lives are going to change, and we need to ruminate on what it all means to us and our underlying psyches, as a family and as individuals."

We ate cold SpaghettiOs out of the tin and a lot of peanut butter.

Not being campers, we didn't have any of the right gear, and we froze our asses off at night when the temperature dropped dramatically even though it was August. But we laughed and laughed.

I had so many mixed memories from that weekend, the kind where enough time has passed, and they're easy to laugh about now. My sister refusing to take off the wool mittens she had found buried under the backseat of the car, left there a season ago. My mother constantly swatting away mosquitoes and horseflies with shock and awe that they would bother her at all while she was so deep in thought. How dare they interrupt her concentration?

We stayed out there until the bitter end of our camping permit and were actually a little sad to see the experience come to an end. I hadn't been camping since, and I never again ate tinned spaghetti. When the three of us had gotten back to the city, the packing up seemed easier that time around. We'd had time to forgive my mother for Toly, for the swift nature of her courtship with Carl, for sticking us in a house that was crammed with kids every other weekend. We arrived back at Carl's with some of the tension surrounding the situation released, and that let my mother concentrate on getting us organized for our new school year.

Here was the crux of the matter: I'd made a decision. It was the right one. Getting married was the right thing to do. I didn't want to think about Garrett anymore. I needed to get him out of my system and recommit myself to Rob. To the life I had chosen. To my future. I needed to show Camille that I was worthy of what Rob and I had together, of him. The Starbucks kitty-corner to the park was open, so I went inside and settled for their acrid, bitter brew. Their coffee always made me agitated and jumpy, but it was warm, and they didn't charge me an arm and a leg for a disposable cup. By the time I re-entered the park, the snow was falling harder, making it difficult to walk, but after multiple coffees my head felt clear for the first time in days.

It was last summer. Rob and I had come back from the cottage, and I was at work for the first time in two solid weeks. Even in the summer, when many of the networks were on repeats, we still had meetings, listings, complaints, and so I hadn't noticed the time when Garrett popped into my cube.

"I'm so glad you're back," he said. "It was murder here without you."

"You're still alive so it can't have been that bad."

"Bored to tears. Beth was off with Raj most of the time, and so I spent lunch hours aimlessly wandering the streets of Toronto."

"I can't imagine it was that bad." I laughed.

"You remember when Oliver sits down in the David Lean version of the movie and the whole city's bustling around him, and he looks all lost and forlorn?"

"Are you comparing yourself to a nineteenth-century street urchin about to be conscripted into a gang?"

"Yes."

"Must have been a terrible couple of weeks, then."

"Brutal. Do you know how lonely it is doing all of our lunch things by myself? People were giving me funny looks, Kel, *looks*."

"I've been on vacation before, you know."

"But I missed you." He paused. "Like, really missed you."

"I'm back now," I said quietly.

"I'm so glad."

There, that was the moment, when it all shifted, and we drifted beyond work and into something else. Because I had missed him, too, desperately. My BlackBerry didn't work up north, and while I'd spent glorious days by the lake in my bathing suit simply dipping my feet into the water and reading, I had been anxious. Rob kept asking me what was wrong, and I couldn't explain—Oh, I can't text Garrett every five minutes, or I'm missing my midweek bibimbap at the noodle place on Yonge. That was the moment where I knew

I was staying at the job because Garrett was there and not because of its viable career opportunities.

The pathways hadn't been cleared yet, and the only people out and about were a few random dog owners desperate for their pets to do their business so they could get back inside. The fresh snowfall had enticed the families who lived near the park to pull out their sleds, racing down the hill side at impossible speeds. I walked in the other direction toward the benches north, near Dundas. I was the only one sitting there. Because rational people were not sitting outside on a park bench on Boxing Day contemplating the rest of their lives.

I sat there, just inside the gates, for what felt like hours, thinking about the two men who defined my life. I felt lucky that I hadn't made too many mistakes. My high school boyfriend, who'd introduced me to the concept of being the other woman. How it messed with my heart, how awful I had been to the other girl, and how I expected romance to be maudlin, mixed up, miserable, because that's how little I thought of myself at the time. Not worth it. Never enough. If I hadn't been through all of that, I would never have known that a man like Rob was even an option. And now I could ruin it all by running off with Garrett, or, really, by daydreaming about having a torrid affair at the hotel across the street from our offices. Because I'd been with Rob for so long I'd avoided a lot of the heartbreak that other women my age suffered through. The constant wondering of will he, won't he commit, or call, or even show up at the prearranged time. I was lucky. My friends were lucky. Beth had Raj. My sister had Jason. Even my mother had it all worked out now. Annie would be Annie forever, but I was sure she would have gotten married again if any one of the six or seven fellows who had asked to marry her over the last decade had remotely interested her.

After Meghan and I had acclimatized to our new high school, I had fallen in with a group of kids in similar home situations to mine. We all had a decided lack of parental control in our lives. We had cars, we had fake IDs, and we spent hours downtown at dance clubs before finally rolling home well into the night. It wasn't like Linda to keep so quiet about my behavior, but she never said a word. My grades never suffered, and also, I was pretty sure Carl told her it was a phase, and that to rein me in would make it all worse. I wasn't rude to him, or to my mother for that matter. I just didn't come home. When I picked a university, I made sure it was as far away as I could get because I needed to be separate from them, away. Plus, I had been such a selfish twit that I needed a fresh start, and I'd convinced myself that Queen's was the answer—the exact opposite of the kids I'd been with at school, who weren't planning on even going to university.

Before the awful boyfriend I had dated, and dated, and dated in high school—a different boy every couple of weeks. I found them abroad on class trips, around the corner at our part-time job among the drivers of the dry-cleaning delivery trucks, in Meghan's math tutoring sessions. They were everywhere, these boys. Preppy, punk, older, younger—I went out with pretty much anyone who asked. Meghan told me to calm down and find someone like Jason. "Uh," I said over and over again, "I don't want to be you."

"Good," she'd retort. "You couldn't have a normal relationship if you tried."

I was constantly burning and flaming out, fighting with my so-called best friend after she slept with my so-called boyfriend. Screaming matches in the parking lot after school. I'm mortified thinking about it now—still, I got straight As and had enough extra-curriculars, mainly organizing the school's many dances, that I got accepted to university.

But just because I got into the school didn't mean I was comfortable there. I'd never been so lonely. Alienated, frustrated . . . and then, somehow, I found Rob. We were so different. Even back then, taking completely opposite classes, but at the end of the night, that didn't matter because we'd be out at the pub, absolutely plastered, come home, and have great sex. Eventually, we fell into each other's lives. His friends were my friends. His world was my world. My sister teased me once she met him, saying that I was settling for straitlaced because I knew he would never hurt me. Who would have thought she was right?

Meghan had listened when my mother told us over and over again, "You get the love you think you deserve, girls. I didn't think I deserved much until I finally got tired of trying so hard. Then, *bam*! Carl. He's the best thing to ever happen to me. Do better than I did."

I had been dangerous in high school in ways I'd never truly understood. It was different with Rob. I was different. I was committed and respected and loved. And yet there was a part of me who was still that girl, that silly fool who wanted to self-destruct.

Those same urges were there when Garrett came by to go out for lunch. The huge difference was that I was no longer a teenager, and both Garrett and I were in committed relationships. I was clinging to the fact that men and women could sometimes be friends with no sexual undertones. I did care about Jen getting hurt, or even about her being hurt by my relationship with Garrett. And I didn't want Rob to think that I had so little respect for him and what we had as to throw myself into an editing closet with Garrett, pull off all his trendy clothes, and fuck him on a desk.

Enough, I thought. *Enough is enough.*

I could have sat on that bench for hours and still be no closer to knowing what the hell I wanted. The air wasn't getting any warmer; and even the pet owners had stopped walking by. My fingertips were so cold now that I could barely feel them, and the snow around the bench was inches deep.

The first time I had realized how different Rob was after school ended, when my mother thought she had thyroid cancer. She called on the eve of my last exam, holding it in so well that I didn't have a clue something was wrong until I heard her voice crack. In the background, Carl whispered something, and she answered, "No, no, I'm okay, darling. Tea, please. Hot as you can make it."

I had eventually hung up the phone and collapsed into Rob's arms, worried, desperate to be home. After calming me down and pulling the whole story out of me, he stayed by my side. The next morning, he walked me to the exam hall and sat there, studying on the cold, concrete floor, waiting until I was done. He wrote his own final exam that afternoon, then packed us both up and drove us straight home to my mother's. He didn't leave my side until the doctor called the next day with my mother's test results and gave her the all clear. She and Carl had waited three whole weeks before telling us anything. Meghan was still furious about all of that. But it had been a blessing in disguise for me. I had learned that Rob would be there for me, no matter what. That was what finally convinced me I'd found the love I deserved.

* * *

By the time I got back to the apartment, Rob had thrown himself back into bed. I could hear him snoring from the front door—he was gearing himself up for our dinner party in his own way, by being well rested. I lay down beside him and put my hand on his wrist, feeling his pulse. I tried to close my eyes, to forget about everything, even just for a minute or two. We slept for much of the afternoon, and it was the best sleep I'd had in ages. My mind was decided. Marriage. It was the only way out. It was the right thing to do.

Chapter 10

HOT, STEAMY, AND delicious, the food arrived right on time. The takeout was expensive but worth it. Not even my mother's culinary skills extended to the complexities of Indian food. Whenever Rob and I tried to make butter chicken at home, it never turned out right. We always resorted to ordering from the place down the street. The deluxe flavor combinations alone would have been the death of me, not to mention the fact that, with my poor culinary skills, I wouldn't know what to do with a coriander if it was dropped right in front of me.

The condo looked festive and fabulous. Our Christmas tree lit up the living room–slash–dining room–slash–everything-in-one, and the expensive Jo Malone scented candles that Camille had given me for Christmas smelled incredible. I wore a little black dress that I had found in a tiny boutique on Queen West; it was cut perfectly to my figure. I wanted to look my best, not just because we were having a dinner party but also because that same dangerous voice inside my head wanted to show Garrett what I looked like outside of work. The dress's neckline skimmed the top of my breasts, and the drop waist accentuated my hips in a way that didn't draw focus to the holiday pounds I'd surely put on. Plus, I'd taken a tip from the fashionistas and double-Spanxed, so there wasn't a crease or a line to be seen anywhere on my torso. I wore completely indulgent black patent leather Louboutins. They made my calves look fabulous—even

Rob seemed impressed when I came out of the bathroom scrubbed, polished, and preened within an inch of my life.

"We should have a dinner party every weekend if it means you'll smell like this." He held me tight around the waist and pulled me close. "Are you going to wear your ring?"

My heart jumped slightly in my chest at the thought of wearing the ring so publicly, and in front of people who weren't our families. But the expression on Rob's face was so warm, so heartfelt that I didn't have it in me to deny him a little happiness. Putting the ring on now made our engagement even more official than it was already. Putting the ring on now meant I'd never be able to take it off.

"Of course," I said. "I didn't want to forget about it when I was in the shower, lose it down the drain and then have to call maintenance to snake the entire building. Could you imagine?"

I walked over to my dresser, a beat-up old thing from my childhood that was made of white pine, marked with crayons, and which still smelled like the sachets I had made at Girl Guide camp in grade school. I pulled the ring box out of my top drawer. Even the box had an intensity as I clicked it open to reveal the ring inside. The light in our bedroom made it sparkle like from a scene in a movie. It all felt ridiculous, but my choices were right, and I was living this life, and so I put it on. I felt the weight of the ring on my finger and fought the urge to twist it around and around as though practicing the kind of magic that might make it disappear.

"How does it look?" I held my hand forward to Rob.

"Perfect." He smiled. "Let's get drunk. Indian food always tastes better when I've had an entire bottle of cold white wine. Then at least my senses are dull enough to enjoy the spices."

"A truer sentence has never been spoken."

We opened the first bottle. The wine headed straight from my empty stomach to my head. I was so tipsy as I set the table that I had to recheck three times that I had enough cutlery. Rob decanted some red wine, and we sat in our warm, lovely home waiting for the doorman to ring up our guests.

"I'm sorry that Marianne and her boyfriend Cash are coming," I said. "I wanted you to spend some time with Garrett. Outside of Beth, he's my best friend at work."

"I wish I knew what that was like," he said. "Sure, we go out for drinks after work, and then there's the bonus celebrations. Still, it's nothing like what you guys have. It's a sport among these guys. They're hungry for a kind of success that I don't care about. I need to get off the floor and into the analyst's chair."

"The right job will come up," I said.

"I just have to be patient," he said. "They party hard, some of my co-workers, but I've never felt comfortable being too loose around people who control so much money, let alone my future at the company. I've got a rep now for being a teetotaler since I don't go out that often. But seeing them drunk and messy would just make me lose respect for them."

"If Garrett or Beth lost any respect for me every time I got tipsy, I wouldn't be able to show my face around them anymore. They're not judgmental of the drunk me—at least, I don't think so."

"No one could be judgmental of the drunk you, Kelly. You're hilarious when you're tipsy." Rob paused. "It's a different industry, a different world. It's not like the world stops if a publicist is hungover at the office."

When what he was saying sank in, I grew irritated. "Are you insinuating that there's no real value to what I do? So, I can just go off and get drunk with my co-workers all the time because television's schlock anyway and what does it matter to the real world?"

Maybe I was more nervous than I wanted to admit, and the few glasses of wine I'd had didn't calm my nerves. They were acting like an incendiary device. My bones felt itchy. I resisted the urge to scratch my dress right off my body.

"That's not what I mean. No, I'm saying I think it's irresponsible for people in my line of work to go out every night and get drunk. You need a clear head to challenge the markets. But, I mean, hey, what would the world do without television listings, eh?"

"You can be such a jerk sometimes. Really," I snapped.

"Come on, Kelly, I'm kidding. Plus, I know you don't want to do that job forever. I know you're not happy there, and you won't always be a publicist shilling other people's projects instead of your own."

"That's not the point!" I was shouting now. "I know my contribution here isn't as much as yours. I know I don't own anything of my own, and I barely subsist from paycheck to paycheck—"

"And spend too much on shoes." He laughed.

"What I do is a real job. I put in the hours and sit at a desk just like you do. You can't mock what I do and then loop back around and be critical just because I have friends and you don't."

"What are you even talking about? I *have* friends. But I keep work at work and home at home. There are no blurred lines."

"Oh please, you can't tell me that the lines between your life at home and at work aren't blurred, not with the hours you work and how hard you have to suck up for any kind of measly promotion to further your career—which is backed, in part, by your parents' generous income.

"Haven't you always said that if this didn't work out you'd just fall back on the law and go work for your father? Your boss is one of your father's golfing buddies. What I've done, I've worked for, and I've landed where I've landed because those were the choices available to me. You've had a hell of a lot better choices in your life, Rob. Don't tell me you haven't."

Rob looked stunned. "Where is this coming from? What are we even fighting about? Because we might as well just toss all the food off the balcony and cancel if you're going to be this much of a bitch."

The phone rang. We both looked at each other. Neither of us stood up to answer it.

"That's them," I said. "I'm sorry. I'm nervous. I didn't mean to fly off the handle with you."

Rob looked tightly wound. He never cried. He never raised his voice. And he never used the b-word. The phone kept beeping. In one angry step, Rob moved off the couch to pick it up from the kitchen island.

"Hi." Pause. "Yes, send them all up, we're expecting them. Yes, we had a great holiday. Hope you did too."

I stood up to take his hand as he hung up. "I know you work hard. I do. I just want you to see that I do too—even if my job is kind of useless sometimes."

"Your job isn't useless," Rob said as he pulled me in tight. "I don't know where all of this is coming from. I don't know what you're thinking."

I squeezed him back, both my arms wrapped around his middle. "I'm a fighter. You've met my mother. But trying to figure out what goes on in my mind, that's a freak show I wouldn't recommend. Fighting is my natural state. I'm not me if I'm not miserable. What do you want from me, from us?"

Rob pulled away and held me at arm's length. "Nothing," he said. "I want nothing. I love you. I don't have to think about it. I love you and that's the end of it. I have my happy and then some. I don't care what you do. I want you to be happy. And you never seem happy."

"So not my natural state! I wouldn't even know what to do with happy. *Sheesh.* Have you even met me?"

There was a quiet knock at the door.

"Let's not be mad all night," he said. "Let's get drunk and show your friends a good time."

I walked to the door and inhaled as deeply as the Spanx permitted.

There was a rush of hot, stuffy hallway air as Garrett, Jen, Marianne, and Cash walked in. Their arms were full of wine and winter flower arrangements and what looked to be honest-to-goodness hostess gifts for me. Jen, who was tiny with dark hair and heavily lined eyes, smiled warmly. Introductions were made all around. I took everyone's coats and hung them up in our tiny front-hall closet.

"Dude!" Garrett said, "your place is awesome and so grown-up. It's as if you pay attention to those design shows." He grabbed Rob's hand and shook it firmly. "Rob, it's nice to meet you, man, I've heard so much about you. Thanks for having us. We've been lonely not visiting the parents this holiday season. I'm homesick, so I've been looking forward to a festive-type meal."

Jen laughed. "You are not homesick. The fact that you had nothing to do this Christmas except sit back and watch *Lord of the Rings* has made you the happiest I've seen you in months."

"That might be true about the *Lord of the Rings* DVD extravaganza, but I still insist that I'm a little sad not to be on the West Coast. Anything to escape the weather and not to have to travel a billion hours to get to a decent ski hill."

Rob said, "Collingwood isn't to your taste? We've skied there for years—it's a great hill if you catch it right."

"Sure," Garrett said, "but I miss fresh Rockies powder."

"I spent a season at Whistler once," Rob said. "Waiting for Kelly to finish undergrad."

"Cool," Garrett said, drifting away.

"Can I get anyone a glass of wine?" Rob offered.

"We've brought some organic wine with us, let me grab it from my bag," Marianne said. "The nitrates in store-bought wine do a number on me—wicked headaches." She grabbed the bag she had dropped by the door and peered into it. "Oh no, Cash, I think I actually forgot it in the car—do you mind?"

"'Course not," he said. "I'll be back in a spliffy-jiffy."

I gave Rob a wide-eyed look at the "spliffy-jiffy" and then handed my keys to Cash. "Here, take my pass key for the parking garage. Then you don't need the concierge to buzz you back in."

Cash smiled. "Thanks, man, be right back."

"All kidding aside," Jen said, "you have a lovely home. I hope this suits—it's just a little something." She handed me a delicately wrapped gift bag. I thanked her and put it aside on the kitchen island, intending to open it later.

"Please open it now," she said. "If you don't like it, I might have a chance to exchange it."

"Of course," I said. "Let's all sit down. Rob can handle the drinks orders."

Sitting down on the couch, I pulled the white tissue paper out of the bag to reveal a tiny crystal figure of a mouse. It was delicate, sparkly, and so completely my taste.

"It's vintage, from the early '80s. I found it in a pawn shop around the corner from our house. It's Swarovski crystal." Jen laughed. "I can never say that name right."

"It's spectacular. I'm going to put it on my bedroom dresser for safekeeping while we have dinner." I paused. "Can you even return stuff to the pawn shop?"

Garrett laughed. "Only if we take a deep discount of fifty percent or more. Jen was being polite about returning it. You'll need to pawn it off on someone else if you hate it."

"I don't hate it, not at all—it's the season for sparkly things, I think." I smiled at Rob. "I might get confused about who I am with all the beautiful presents I've received this Christmas. I'm feeling very spoiled, indeed. Thank you both for being so thoughtful."

My voice had an odd tremor in it that didn't feel entirely authentic because I was talking too quickly. I stood up and took the gift to my bedroom so I could both get away from the living room for a moment and stop myself from staring at Jen, from scrutinizing her from the tips of her shoes to the ends of her neatly bobbed hair. My first impression of her was that she was lovely, considerate, and sweet. Exactly the kind of girl I could imagine Garrett with. Exactly the kind of girl that he would settle down with for life.

When I came back into the room, Marianne and Jen had slipped easily into conversation, holding their heads close together in that way that women do, with a sense of camaraderie that made me long for my sister. I should have invited them to dinner too. At least then I would have had Meghan to lean on throughout, and no one could break a tense situation like Jason. He was impossible to embarrass and would say anything that came to his mind. Or I could have invited more people and turned this into a drinks thing with just appetizers so the crowd could conceal my ulterior motives.

Marianne was rattling off news from Banff about old friends having babies, getting married, and getting divorced—all the little things that make up casual conversation between two friends who are familiar with each other but not often in contact. I hated Jen for a moment, for being so small, for her pixie-like hair, for her quiet, gentle voice, for the determined way she sat on my couch with her legs crossed, already comfortable, already in command of the social situation.

Rob and Garrett were talking by the sliding doors that led out to the balcony. I heard the words *Leafs* and *embarrassment to hockey*.

"Rob!" I shouted. "You didn't get Jen any wine!"

"She declined," Rob said. "Has she changed her mind?"

"Oh, no, thanks," Jen said. "I'm not drinking tonight. I'm the designated driver."

Marianne laughed. "You always get stuck being the DD, don't you? Let your hair down! I'm sure we'll be here long enough that you can have a couple of glasses."

Cash came back into the apartment then carrying the bag that Marianne had forgotten in the car. "Putting your key in this key-happy bowl right here, Kelly, okay?"

"Sure."

Marianne pressed the issue. "Why don't you have some organic wine? I'm telling you, it'll change your life. Hangovers are half of what they might be on the regular stuff."

"No, I'm fine, really," Jen insisted. She looked flushed for a moment, like she didn't know quite what to say to put an end to Marianne's pressure.

I knew why in an instant. Without thinking, I blurted, "You're pregnant."

The air in the room stopped circulating for a single second, and then another. No one moved. Jen turned an awkward shade of pink and said quietly, "No, no, that's not it, I promise. I'm taking antibiotics, and you're not supposed to mix them with alcohol."

"Thank god," I said.

Jen looked a little mortified, and I stumbled further over my words. "My foot couldn't have been any bigger in my mouth. Everyone I know is pregnant, and it's got me all muddled."

It was an awful, uncomfortable moment, and it caught me completely off guard. I stumbled away from the couch and leaned against the island. Making assumptions about other people, about their lives—letting the thoughts spill out of my mouth without any self-control. That's how I hurt people.

"Oh man," Garrett said. "That would have been an odd way to find out I was becoming a dad." Trying to lighten the mood. Trying to cover up for my being so impossibly rude.

"Is there a bathroom around?" Jen asked. Tears were threatening, I could tell. I knew the feeling well.

"Use the one in our room," I said. "Here, I'll show you. Come on with me." I put my hand on Jen's back as she held back tears and shook a little. I felt big, gruff, ruthless, and lacking tenderness.

"I'm so sorry," I said, leading her into the bedroom, and turning on the lights in our bathroom, then handing over a box of tissues.

"I don't even know what to say. It just came out. Rob's sister, my sister, they're both pregnant. A couple of glasses of wine and nonsense pops out of my mouth—"

"It's okay," Jen said. "It's not your fault. Garrett and I have been fighting about kids for weeks. I want them, he doesn't." She laughed a little. "Sometimes I wish Marianne would learn to shut up."

"She *really* has a problem with that," I said.

"She does, right?" Jen said. "Can you give me a minute?"

"Of course, I'll wait out here."

The water ran in the sink. I thought of all the times Rob had been in there shaving in the morning, the sound of the tap turning off and on as he shaved, rinsed the blade, shaved, rinsed the blade. I wished my furniture in the bedroom wasn't so beaten up, wished that I hadn't thrown all my rejected outfits all over the floor. Jen came out of the bathroom a moment later, and saw me sitting on the bed.

"Sorry about this mess."

"Kelly, good grief, please don't even worry about it. You've never seen our place, but I can assure you, it's piles of video games, DVDs, tapes, various chips bags, and now the mess from the presents Garrett's family sent. He's dumped it all in a pile in the living room while he watched *Lord of the Rings*."

"Are you sure you're okay? Did you spoil your makeup? I've got cotton and makeup remover—"

"Please, don't fuss," Jen said. "I'll be fine."

She sat down on the bed, near the foot. The space between us was awkward and odd—it's not like I imagined having a serious heart-to-heart with Garrett's girlfriend tonight.

"It's such a sore spot, us wanting different things."

"It might not seem like it, but I do know how you feel," I said.

"We had a huge blowout on Boxing Day. I've been sick. This bronchitis that won't go away. I want to go back home, hate this city, hate the weather. Get married, start our *real* lives."

Jen smoothed the folds on her jeans, pulled her sweater down. I didn't know what to say, and absolutely didn't want to put my foot in it again.

"If he was remotely interested in having kids, which he's not—it's all one big mess," she said. "At least you're getting married."

"I'm not sure I want to get married," I said.

"You don't?"

"I'm living with it for now." Admitting it seemed easy. But the rumble of emotions underneath threated to sweep me away. Rob and Jen were the same, and if it wasn't so ironic, it might actually be funny to swap, set them up. What the hell was I thinking?

"You seem so settled here."

"The condo's a good investment. Rob's nothing if not a very practical man when it comes to finances. Being settled is easy; a permanent, legal, binding commitment is much harder." I rummaged through my side table. "Here you go." I handed over my spare makeup bag. "If you need powder or anything, help yourself—there's tons of samples in here. I collect them unnecessarily."

"Thanks Kelly, you're"—she sighed—"being too nice."

"Hey! No tears, remember. It'll all work itself out. I'm going to head back out there. Take as much time as you need."

Garrett came into the bedroom as I walked out. He held a tumbler of wine tightly in his hand. I wanted to reach out and grab him, clutch him tightly to me like in the best drunken hugs.

"She's all right," I said. "She's not used to the asshole Kelly."

"You're not an asshole," he said quietly.

Not surprisingly, none of the daydreams I'd had over the last few months about finding myself in my bedroom with Garrett included him being mute with shock over the fact that his girlfriend had burst into tears at a dinner party. My sister, Rob's sister, Jen wanting a baby and not being able to have it. I didn't get it. My mother warned me my biological clock would tick into oblivion the more I ignored it, and no amount of me telling her it was simply absent made her believe I was being truthful. Still, I made a mental note to double check my birth control pills and perhaps abstain. The last thing Rob and I needed was to throw a baby into this mix.

I closed our bedroom door to give them a bit of privacy. Every bit of me wanted to hover outside and listen, see how he was reacting, listen to what they were saying, just *know* what was going on, but I'd interfered enough. The whole episode had a bad soap opera tinge to it, like something my mother might see on *Coronation Street*. First dinner party: ruined.

Back in the living room, Rob was making small talk with Cash, and Marianne was sitting on the couch, sipping her wine, and looking off into space.

"I think I should go in there, you know, offer Jen some moral support," she said.

"No," I grabbed the wine and poured myself a huge glass. "Let's leave them alone. They'll come out when they're ready. You can help me get the food."

"Sure." Marianne sounded distracted. "I'd love to help."

We stood up, and I deliberately turned the stereo up a bit louder, then yelled over to Rob, "We're going to get dinner on the table."

He raised his eyebrows at me and nodded, as shell-shocked as the rest of us. Kudos to us. We had now thrown the most awkward gathering of the holidays. We were used to the heightened emotions of my family. Crying wasn't unheard of even when everyone was happy. But you were supposed to be able to get drunk and happy with your friends out of relief that they were *nothing* like your family.

As I put on the oven mitts to take the food out, Marianne exclaimed, "Holy shit! What is that on your finger?"

"Rob and I got engaged," I answered as casually as I could. "It's his grandmother's ring. Pretty, isn't it?"

She grabbed my hand and pulled the ring off my finger—it happened so quickly that I barely registered it wasn't on my hand anymore. "Oh my god, it's gorgeous!" She held it up to the light. "What perfect cut and clarity!" She shouted, "Cash, this is an *engagement* party! We should have brought champagne too." She turned back to me. "Why didn't you tell me?"

"It's not a big deal. We've been living together forever."

The warmth from the oven exploded onto my face, and I wondered if I'd be more comfortable at the top of a volcano than having this conversation with Marianne.

"I thought you hated marriage. Aren't you and Beth always going head-to-head about it? The pair of you are always blabbing on about how you couldn't possibly handle the pressure of something so 'totally serious.'"

"Beth got engaged, too, last week, and I'm coming around to the idea," I said. "But I need the ring back."

"Oh, right, sorry, here you go." Marianne handed it to me as Garrett and Jen came out of our room and rejoined the party. Marianne rushed from behind the island and gathered Jen up like she was a bunch of fresh-cut flowers—gently and tenderly—and whisper-yelled, "He'll come around," with Garrett standing *right there* hearing everything.

"Let's eat!" Cash said. "That smells so delicious, Kelly. I don't know how you could possibly manage to cook Indian food from scratch with everything else going on during the holidays. When I'm attempting a curry, I always give myself a good two days to get it right."

Rob laughed. "We didn't make any of this food. We ordered from down the street. Awesome takeout. Here, let me help you, Kelly."

We got the food on the table, poured some more wine, and everyone sat down. Our table was big enough for all six of us to comfortably sit around it, surrounded by serving dishes filled to the brim with aloo gobi and dal, spice-dusted cauliflower, and delicious-smelling buttery naan. Conversation during the start of the meal was mainly Marianne oversharing about her intense family, who had moved to Banff to live as close to the mountains as possible, give up all their worldly possessions, and "tent it," as she called it, for the first two years there—winters included. "I've got cold bones!" She laughed at her own jokes and generally sucked all of the air out of the room.

I drank. And drank some more. Watched Rob from the other side of the table as he and Garrett went deep diving into the differences between the films and books. Garrett was in his element defending how much richer the worlds were on celluloid. And Rob backing up the predictable "the book is always better" line about Tolkien. Deep down, I should be happy they were getting along. Deep down, I shouldn't think about throwing away the hope of a life with Garrett because we wanted the same things. Deep down, I shouldn't want the people I love to hurt in any way.

And then I settled into a melancholy that rested on the fact that I had to get the fantasies about me and Garrett out of my head, forever. There was to be no realization that we should run off together and start again in New York or somewhere equally exotic. Deep into a bottle of wine and even deeper in my own bitterness, I couldn't see my selfishness. If he and Jen moved back west, that would take Garrett even farther away from me and pull him into proper adulthood. Not the playing at adults we did every day at work, but late nights, responsibility, and eventually supporting a family. I was being ridiculous. I had a gorgeous engagement ring and an equally gorgeous man, and I, too, was about to cross a bridge that would collapse as soon as I landed on the other side. If I was in it with Rob, I was in it for the long haul.

"Kelly," Rob said from across the table, "you've barely touched your food. You'd better get in there before I start in on seconds."

He turned back to Jen and politely asked about her job, whether she enjoyed it or not, how she had come to work for the nonprofit industry.

"I hate it," she answered. "I'm doing cold calls, always asking people for money. It's a good cause, but it's not like I'm dying to go back after the Christmas holidays. I was an outdoor rafting guide back home on the Kicking Horse."

The tension fell again. But Marianne lightened the mood. "That's not a safe career, Jen."

"I love being outside. I miss the mountains."

"I know," Garrett said, a bit sharply. "But the industry is better for me here."

Marianne piped up. "Cash worked for a rafting company for a while, too, didn't you babe?"

Babe.

Cash cut the tension by telling some stories about the kind of tourist who would come to the river completely unprepared for the adventure. How they lost themselves, and were shocked when the boat would bounce them into the river. He told us one completely sobering story about how they almost lost someone who got stuck *under* the boat. Then Garrett piped up about a documentary he was working on, his first acquisition, about the history of mountaineering on Everest. "They've even got Peter Hillary and Jon Krakauer as talking heads. Do you know how much garbage is on the mountain? They've got expeditions to clean it up. The world's most dangerous garbage collection."

"We were going to go to base camp," Jen said. "Now you're making videos instead of doing the thing. You know what, Kelly? Pass me the white."

I could read the look on Garrett's face. One part anger, the other embarrassment. I passed the bottle down the table. Jen was on Rob's right, Garrett on his left. He looked down the table at me with an expression I could easily read as *what the absolute fuck is going on* and *who are these people?*

"You were," Marianne interjected, "going to go to base camp after university, I remember that now."

Marianne was the least socially cognizant person I think I've ever known. She was sitting to my right, Cash on my left. He was on his third plate of food and was surprisingly fun to talk to; my go-to party question of apocalypse survival was enthusiastically received. Turns out he had a whole escape plan mapped out, which even rivaled mine and Meghan's.

"Okay, so fight or flee? What would you do in a zombie apocalypse?"

"Not this again," Rob said, his voice light.

"Not you," I teased. "I already know your plans."

"Which are?" Cash asked.

"He's going on foot to his cottage. We've been arguing for years about the ability of zombies to survive underwater."

"They absolutely can," Garrett said.

"They absolutely can't," Jen added.

"Oh, a debate!" Cash laughed. "They don't breathe, man."

"But they are still skin and bones," Jen argued, her face flushed from the wine. She must be a cheap drunk because she'd barely had half a glass. "Which would get waterlogged, and they'd simply expand. The water would rot them away."

"You can't win against water," Rob said.

"They'd simply walk along the bottom of the lake and then pop out the other side," Garrett argued.

"Exactly!" I said. "See, Garrett gets it."

"Of course he does," Jen said.

Rob tried to steer the conversation back to lighthearted. "You are all welcome at our cottage if the zombies do hit."

"Except we'd all probably starve," I joked. "Because neither of us know how to forage or garden."

Cash added, "I've got you both covered."

Garrett looked at Jen, tried to get her to meet his eyes, soften whatever was between them and turn the night around. That moment, that small, teeny instant—it tied up everything you could know about them. They lived in each other. They were each other. I couldn't compete with that.

My wine glass was empty. I filled it up.

Rob stood up. "Phew, that dish is hot! I hit a pocket of spice, my mouth is on fire Anyone else need water? Kelly?"

"I'm fine, thanks." I was pushing the food around on my plate, nibbling every now and again on a piece of naan.

Rob brought a pitcher of water to the table as the conversation drifted to families and Christmas. He poured a glass of water and set it down in front of me. I gave him a look, and he raised his eyebrows. I took an obligatory sip.

Marianne told a story about how her father would pick their tree, the one that "spoke" to him after meditating in the woods. "It was quite simply the best symbol a girl could have growing up. It defined not just the season but what it meant to be home, knowing that he spent that much time picking a tree to cull from our property."

Cash explained how, being Jewish, he judged the season by the quality of the movies in the theaters, and how they'd sometimes see three in a row on Christmas Day, to stay out of the house.

"My mother packed an amazing picnic. To this day, I have no idea how she'd get soup and crackers and rock-hard toast into the theater, or how we didn't make an absolute mess eating it."

The amount of wine I had had caught up to me. The room wobbled. If I didn't get some fresh air, I might pass out headfirst in my curry. "I'm too full," I said. "I'm going to head out to the balcony for some air before dessert." The table tipped ever so slightly as I stood up.

Rob steadied it. "Grab a coat at least," he said.

I grabbed a bottle of wine instead.

The temperature was crisp, which made the chill brilliant. Standing outside on the tiny speck of concrete that posed as our balcony, I took deep breaths. *Rob. Rob. Rob*, I kept repeating in my head. *I'm going to marry Rob. Rob. Rob.*

The door slid open behind me and Garrett appeared. "Hey. It's intense in there. Marianne will not let the conversation slip to anyone else. She's gone from her perfect fucking holiday tree to some inane story about meeting Sarah McLachlan wearing rollerblades when she stopped in Banff during a tour."

"Marianne was on rollerblades?"

"No, Sarah McLachlan was, apparently, rolling up and down Banff Avenue decked out in knee pads but no helmet, her tour manager or band whatever holding her up. I can't believe I cared enough to remember that much detail."

As much as I didn't want to talk around what had happened in my living room, I couldn't *not* talk about it either.

"I don't know what to do." Garrett emptied his wine glass and set it down on our outside table. "Except get drunker."

I handed him the bottle in my hand and looked out toward the lake. As we stood there with the cold encircling us, Garrett said, "What happens now?"

He leaned against the railing on his forearms and pulled his hands into his sweatshirt sleeves. "I don't know what to say to her. Everything is wrong."

"How about: I love you, and, we'll work it out might be a good place to start."

"What if—"

"Nope. That's why I'm a publicist. I'm very good with good-sounding words."

"So, you're going to marry *that* guy?"

"So, you're moving back west with that girl?" I retorted.

"Touché."

I leaned in, resting slightly against him. "I'm swaying."

"No, Kelly," he said, "you're drunk. You know how to be drunk. Get it together. You've got another few hours of listening to Marianne and knowing that my life is in shambles to get through. We haven't even gotten to the messiest part of dessert, when all the shameful secrets come out and we start playing truth or dare, because you know Marianne's going to suggest it. It's her favorite party trick. I've been putting up with it since high school. And since we don't all know each other that well, it'll be carnage."

"We hit the truth on the head already tonight."

Garrett laughed. "We sure did."

"Plus, I need to be drunk to face the reality of my life."

"You know you can leave him anytime you want. What's next for me? My own fucking wedding? A baby? It's a whole life that I never expected to be leading. She knows this."

"Truth and dare," I mumbled.

"What?"

"I think I love you."

Garrett stood there without moving. It was as if the city stopped. The CN Tower refused to blink. The stars paused. The temperature dropped even lower. He said, "I know."

"Well, that's one answer."

"It's complicated."

"It's not. I leave him. You leave her. We leave together."

"You're not thinking straight, and I'm drunk, and you're drunk, and when we get back after the break, things will be normal and we can have lunch, and this night won't have happened, and you won't have told me what I already knew, and I won't have to break up with Jen, and you won't be marrying *that guy*, and we can pretend that we can just be friends, because that's the only way I can function."

"In complete and utter denial."

"In complete and utter denial."

I put my head on Garrett's shoulder. "We should go back inside."

"Just one more minute. I like the weight of your head there."
After a moment, I heard Marianne whoop with laughter and turned around to see Rob illuminated through the glass doors. My living room was bright and festive, but the look on his face was decidedly neither of those things. He had seen Garrett and me standing there, tangled up in one another, and did not look happy.

"We'd better get back inside," I said.

"In a minute," Garrett said. "I want to stand here with you imagining this is our place, and it's our future."

"This is crazy."

"One minute."

Turning away, I picked up the wine bottle from the snow-covered deck table and went back inside. I brushed by him—not facing it. Him. That was my strategy. The dining table was a mess, and so I picked up the used napkins, the empty containers, blew out the candles. I didn't want to do this anymore.

When I came back to the couch where everyone was sitting, Garrett was back inside.

"Marianne's suggesting we play a juvenile game of truth or dare," Rob said.

I burst out laughing, then crumbled into the couch with Garrett, and he caught me in his arms.

"What's so funny?" Rob asked.

"Nothing, really," I said.

"It's just a dumb inside joke. Marianne," I shouted, "we are not playing truth or dare. We are all almost thirty years old, some older—ahem—and if we're playing any parlor games, then my vote's for Apples to Apples."

Garrett giggled, snorted a bit, and spilled his wine on the couch.

Jen sat down beside him on the other side and said, "I'm getting tired. Would it be okay if we left soon?"

"Dessert!" I shouted. "You can't leave until you have dessert, and it's chocolate, and delicious."

The room swooped around me when I stood up, but it didn't matter. I was now on a mission to provide dessert to my guests, and nothing could stop me. Not even Rob gently pulling me away from the kitchen. Not even Marianne saying something about her dessert and Cash swearing off sugar, and didn't I want to serve her fruit-only apple crumble?

"I'm getting the dessert. And you guests can decide if you want to eat it."

I shook Rob off and clattered back to the table with a container of Christmas cookies from my mother's and ice cream, and then dropped them in the center of the table. "Look," I said, "I even have a proper scooper. And I have great form."

"No one wants any ice cream, Kelly," Rob said.

"I want some ice cream. Fuck you all if you don't."

"Kelly," Rob said quietly. "You need coffee, water, and no more booze; you don't need ice cream. It might be time for us all to call it a night."

"What's your fucking problem? It's ice cream. A dinner party deserves dessert. Even if it's already been ruined by—every time I turn around someone's moving on with their fucking life. Oh, marriage, oh, babies, oh, let's everyone be together and be *happy*. And then I'm the bad guy because I like things the way they are, and that's me not wanting to move on with my life. Yawn, fucking yawn."

I pulled out a chair, sat down, and began to eat the ice cream directly from the carton. "There, now it has my germs all over it. Kelly's contagious—ruining lives left right and center, and now, spoiling the dessert."

Jen didn't say a word as she walked past me. Garrett moved to join her. He kissed the top of my head. "Kelly, it's been a ride. Rob, thanks for dinner. I'll leave this mess to you both, and now, I'm going to dutifully go home and discuss my own."

Marianne and Cash were already by the front door, holding court with Jen, who seemed frail and tiny.

"Well, it's turned out like a family holiday anyway," I said. "Complete with the drunk one drowning her sorrows. Have a wonderful evening, everyone." I started to sing the Talking Heads. Because this was not a beautiful life.

The evening spiraled deep down into that place I went whenever I felt cornered. The tide of regret rose up like bile—every awful fight I'd ever had with my mother, with Rob. The result was always the same: a giant chasm in the road that was my life.

There were quiet murmurs as jackets were passed from the hallway closet to their owners. Rob apologized on my behalf and then locked the door once everyone had gone.

Garrett says not to marry him. But I *am* getting married.

Rob didn't say a word. Instead, he started picking up the plates, crashing around in the kitchen, rinsing, loading the dishwasher. I angled my anger in his direction, letting it drip like the melting ice cream, not knowing how to stop the words once they started.

"Way to back me up there!" I shouted. "As usual, when I need you, you're not there. When you want something to happen, it's a big fucking deal. Like a proposal for a marriage I never wanted, in the middle of Christmas with your hawk-eyed mother there to swoop in and tell me, yet again, that I don't deserve you. And, here I go, just proving it, didn't I? A big 'Oh, she's off again, Kelly's drunk and stupid, and it's all her fault the party got ruined.'"

Rob wiped down the table, and left me sitting there as he put the room back to normal.

"You're drunk," he said. "You're going to hate yourself tomorrow for the things you've said. For what you've done. How mean you were to that girl. She's not the kind of girl you go around hurting, Kelly. She's not like you. She seems kind, nice, and genuine."

"And I'm none of those things?"

"You're the opposite of those things when you're like this. I don't like it, but you won't remember that in the morning. You won't remember any of it in the morning."

"It's a good thing there are so many hours left in the night, since the party broke up so soon. There's plenty of time for me not to remember things."

"Enough," Rob said. "That's enough."

"I don't want to do this anymore," I said, my voice cracking.

"You don't want to do what anymore? Get so drunk that you embarrass me and all your friends? Make a fool out of yourself? Throw yourself at Garrett in front of me, in front of his *girlfriend*? Make a mockery of our life, like I mean nothing to you? Like it didn't take every ounce of my courage to get that fucking ring out, to convince my mother that you were worth a lifetime together, that I know you better than you know yourself, and that we'll have an amazing life if you could just open your stupid eyes and give it all a chance?"

"It's too hard."

"You make it hard!" he shouted. "It is the opposite of hard. All we have to do is love each other, and it's fine."

"No, it's only fine if I fall in line—it's not enough that we love each other, because everyone expects a next step. A giant wedding. A huge house in their neighborhood, on their dime, the life they see for you. A baby. Then another. Moving forward in some way. Everyone assumes that's what's going to keep us happy. Falling in line with what society expects, and then—"

"Kelly, there's nothing that says we have to get married the way my mother sees it. There's nothing that says we need to have babies. There's no pressure. I *want* to be married. I couldn't care less if we have a big wedding or if we go off and elope to a beach somewhere. I'm showing you that I need it in my life. The forever-ness of it. Serious. Adult."

"There's the rub."

"You"—he couldn't even get the words out right—"you need to figure it out. Be here if you want to be here. Go if you want to go, but stop telling me you love me and then making it painfully obvious that you would fuck that guy sideways if I wasn't looking. I'm going to bed. You're welcome to sleep out here."

"Fine."

I wish I could say I went after him to apologize. I wish I could say that he forgave me, and we spent the next day cuddled up, having great make-up sex all afternoon on that same couch where Garrett and I had collapsed in the drunken laughter that had proven to be the beginning of the end of the entire evening. But all I did was grab my BlackBerry, tugging the cord out of the wall so hard that I snapped back and bruised myself on the marble island that separated our kitchen from the dining room, and then stumbled back onto the couch.

Chapter 11

I DIDN'T WAKE UP on the couch but on top of various pairs of relatively expensive, now completely crushed shoes, with my mother standing over me. "For goodness' sake, get out of the closet. You aren't Sylvia Plath, and this isn't *The Bell Jar*, so stop being so bloody melodramatic. There's a perfectly good bed over there. Who passes out in the closet?"

My sister was here too. They must have used her spare keys. From the looks on their faces I knew it must be very early in the morning. I was sure that I looked terrible; I was more hungover than I had been in ages. I could feel the makeup caked on my face and gluing my eyelashes together as I tried to open my eyes fully.

I crawled out of the closet and felt my entire body swoosh to one side and then the other. "What are you doing here?"

"You called me," my sister said. "At three in the morning, bawling, because you had a terrible fight with Rob. You told me the whole thing was over, that you were over the barrel about Garrett. And then you asked me to get Mom to take you home today. So here we are. I called in sick to work."

"I don't need to go home, Mom. I'm sorry. I—" Standing up was proving near impossible, so I crawled over to the front end of the bed and leaned against it. "I had too much to drink."

"Obviously," my sister said, yawning. "Your place is a disaster.

There are bottles all over your kitchen that need to be rinsed out, and it smells like a curry house."

"It's not that bad," my mother said. "Your sister has a sensitive nose from being pregnant. I remember not being able to go anywhere near your diapers when I was pregnant with her. Oh, I threw up so much."

"We had that dinner party," I said as I pulled off first my tights and then the awful Spanx that had cut off my circulation. My stomach and legs had deep red welts where the elastic had bitten into them. The apartment was cold. Or maybe I was just shivering.

"You need a hot shower. Come on, get up." My mother bent down and tried to tug me upward, like I was a toddler unsteady on her feet. She eventually gave up and said, "I'm going to get you some comfortable clothes. If you aren't going to have a shower you at least need to get out of a dress that looks covered in sick."

"No." I needed to sleep. "Seriously, I'm fine. We had a fight. It'll be okay. I'm sorry I drunk dialed you, Meghan, and you really didn't need to call Mom. God, my head hurts."

"How much did you have to drink?" Meghan asked.

"I don't actually remember." I tried to swallow, but my spit was tacky and it stuck in my throat. "Bottles, plural. And I didn't eat anything. I'm pretty sure I had lunch, but I'm almost positive that I didn't eat much dinner. Did I at least throw up in the bathroom?"

"As far as I can tell. You don't smell too badly of puke," Meghan answered.

"Here." My mom handed me a pair of Rob's jogging pants and one of our old Queen's sweatshirts. "Put those on. I'm going to tidy up."

"What happened?" Meghan sat behind me on the bed, and I rested my head on her legs.

"My friends from work came as planned. Garrett was fighting

with his girlfriend, and then I think Rob and I broke up. There was drama. Rob thought I was acting ridiculous."

"You drink too much, Kelly," Meghan said.

"Tell me something I don't already regret. Can you get me a glass of water?"

"Yes. But then I think Mom's going to force you to come home for a bit to dry out. She may have already talked to Rob."

"She did what?"

"They had a long talk this morning about all kinds of things, and he said it'd be best if you went home for a few days to 'sort stuff out.' He told her he'd be at the gym after work, and for us to come and get you. He doesn't want you at home when he gets back."

"Oh god."

"Indeed." Meghan laughed. "When you screw up, you certainly don't do it any way but royally."

My mother returned with my old leather overnight bag in her hands. "I grabbed this from the front hall closet. Please, get some other clothes on. I am not taking you in the car smelling like that."

She started to tug at my dress but I batted her hands away. "For fuck's sake, Mother, I can dress myself."

"Don't swear at me. It's as if we're living that god-awful prom night all over again. Aren't you at least a decade older now? Have you learned nothing in your years on the earth?"

"It's nothing like that prom night. Everything's going to be fine. I don't need to leave. I need to sort stuff out with Rob. I'm sure I need to apologize."

"He doesn't want to hear it," my mother stated with a sense of finality that honestly scared me. "Pack a bag, and that is that. Let's go."

I threw my hands up into the air. "I can't fight you. I'll go take a shower. I'll put on those clothes. If we're leaving, then you pack. Please don't forget to pack me some underwear. You always forget something important when you're packing. Despite how much practice you've had."

My mother gave me a look that said *Too far. Don't push your luck.*

* * *

Hot. The shower had to be as hot as I could stand it. I was too woozy even to stand, so I sat down and let the steam swirl around me. What had I done? Bits and pieces were coming back to me. Drinking a bit more wine. Furiously typing *something* on my BlackBerry. Screaming at Rob, him going to bed, and me closing myself in our closet and crying. But I can't believe he left me here. I must have said some things that were truly unforgiveable. We'd never fought this much or this intensely before. And I was scared. But was I more scared of being on my own or being without Rob? If I was honest with myself, I didn't know.

The bathroom was steamy, which made my stomach even more queasy. Wiping the condensation away with a towel, I took a good hard look at myself. Black mascara was mixed with the bags under my eyes. My complexion was pale, paler than normal. And my eyes were dull. My highlights needed a touch-up, and my hair needed a good trim. What my life needed right now was that makeover montage in every rom-com I'd ever watched with Meghan.

"We're leaving in five minutes, Kelly," my mother shouted. "Hurry up. I'm going to make you some coffee."

As I stepped out of the bathroom, Meghan came into the bedroom. "Is she ever mad at you," she said. "You probably didn't need that crack about packing."

"No, probably not." I collapsed onto my bed and immediately felt that all-too-familiar day-after dizziness spread from one end of my body to the other. "I'm going to be sick."

"Try to make it to the bathroom, at least. If you start puking, I am for sure going to start puking too."

I did make it to the bathroom and managed to vomit the bilious contents of my stomach into the toilet without much mess. I splashed cold water on my face and changed into the clothes my mother had handed me. By the time I got out of the bathroom, she and my sister had their coats on and were waiting by the front door with my bag.

"I need a minute," I said. "Is Rob really not going to at least be here to say good-bye? You're sure he doesn't want to talk to me, like, at all?"

"Not at all," my mother confirmed. "You have one minute to write a note. We'll be in the car, with the engine running. You'll be responsible for ruining the earth if you don't get your ass downstairs."

The ice cream from last night had melted into a sad, sticky puddle all over our dining-room table. It smelled old and off. Rob was right about everything. I felt like the most horrible person in the world. I let the water in the kitchen sink run as hot as it went, filled a bowl, and found a sponge. Without rubber gloves, I plunged the sponge into the hot water and wiped down the table until there was no more evidence of last night—on that surface, anyway—and then I went down to join my family, waiting for me in the car. My mother silently handed me a cup of coffee in a travel mug, and I burst into tears for the second time in three days. I don't know if I'd ever cried this much in all my twenty-eight years of being alive.

* * *

My mother drove carefully out onto Queen Street and through the neighborhoods in relative peace and quiet until we turned off Spadina to get on the highway, the quickest way back to Etobicoke.

The car was too silent. My mother was brewing, like a rich cup of tea, and it wouldn't be long before she poured out her opinions.

"This is an intervention," my mother said. I burrowed deep down into my coat in the backseat, wiped my eyes, and attempted to concentrate on the radio show playing on the CBC. My sister, who was sitting up front in her giant, puffy down coat, was trying very hard not to giggle.

"What do you mean, intervention? Did I suddenly pick up a heroin habit over the holidays? You've been watching too much A&E, Mother. Did you and Carl watch some sort of twenty-four-hour supermarathon once all the festivities were finished?"

"This is a you are ruining your life intervention. Mooning over some man you work with, ignoring your—ahem—fiancé, shitting all over your perfectly good job? You need to get it together, Kelly. You're drinking too much, and you look sallow and depressed. So, intervention."

"I do not look sallow and depressed."

My mother glared at me in the rearview mirror. "Yes, you do."

"I do not."

My sister put her hands up. They brushed against the roof of my mother's hatchback. "Enough!"

"You're going to lose everything at this rate," my mother said. "Is it worth it?"

"First of all, Meghan, I'm going to kill you for telling Mom about Garrett. Second of all, I'm an adult, and it's all mine to lose. And third of all—is that even a saying? Whatever—kidnapping me from my home isn't going to help me fix what I've screwed up."

Judging from the way she was gripping the steering wheel tightly through her black leather gloves and pursing her lips, my mother wasn't buying it. "You can't string Rob along if you don't want to be with him. Look, the last thing you'd ever want from me is advice, I know that—"

"Doesn't stop you from giving it."

"Don't interrupt me, Kelly. So help me, I'll pull over on Lake Shore and leave you by the side of the road like the ladies of the night who work this stretch."

"Mother!" Meghan cried.

"I'm serious." My mother continued her tirade, "You've been with him for ages. We adore him. The first time you brought him home I told Carl I thought he was a lovely boy with such nice manners and clean collars. And he's grown into a wonderful man with a steady job and an exacting sense of what he wants from the world. And as Rob's found himself, grown successful, and, well, grown up, I've been watching you wither away.

"You moved into that sterile condo. You've turned pale. You seem stuck in that job, and you're not making any moves to try to find something else. *Pale.* You've been telling me for ages you're going to finish your film classes, and it's really not about the debt anymore, you're not motivated. *Pale.* I realize it's not a particularly good metaphor but you are colorful Kelly—you do not have the washed-out beige personality I see when you describe what you're doing.

"Now you're mooning over this Garrett fellow, which is the worst kind of affair—trust me, I've been there. And I keep thinking that you just need to time to sit and think, to make up your mind. You need to stew in your juices for a while. The boys have gone back to school early. Carl is off at his annual work retreat in Niagara Falls until New Year's Eve. And you and I are going to hash this out once and for all. I'm going to sort you out whether you like it or not."

There was no arguing with my mother when she had her mind set on mothering. I stared out the window as wet snow smashed up against it, and I realized that I hated the fact that she was right. I didn't know what I was doing. I didn't know what I wanted to do. I hadn't even admitted to myself that things were so off course with Rob that I didn't know how to correct anything.

"This isn't about me being right, and people getting hurt when you ruin things," my mother said, softening a bit. "You can't solve your problems by being so awful that other people take action instead of you. There's no reason for you to stay on a course that's not making you happy."

"Things might not be perfect right now, but overall, I'm not unhappy, Mother. Maybe I'm a little unsatisfied, but who isn't at my age?"

"You're stranded. We're your lifeboat. You need to leap off the ship. It's sinking."

"Dear god, Mother," Meghan said. "All the self-help metaphors, interventions, and lifeboats—make sure you throw her an oar so she can paddle up to shore once in a while for a conversation that won't have her rolling her eyes and not taking you seriously."

That did it. The tension broke despite everything, and then we settled into silence cut by the CBC that drifted along until we got home. Meghan said she would walk home, and I surrendered to the "intervention," which, for the moment, meant grilled cheese sandwiches and Campbell's tomato soup. I couldn't remember when, in the past few days, I'd had a better meal.

"So." My mother handed me a chocolate chip cookie. "Tell me what's going on. Start at the beginning. No, tell it to me straight: Are you having an affair?"

"No, don't be ridiculous, nothing's happened. Nothing will happen. Garrett is a friend. I'll admit my feelings for him are out of control, but I've hurt Rob's feelings enough. I have to make this better. I love Rob."

"I'm not sure you do, darling."

I reached over to brush away a light dusting of crumbs on my mother's chin, and she continued thoughtfully. "You've got psychological scarring from all the back and forth growing up. I know your father was, and continues to be, ridiculous, but you can't tie yourself into a serious relationship you don't want to be in just because you don't want to end up like me, bouncing around until I was in my late thirties, and then finally finding the one. You can't spit shine Rob and turn him into the one. It's okay not to be together forever. It's okay if you never want to get married. It's okay if you never want to have kids. I'm sorry if I ever made you feel like you had to conform to any of those ideals."

"It's not about conforming, it's really not," I replied, taking a sip of hot tea. "I want to want to marry him. I want to want to have kids. I want to want all of it, but deep down there's a quagmire of doubt about everything. I can't put my finger on it. And Garrett's just there. He's funny and smart, and we have so much in common, and Rob's so busy, I don't know. Garrett is like a raw energy I can't stop. I find myself doing stupid things, wearing too-short skirts and getting too comfortable."

"Men and women can't be friends."

"Oh, they can. But not with Garrett. I think I love him."

"Absolutely not."

"What do you mean, 'absolutely not'?"

"You're projecting."

"Projecting what?"

"What's lacking. More precisely, what you see Rob as lacking— that artistic, romantic, Byronesque shit that drives you crazy. This Garrett has all of it. The question isn't whether you think you love him. More to the point, it's why are you thinking about it at all? If you were happy with Rob, a crush would stay a crush. It would not end up with you a soppy mess in the bottom of your closet, letting your face turn the shape of your shoes."

Sometimes, it was impossible to get a word in edgewise with my mother. She was opinionated. She was stubborn. She was smart and sassy. But she was always right.

My mother kicked off her shoes and started to rub her foot.

I could hear her nylons rustling, her toes cracking. "There's nothing worse than being shocked into a relationship. You were shell-shocked at that university of yours. You stuck to Rob because on some level, you knew he'd never leave you."

"Oh, he's probably left me."

"What if you went home, confessed, and told him the truth, Kelly? The real truth? The whats-its swirling around, how terrified you are of the realness of this whole engagement, of marriage, of children? I'm convinced he'd want to work it out." She put her foot down and switched to the other. "He'd wait until you made up your mind. But I'm convinced you don't want to make up your mind. You want someone else to make it up for you—and that's not fair. You can't keep treating Rob like a fallback position when he's sleeping next to you in bed night after night."

I couldn't look at my mother, and she was waiting for me to meet her eyes. "First," she continued, "your hair is too blond. I don't like it on you."

"*Mother.*"

"Second, you need to figure out what you're doing at that job."

"I'm making a living."

"Third, you're drinking too much."

"Look, I had a bad night—it's embarrassing. It's approaching pathetic, but I don't need this intervention. It's the holidays. And I know you noticed, otherwise I wouldn't be here and you wouldn't be sitting there, but my relationship's a mess at the moment. How do I fix it? Can we concentrate on that?"

"You won't." My mother sighed. It was such a familiar response—she pursed her lips, squinted, sighed. These were all signs that she was less than impressed by whatever conversation we were having. Like I was missing the point. Maybe I was; maybe I needed to take a moment and think, deep down, about stopping my life right in its tracks and changing direction.

"What I meant to say is this: you *don't* fix it, Kelly," my mother said again. "You get out and move on. Stay here for a while. Then start again. Don't wait another five years, ten years, until after you've got two kids and the relationships hasn't worked in a couple of years—because, tell me, is he going to be the one to stay home? You're not trapped now. You just feel like you are."

"I don't think I feel trapped."

"You wouldn't be acting this way if you didn't feel trapped."

"Not trapped. Foolish, maybe, expecting to run away with Garrett." My mother was about to say something. "Don't," I said. "Don't bring up the whole people always say and act the truth when they're drinking crap."

The look my mother gave me could have stopped a clock dead. "You're using alcohol as therapy, as an escape, and it's not healthy. I know you can't hear me sometimes. Or you just stop listening. But your father—"

"I'm not my father. I don't even know my father, how can I be anything like him?"

"Sweetheart." My mother's tone softened. "I don't want to raise old ghosts or talk about the emotional implications of your father leaving us so early. It's not something that you've ever dealt with—you think that you have dealt with it by pushing it all down and being strong and making your way in the world. But hear me out.

"The minute that the going got tough—and trust me when I say that it was tough with two kids under the age of three, no money, and no support from either of our parents—your father checked out. Eventually, he left, but for an entire year before he decided to go, he was already gone. Drunk all the time. Lazy. Absolutely no help with either of you. I don't just mean changing a diaper or letting me take a nap, which would have been nice, but the way-down-deep stuff that makes a relationship work. The connecting tissues of it all. He gave up. And that was worse. The giving up months were so much harder than after he left. Because at least once he was gone, I knew what I was dealing with."

My eyes welled up and my throat got tight; all the words that were always so quick to come to the tip of my tongue just disappeared as my mother continued.

"Call it what you will—trapped, stuck, unhappy—you've been giving up for the last year. I've been watching it happen and biting my tongue."

"This is biting your tongue?"

"You need to change your life, Kelly. That's the point. Change now, before you regret it."

Our conversation continued, the back and forth, my mother providing more and more examples and instructions about how to fix what was broken. I listened for a while, tuned out for some, sat at the kitchen table until I could barely feel my legs, drank tea, and when I was done, when I couldn't hear anymore, I laid my head on my arms. Without hesitation, my mother stroked my hair like I was three again, sitting in her lap, totally disappointed, bawling, because I had dropped my ice-cream cone in the sand at the park and the truck had already driven away. It was my earliest memory. The only thing that comforted me to this day was knowing that the minute I put my head down in front of my mother, she would stop whatever she was doing and move her hands up and down, back and forth, for hours, if I needed it.

"Everyone's having babies. Getting married. It's too adult for me. I'm not ready for it."

She carefully considered her words. "It's the idea that your life, along with the lives of so many people around you, has finally transitioned into proper adulthood. That's what's causing you so much anxiety. Maybe some of this has to do with the stress of worrying that when the baby arrives you and Meghan won't be so close anymore. You won't be able to drunk dial her at three a.m. when she's got a newborn. She'll be drowning in that baby for months and not be able to get to the surface."

"I'm so happy for Meghan, I am. But it's not what I want. I need you to know that."

"I promise I'll try to hear you better. And stop pressuring you. I know you're not Meghan."

"And if I don't want to *be* with Rob, how come I can't imagine being without him? The only way I'm holding it together right now is by not thinking about how badly I've hurt him."

"You'll either stay together or you won't. It's that simple. Rob's said it. I've said it. If Carl was here, he would say it."

"Every sensible part of my brain is screaming at me right now to go fix what I've broken. Not a single part of me can imagine that I might have broken it for a reason. I'm the worst person in the world."

The tears were unstoppable now.

"Oh, Kelly." My mother sighed. "You're hardly the worst person in the world. Maybe"—she paused—"you're the seventy-seventh."

And we both laughed. I would have bet that if I'd asked my mother to list the seventy-six she imagined were worse than me, she would have, if only to take my mind off of it all.

At that moment, I didn't feel my age. I didn't feel like an adult with a home and an almost husband. I didn't feel like someone who knew where she was going or what she was doing, who had her head on straight. My mother hadn't been kidding—she knew me so well.

"I need some proper sleep," I said, drying my eyes with a tea towel. "I need to curl up and sleep for a week."

"Spare room's all ready. Fresh sheets and all."

Carl and my mother had turned my bedroom into their spare room the minute I left for Queen's. The room was covered in various bits and pieces of my mother's projects—embroidery, sewing, odd bits of stuffing for crafts she was making for the baby, the pieces of what looked like the start of a beautiful mobile. My posters were long gone. My life had moved out and been packed up a decade ago. Anything that was not with me at the condo had been lost forever to the funeral march of impermanent housing.

Every now and again, I felt nostalgic for the concert shirts I'd bought at shows I still remembered attending. I wanted to pull out the photo albums filled with grainy pictures of blurry people at house parties that I had stuffed into the side drawer of my old desk alongside the odd earring or two and the liner notes from a Pogues CD that I didn't remember buying or being given.

When I left for Kingston, I had thought I was starting over, that I could be a different version of myself, and so I left so much behind—all the odds and ends of my teenage life that felt important, and now I looked around and remembered them, probably because I was now struggling to know who I was at all. If Rob and I broke up for good, for real—the thought of it was too hard to even imagine—I'd be back here for a while, living in my old room. Sleeping in my old bed. How could you do that and not feel like a complete failure? Could I stuff my clothes back into the drawers of a dusty old dresser and shake out the cobwebs of the life I thought I'd left behind?

Maybe I didn't want to be with Rob. Deep, deep down, so far down that I wasn't sure I could see the bottom, the well of my emotions was unable to comprehend the lowest I'd ever gone when it came to hurting someone, the most selfish, the most horrible, the most devastating things I'd ever been. I knew at some level that I didn't want to be back here in my room, mooning over him. I didn't want to hurt because Garrett was probably going to end up back on the West Coast with Jen. I didn't want to feel so deeply betrayed and rejected. If that was what I had done to Rob with Garrett, I wasn't sure how I could live with knowing I'd hurt someone who loved me so much.

But maybe my mother was right; I was still angry with my father. After all these years the pain of his abandonment still reverberated, was still a feedback loop ringing in my ears. My options right now were here or home. Did I want Rob—fully, completely? I didn't know. Maybe I'd just empty my bank account and disappear into the moors, like in those great shots of Austen as interpreted by Hollywood. The wind swept the heroine's problems away and she'd be left standing in front of the hero at the exact moment it threatened to rain.

Chapter 12

THE NEXT FEW days were a blur of wandering around my mother's house in jogging pants, trying desperately to avoid her whispering to Carl on the phone, worrying about me and the state of my relationship. Their phone rang but I didn't answer it. My BlackBerry was shockingly silent. I sent one quick note to Rob letting him know where I was and not to worry. But there was no way I could properly apologize for what had happened in a text message. I sent something simple but inadequate.

Please keep an open heart, and I will try to make this better.

He didn't reply.

The house was quiet with my stepbrothers back at school and Annie not dropping in every now and again. Carl was at his retreat, and my mother headed to the office the day following my intervention. I sat around their house feeling eighteen again, like I was skipping school to watch too much daytime TV and eat terrible food. Late-night talk shows were a distraction too. I could have talked to my sister or called Beth, but I didn't want to make the situation worse by talking it to death. Even going over what I remembered made my stomach revolt, tossing and turning like a ship at sea until I couldn't bear it and had to take something to make it settle. Other than the quick note to let him know where I was, I didn't call Rob. I desperately wanted to, though. I wanted to prove to him that I was worthy of this life for us that he was working toward by making some grand gesture—a surprise wedding at city hall? A last-minute beach vacation where we could wash away all our sins during the day and then eat them up again at the buffet table in the evening? Nothing rang true, so I lay around convincing myself that if I just let the situation air out the stain might lift, and then everything would be back to normal.

And then it was New Year's Eve proper—Beth's big party night. I couldn't avoid my life any longer. I had to go home and then head over to help her at the venue. My mother spent much of the day calling me and begging me not go, to just call in sick. But I had promised Beth, and I couldn't let her down. Nor did I want to hear what Siobhan might say if I dared skip out on the biggest party our department had ever thrown. My mother came home over lunch to find me packing clothes back into my duffel bag. She gave me a look.

"I have to go," I said.

"You don't have to," she said. "This is a crisis situation. Your life is falling apart. A party doesn't mean anything."

"I can't let Beth down," I said. "Regardless of the shambles my life is in, I can't make a shambles of this for her—her career is on the line. If this goes off without a hitch, she gets a great promotion. I don't want to be the reason something else goes wrong."

The tears fell. My mother rushed to me and held me tight, wrapping her arms around me as she'd done countless times. "You haven't made a mess; you've made a mistake. All of this was born out of you not wanting to hurt someone you love; it's just bubbled to the surface in the worst way possible."

"Way to make me feel better, Mother." I laughed as I pulled away from her and grabbed a tissue to wipe my eyes and nose. "Okay, I think I've got everything. Who knows? I might be back tomorrow if Rob's kicked me out for good."

"The end of a relationship is not the end of the world. If I've taught you anything—"

"You've taught me that. Trial and errored that one to death, I believe, my darling mater."

"Kelly . . ."

"Mother . . ."

"I'll call you tomorrow from wherever I land," I said, heading down the stairs.

"Tonight!" my mother shouted after me. "Call me tonight!"

* * *

Luckily for me, the TTC worked in my favor. As I opened the condo door, I was terrified of running into Rob. I knew he'd be at work until at least the early afternoon, so I had an hour to shower, grab my dress, and head off again to meet Beth downtown. My role tonight was support, plain and simple: to keep people organized and on track, to make sure the decorations were up, to check off the guest lists, and do anything else she needed.

The apartment was almost exactly as I had left it. Our tree was still up. Unlit, it looked out of place, like it had realized that the season had come to an end and no one needed it to be festive any longer. Heading into our bedroom, I couldn't help but notice that our bed was impeccably made—crisp white sheets, pillows placed exactly right—as if Rob hadn't even slept there either. I didn't want to think about it. Shower, hair, makeup—the routine was second nature, and I had it down to an art form. Pulling out an old garment bag of Rob's, I tossed my shoes into the bottom and then zipped it up around my dress.

Halfway out the door, I changed my mind and stopped to leave Rob a note.

Heading out to Beth's gig. I hope you have a good New Year's with the boys. I hope I can see you late, late, late for the midnight kiss that I'll miss. Sorry doesn't even begin to make up for what happened. A note isn't enough.

Outside, on Queen Street, I was lucky enough to find a cab—a miracle on New Year's Eve. A part of me was relieved not to have seen Rob. Relieved not to have had to find the words I wasn't even sure were there yet. Relieved not to have had to explain how I was feeling or not feeling—that might have been the most honest way to describe the mess that was in my mind.

Scanning my messages, I saw that Beth had already sent me a handful of texts worrying about the details of the party. I sent one blanket reply letting her know I'd be there in about fifteen minutes if the cab cooperated. We were good at our jobs. I had confidence that all our hard work and preparations would pay off.

Our high-profile guests were scheduled to arrive at nine or shortly thereafter, making an entrance along a red carpet set up at the Bloor Street entrance of the Royal Ontario Museum. Their personal publicists and managers had all confirmed, and many of them were having dinner beforehand with Siobhan and other senior members of our company.

I could feel the city slowly waking up to the excitement of the biggest night of the year. People were scattered around the sidewalks already, heading to early dinner reservations or racing home to get ready for a party at a friend's. Ever since I'd gotten together with Rob, New Year's had been my favorite holiday. With the stress of Christmas finally over, I could leave it all behind. We'd head out to dinner and a show. Sometimes we'd celebrate intimately, just the two of us at home with a bottle of champagne and a great film that he would do his best to enjoy for my sake. Some of my fondest memories were of us packed into the Horseshoe with hundreds of other people, dancing like mad to a great band. The focus and energy of a New Year's party were addictive; everyone rode the crest of good fortune to make it to another year. Every minute was filled with the potential of the new year, not bogged down by failed resolutions or the stress of the everyday workweek.

By the time I arrived at the museum, the velvet ropes were already up, and the carpet was already down. The weather had held; it was cold but not snowing. I crossed my fingers that it would stay like that, saving our shoes and ensuring a full house.

Beth was upstairs where the restaurant was, holding court. The room had an amazing view of the city from inside the Crystal, the bizarre-looking section of the building that jutted out of the older architecture like a massive, windowed Rubik's Cube. The venue was close to the office, and we threw a lot of parties there, especially when we needed to impress our American counterparts and make a statement to the industry. Beth was looking over a clipboard, surrounded by some of our co-workers. She looked calm and in control, and just seeing her made me want to burst into tears. Marianne was nowhere to be seen. I was so relieved I didn't have to face her just yet.

"What can I do?" I asked, approaching Beth.

She threw her arms around me and clutched me and the clipboard tight together. "I am so happy you're here. It's been a nightmare. The food's behind—the kitchen couldn't get in until an hour ago—so we're having cold hors d'oeuvres to start, and the signage was all wrong, so I had to have one of the juniors head back to the office to quickly print up some new ones that look terrible but will have to do, and—"

"What can I do?" I repeated, laughing. "It's all going to be fine. We've got three hours. Have you had anything to eat?"

"Not hungry."

"That's what I'm going to do first—let me stash my stuff and then I'll head across the street and get a couple of burritos."

"Just hearing the word burrito makes me nervous—last thing I need tonight is to be gassy."

"Gassy?" I said.

"Gassy."

"But so delicious." I nudged Beth gently with my hip. "You need to eat or this night will wear you down completely."

She sighed and conceded. "I need a burrito."

"Yes, you do."

"Hey!" Beth shouted over at one of our assistants. "Don't stack those glasses there—there's no champagne flute tower tonight. Please, get some trays and sort it out in the kitchen. We'll serve champagne at quarter to twelve and no sooner—I don't want people mistaking this for a wedding reception circa 1985." She rolled her eyes at me. "How can they be so inexperienced?"

"They're young. We were once too."

"You're too kind." Beth pushed her hair off her forehead. "Fuck, they'd better get the climate under control in here. If it's this hot right now, it'll be a sauna by the time everyone gets here."

"I'm going to dump my stuff. I'll be ten minutes, and then you need to eat. You're getting hangry."

"I'm not—holy shit, is that an *ice sculpture*?"

I left Beth to deal with the massive unwanted ice sculpture that someone from the museum had just rolled out of the elevator. I narrowly avoided Marianne squeaking into the room behind it and the delivery guy. She was busy giving him directions about where to put the sculpture, while Beth was trying to send them both back downstairs, convinced they had confused the order with another event taking place on the lower floors that evening, some sort of hospital fundraiser. Finally, Beth shouted, "Marianne, *listen to what I am saying*. We did not order an ice sculpture; it's not something Siobhan approved last minute. You do not know what's going on, so please shut the hell up for once and let me do my job."

Beth turned to the delivery guy, who wore a cute smirk on his face. "Please take it downstairs. There's another party in the main area of the museum, some benefit—this feels very benefit-y to me."

Safe in the elevator without Marianne spotting me, I tapped my toes and wondered if getting stuck in it wouldn't be the best way to spend tonight. Eventually, she would find me. Eventually, she'd give me a piece of her mind. Eventually, I'd have to tell Beth the whole sordid story of the past few days. I desperately wanted to talk to Rob at that moment, but I couldn't bring myself to call him.

Our favorite burrito place was jammed with people filling their stomachs with delicious beans and cheese before heading out and pummeling themselves with gin and juice. I was standing there, checking my phone, when someone behind me said, "Hungry?"

"Pardon me?"

"I asked if you were hungry." It took me a minute to place him now that he was out of his suit and dressed down in jeans and Adidas. It was the winker from the streetcar that day after our work party. His hair lacked product, and he seemed less put together, but it was him.

"Oh, hey, um, yeah, I'm just picking up something for me and a friend. We're running an event across the street tonight."

"In the cube? I saw the carpet and wondered."

"Yes," I replied, "in the cube."

I desperately wanted to turn back around and avoid making conversation with this person. There were four people in front of me, though, so there was no way out of it.

"Room on the guest list for one more?" he asked.

"What, you're telling me you haven't got at least three ladies queued up and six clubs to hit tonight? It's the biggest party night of the year."

He laughed. "I'm lying low. I was visiting my dad. He lives in a building around the corner."

"Burritos to go for both of you? A dinner fit for two bachelors, am I right?"

He laughed again. "Something like that. This party, you'll be there?"

"Wasn't that implied by the 'running it' part of me explaining why I'm here?"

"Right."

Two more people ahead of me in line.

"So, maybe I should know your name if we're going to keep running into each other," he said.

"Kelly."

"Evan." He held out his hand. "Nice to meet you." It was cold but not clammy, and his handshake was stronger than I had thought it would be.

"Nice to meet you too."

"Think I could get on that guest list?"

"Um, sure, I'll make a note. Last name?"

"Crawford."

Finally, the line moved up, and it was my turn to order. I turned my attention to the person behind the counter, hoping I wouldn't have to answer any more awkward questions or field any more requests to attend a party at which I would already be trying to apologize to Garrett, Jen (if she even came), and Marianne without also having to fend off some fellow I couldn't stop running into whose name I now knew was Evan.

* * *

Where was Rob? In that instant between ordering and standing there waiting to tell the burrito guy which toppings I wanted, the tears swelled in my eyes, *again*. I couldn't believe how badly I'd messed everything up. I'd left the ring at home. The ring would have explained everything to this Evan character without me having to say a word. I felt Evan kick me gently on the side of my foot. "Move it along there, Kelly. Some of us need extra cheese and guac for tonight."

"Sorry, miles away."

"I could see that."

The burritos were now at least being grilled, and I was about three minutes away from being free of this situation and this conversation. "Fight with my boyfriend," I said.

"Ahh, the stress of the decision about what to do tonight. Many a relationship can't weather that storm."

I laughed despite myself. "You're right, we're over because he couldn't stand to come to my stuffy corporate party, and he's going off the rails with the boys tonight."

The server called my order number. "Thirty-six?"

"That's my order," I said to Evan. "I'll drop you on the guest list, Evan Crawford, but I can guarantee you'll find something better to do between now and finishing your meal."

"I'll see you later, Kelly. Wait, Kelly what?"

I shrugged as I grabbed my food and slipped past him. "Just Kelly, for now."

* * *

Beth devoured the burrito in about five bites and was wiping refried beans off her chin before I'd even finished half of mine. "Sure, you weren't hungry," I said. "You swooped on that like a seagull on a fry at the beach."

"Squawk. That was *delicious*." She took a deep breath and crumpled the wax paper into a ball. "What is up with you? You look terrible."

"I don't look terrible. The lighting in here is bad—people always look worse at the beginning of a party, before they turn the lights down. Come to think of it, it's almost as bad as people look at the end, when they turn the lights up."

"You're dancing pretty hard there, Kelly."

"I know." I took another bite. "I don't want to confess. It's all too awful."

"We're going to get pretty busy in about fifteen minutes, so you had better spill now."

"I got engaged. On Christmas Eve, in front of Rob's parents when he gave me an antique ring worth more than my postsecondary education. Oh, and then his mother gave me this watch that's also so far above my pay grade that I'm not even comfortable looking at it, let alone wearing it. The dinner party was a complete disaster; I got drunk and hit on Garrett in front of his girlfriend; Rob exploded, rightfully; I told him he was pretty much pathetic for even staying with me; then I drunk dialed my mother and sister, who performed an intervention the next day, basically locking me up in Etobicoke, with very little booze and a *lot* of lecturing, until today."

Beth looked at me for a long moment. "Wow." Pause. "Sounds about right for you."

"I'd have been surprised if it had turned out any other way."

"The minute Marianne misunderstood her invitation," Beth said, "I had a feeling something might go wrong—but wrong like you finally telling her off for doing aerobics at work, not like, oh, I don't know, you *getting engaged* and *freaking out*." She reached across the table and grabbed my hands. "Seriously, you hit on Garrett in front of his *girlfriend?*"

She continued, "Kelly, the rules about work boyfriends are terrifically clear—they are not and never will be *real* boyfriends."

I nodded, mouth full. Another assistant wandered up to us and asked where the coat racks should go. Someone had called to say the racks were on their way up. I looked up at the assistant and pointed to the COAT CHECK sign that Beth had put up in the cubby-slash-hallway one flight of stairs down to the left of the elevator. "Over there."

"That makes sense," she said and wandered away.

"If only they would use their eyes before their mouths," I said. "They just like wearing the walkie-talkies."

"You're changing the subject."

"I know, but it was utterly rotten. I don't know what happened. No, I'm lying, I know exactly what happened. Rob made a perfectly reasonable request that I consider getting married. We've been together for years, it makes sense. Only it doesn't make sense to me—at least, I don't think it's what I want. And I love him, so much, but now I think I've ruined the best thing that ever happened in my life. I'll never have my two-weddings wedding like you."

"You're changing the subject again. We aren't talking about me. Are you sure you're okay? I can manage tonight if you need to go."

"I'm not okay, no. But there are bigger things to worry about. I'm not abandoning you at this party. I'll find a way to have a serious conversation with Rob that may or may not end our relationship. And on that note—it's time I got changed."

Beth looked at her watch, which was giant on her thin, pale arm. "We still have a few minutes."

"There's not a lot more to say. I haven't talked to Rob since my mother took me home, and I'm not sure what's going to happen tomorrow. I might end up on your couch for the next month until I can find a new place to live."

"It's not going to come to that," Beth said.

I shrugged. "It might."

The coat-check assistant was back now, wondering if Beth had a schedule for all the guests arriving so she could make sure there was enough room for their coats on the rack.

Beth had a perfect look of disdain, and stood up. "If we run out of coat racks, we can call downstairs for more. There are always more coat racks. Counting coats before they arrive might not be the best use of your time. Have you checked to see if you have enough change? It's two dollars a coat, and all the money is going to the talent's inner-city charity for sustainable housing, so we need to be careful collecting the change. Do you even have the cash box?"

The intern looked shell-shocked. "Um, no?"

"No, you don't have the cash box or no, you haven't checked it?" Beth asked.

"Neither? Both?"

Beth took a deep breath and turned her attention back to me. "This conversation is not over."

"Go deal with the situation. I'm going to get changed and then get the greeters downstairs organized for the early birds. Oh, and I need to add someone to the list—Evan Crawford."

"Who is Evan Crawford?" Beth asked.

The lie escaped my lips so easily. "I got a text from Siobhan, he's a friend of hers—decided to come at the last minute."

What in the world was going on with me, lying to my friend, talking up strangers while in line for burritos, and not speaking to the man who had loved me for the better part of the last ten years?

Loud noise crackled through the speakers, and Beth looked like she would pass out. "I'll fix it," I said to her. "It's going to be fine."

I wished I believed myself when I said those words. And then there she was, standing right in front of me wearing a bandage dress and insane heels: Marianne.

"You're a bitch," she said. "You know?"

"Not right now, Marianne. I've got to get the sound check under control, then organize the greeters downstairs, then get changed. You look great, by the way."

"Don't butter me up, Kelly," she said as I stepped around her. "It's not going to work. You'll get a piece of my mind tonight."

"I don't doubt it. I don't—I'm happy to stand in front of you for a dressing-down, or whatever you plan to say to me. I deserve it. But right now, I've got things to do."

In my head I was screaming "Whatever," and snapping my fingers in a blah-blah-blah motion. *Like you've never made a mistake, Marianne. You're with a guy named Cash who is broke and seriously hits up the bong when you're not around. It was wafting off his coat. Wafting.* And then I resented myself for being so mean because I *was* terrible. The party *had* been a disaster. And ruining my friendship with Garrett was one thing, but breaking Rob's heart in the process, that was a sadness that felt unparalleled.

Without music to fill up the room, the entire venue felt too big, too alienating, akin to that moment at the end of the night when you're at a rock show and they turn the lights on. The magic evaporates into trash on the floor, sticky feet from all the spilled beer, and a prehangover because it's about an hour after last call. I found Beth wrestling with a giant banner celebrating the network and asked her when she wanted the DJ to start up, considering we were inching toward open doors, and I wanted the early birds to feel welcome.

Beth had hired young people who usually made their living as extras on film sets to fill out the club in case of an empty-venue emergency. They were always half starved and anxious, but they wore the best clothes they could afford on their shoestring budgets and they showed up early. They charged by the hour, sipped a maximum of two drinks (with the tickets we provided), and hovered around the venue trying to look like they fit in. I had a soft spot for these guests. I always tried to make them feel welcome, not just a part of the scenery. It wasn't an easy job, and acting was an even harder industry to break into. And we were the lower end of the spectrum; a party celebrating cable design-show stars was certainly not the Academy Awards.

"Sound check was good, the DJ's ready to go," I told Beth. "I have a feeling things will start closer to on time than not. The music's going to start up in a minute, okay?"

"Yes," Beth called down to me from atop a rickety-looking chair.

"Be careful, that chair doesn't look steady."

"Don't worry. I've got good balance, even in these shoes."

I laughed and went back to the DJ booth. At last, the music was a solid distraction. The whole atmosphere of the place lifted, and there was a nice, fluttery anticipation of a solid New Year's celebration and that it was all going to be worth it when the clock counted down to midnight and the VIPs smooched their way into the hearts of the masses.

* * *

The doors were open, the celebrity guests were roped off and ensconced in their proper place, having done their duty of introducing the party and each other to the giant crowd of fans, network guests, and advertising clients, and the place was packed. The turnout was even better than expected. I didn't doubt that Beth had worked hard in the weeks leading up the party, selling it to everyone on her contact list. She had called in every favor; anyone who owed her even the slightest bit of payback had been told to put aside their plans tonight so we could fill out the room. It was the most expensive event our company had ever put on, and even though I was busy running from one end of the building to the other, I felt pleased that we had pulled it off.

The jumbled mess of my mind was forgotten for a while; I had something to do every minute, whether it was supporting Beth, chasing down the junior staffers to make sure they were on top of the menial tasks, or keeping our valued special guests well lubricated so that anyone looking at them (especially the press snapping shots for *Toronto Life*) would see they were having a fabulous time. In between, I was guzzling as much water as I could manage without having to use the bathroom every five minutes. I'd decided to stay sober even though it *was* New Year's Eve, after all. I'd decided that the only drink I'd have tonight was the champagne at midnight.

Beth grabbed me as I walked by her on my way to the bathroom. "Siobhan has lost her evening bag."

"Like, someone took it?"

"She doesn't know. She thought she left it at her table when she went dancing, but it's not there now, and she wants to go, but her car keys are in it. You know the drill—she's asking us to find it for her."

"I want to give you a look right now that says exactly what I am thinking," I said. "Rolling my eyes doesn't seem quite enough."

Beth laughed. "I'm thinking the same thing. Can you get one of the juniors to look for it at the coat check? I'll bet she checked it and doesn't remember, sloppy drunk that she is."

"Every party, it's the same. I wonder if she's making out with the marketing director again."

"I hope not, mainly because her husband's here."

I raised my eyebrows. "He's usually so elusive, I thought he didn't exist. Okay, I'll go down myself and ask. Did she give you her ticket?"

Beth handed it over and waved to her favorite of the publicity assistants. The poor girl was tasked with looking under and on top of tables and chairs for the missing evening bag.

People were milling about on the stairway that led down to the coat check, which was a good sign. Tipsy couples were entwined, there was lots of laughter, raucous and jovial people were stumbling slightly but never falling—these were movie-perfect moments that made me feel proud of what Beth had accomplished. I was having a good time despite the events of the past few days crashing around in my mind. I was lucky that good New Year's Eve celebrations with Rob far, far outweighed the one truly horrible one I could remember.

* * *

The first New Year's that I had spent with Rob we went to a horrible house party way outside of the city, in a small town north of Toronto where Tanya lived. We slipped and slid all the way there in his car, with the snow barreling down and making me scared we'd crash at any moment. I was worried about getting there and equally worried about getting home. No, knowing that I probably *wouldn't* get home that night, I was worried about thinking up an excuse that my mother would believe. I didn't understand why we had to go all the way out of town to be together. There were New Year's parties all over the city that we could have crashed, or, better yet, have accepted invitations to. Instead, we ended up driving out of town in a snowstorm.

Rob had said, convincingly, "Tanya's friend's parents are in Florida. There'll be good drugs and soft beds. It'll be fun, trust me. There'll be a bunch of her high school friends there, who are cool. Like you, you know, not preppy. Not Queen's kids. You can talk shop. Plus," he added, squeezing my shoulders, "we can be together, properly, at midnight. A whole new start to the year."

I had told my mother that I'd be going out to spend New Year's at a local party, because if she had known we were going so far away and most likely not coming home until the next morning she might not have let me go—the weather was that bad.

When Rob picked me up I hadn't yet warmed up properly from a long walk I'd just taken along the lakeshore with my sister. I made him blast the heat, and he complained about it the whole way there.

We turned the music up too loud on the way out of town. Our singing along was more like shouting as the car sped along Highway 50.

We arrived early, and the party took forever to get going. Tanya
was three sheets to the wind, but it was good to see her. The house
was filled to the brim with people. An old-fashioned house party.
My high school friends and I were more the type to hit an indie rock
club than a house party, but I was trying my best to fit in. Sloan was
at least playing on the stereo. Still, I didn't have anyone except Rob
and Tanya to talk to, until I sat down on a plaid couch and someone
joined me. She had long, dark hair that was pin straight; she was rail
thin and gorgeous, her light-blue eyes were stunning, and she had
amazing cheekbones.

We ambled through a mildly friendly conversation for a while.
I could not understand how or why she would want to smell like
cake, but she did. And she was smart—I could tell from the kinds of
questions she asked and the disdain she expressed for what she didn't
like. Rob and Tanya were playing some stoner game of charades that
only they found funny—there was the similarity in their mannerisms,
their sense of humor—and it got me thinking about family traits hiding away in the corners of a person, and how Meghan and I were the
same, similar to each other in ways that only we would notice.

"I thought you'd look different," she said.

"I'm sorry? Different from what?"

"From this."

My expression, I'm sure, was confused. I didn't know her, but
how did she know me—and then it hit me. This was Carys, Rob's
ex-girlfriend.

"You're gorgeous," I said.

"Yeah, it makes you wonder, doesn't it?"

My heart stopped for a moment, and I stood up quickly. "Excuse
me, I'm going to find a drink."

I wandered around the house, away from the center of the party, and spent time poking around the rooms that were off limits by unspoken rule. Sat by myself in an unused office for a while and wondered if Rob had known she would be here. If he had known and hadn't told me because for sure I wouldn't have come. And when I finally ended up back in the living room, bored, I saw Rob sitting on the couch and Carys leaning over him, her hands on his knees. He was holding her hair away from her ear and saying something to her that was making them both laugh conspiratorially. I didn't need to know the details. He didn't see me. She did, but she didn't break away from him.

For a second, only one, I almost stepped forward and pulled them apart. In the next second, I had had enough. I went to find our coats and my bag. I took every last penny of the money Rob had in his wallet and walked out the door into the bitter air. We were in Bolton, a suburb off the main road, and I couldn't walk all the way back to Etobicoke. I found a convenience store still open, and they called me a cab. The driver took me to the subway for a flat fee, which turned out to be every dollar I had minus my subway fare, and I was okay with that. A calmness hovered underneath me—not staying was never something I had considered before. Shouting, tearing through my emotions like they were tissue paper and leaving the shreds at his feet, yes. Throwing anything to hand, sure. But calmly saying no and walking away, then finding a way home from a place I had never even wanted to come, was liberating.

I was home well before midnight. I slept well—really well—and woke up the next day to my mother's delicious waffles. She had made an amazing strawberry sauce from the berries she'd frozen during the summer and delicately put away for this New Year's Day, when Meghan and I devoured them without taking a breath.

"I thought you weren't coming home," Meghan whispered.

"The party wasn't what it was cracked up to be. I was bored so I came home. New Year's is so pointless."

Meghan punched me in the shoulder. "Bullshit. It's your favorite holiday. You still need to make your resolutions because it won't be a new year unless we have our one-to-one competition. I'm still ahead. I stuck with swimming this year, but you did not, I repeat, *not* excel at not losing your temper. Tell me what really happened."

"Nothing," I said. "I didn't want to be there."

I wanted to tell my sister that Rob had abandoned me midparty. But I also didn't want to tell her. Rob was the nice one. Rob didn't do things like that at parties. He called later in the morning, when he could be sure he wouldn't wake anyone up, wondering what happened, worried, concerned.

"I saw you," I said.

"I don't know what you're talking about, Kel, what's going on? You just took off. I couldn't find you, and I've been worried sick."

"I'm fine, I took a cab home. Look, I don't want to talk to you right now. I'll see you when we're both back in Kingston next week."

Rob cried when I finally told him how that night had made me feel. He promised nothing happened, and I told him it was okay if it did—they had history. *But you're my future*. And I'd felt that way for all this time. Like being his future made me safe. In the end it didn't, because people change and grow and evolve and adapt, even if you love each other.

Carys ended up transferring to Queen's. We had a few classes together, and one drunken night in fourth year, I ran into her at Alfie's. Her hair was shorter by then, but she still had those piercing eyes. Drunk but not sloppy—perhaps overly friendly—she apologized in her girlish way for being so mean that New Year's. She hadn't known me, and I hadn't known her, not really.

Rob had wandered over then, swaying slightly, his eyes glassy, his baseball cap askew. "Oh no—" he said.

"Don't worry. We're fine. Future me trusts you."

* * *

All these years later, maybe finally understanding that I needed to make a choice that could make me walk out into the cold night alone on New Year's. This time, though, the other woman in my life was Beth, and there was no way I would abandon her.

On my way down to see if I could find Siobhan's purse, my heel got stuck in the metal grating on the stairs. How ironic, the anti-trip-guard had tripped me up. When I righted myself, there was Garrett, holding out a hand to steady me.

"Hey," he said, "you all right?"

"Fine, thanks for the hand. Wait here, I have to see if Siobhan checked her purse. Beth sent me on a mission to find it. At a party like this we're all Siobhan's assistants."

Garrett nodded and stood off to the side, leaning against the red wall, his hoodie zipped up tight.

The intern working the coat check and I fumbled around for a minute and, miracle of miracles, Siobhan's clutch was there, tucked deep in the interior pocket of her vintage fur coat, which I pulled off the hanger and took with me.

"Come on upstairs with me while I get Siobhan sorted," I said. "And then we can talk. Or rather, I can apologize properly because I am so sorry. Is Jen not with you? I know she's probably not at all interested in talking to me, but I'd like to apologize to her anyway."

"Jen's at home." He didn't move, even though I had started up the stairs. He pulled at my arm. "She's packing now to go back to Vancouver for a bit, asked for some time off of work, time away from me—she doesn't know about anything right now."

And as we stood there on the stairs, happy people coming and going, I held him, as I had always wanted to. But what with everything that was happening, I knew he wasn't mine to want. There was sadness in every part of him as he leaned into me, and while he wasn't crying, he was heavy, weighted, pulled down in a way I had never seen him before. Garrett was the life of the party, always making light of every situation, trumping a punchline with something funnier, at ease with himself and with other people.

"I didn't realize how much I wanted out until it wasn't fair anymore," he said.

The right response would have been to tell them to try again. Now they knew what they wanted, it would be easier than breaking up. That he was strong and such a good person, and that they were so lucky to have each other. But the selfish part of me stood there, barely out of my own relationship, holding him.

"I didn't tell you at your house, I couldn't even admit it. But I feel the same way about you. But I'm such a mess," he said. "I can't go from one to the other. I can't jump from Jen to you, and we can't run away together."

"I know," I said as I pulled away, tucked his arm in mine. "Let's get you a stiff drink."

Relief washed over me as I realized that I hadn't ruined what I needed more than anything now—friendship. I managed to get Garrett a spot at an out of the way table in the VIP section so he could just sit and sip in peace the giant glass of scotch I left with him.

Then I noticed that Marianne had seen us. She stormed over, a hurricane of misspent energy and misunderstanding. I stood in her way before she could get to Garrett.

"You are pathetic," she said. "Simply pathetic. You're a selfish, self-centered whore who doesn't deserve him."

"Get it all out, Marianne. Say what you need to because it doesn't matter to me. All that matters is what he thinks of me, and that he knows my intentions are good. You can hurl all the words that you want at me, but right now I've got to get Siobhan's clutch back to her before Beth loses her shit. And then I'm going to sit and spend the rest of the night talking to Garrett, whether you like it or not."

Marianne elbowed past me, knocking me off balance slightly on her way to Garrett's table. Days ago, I would have raced after her, jealous of anyone else being around him without me, jealous of their history, their growing up together. Who knew that New Year's Eve could be a night of clarity and understanding? New beginnings, sure—but how about understanding your love life in one crystal-clear moment, just like when I had walked out of that party. When I had held Garrett in that hug, I had known, just known, that all my feelings for him were real, but they were also just another way of not dealing with what I *should* have been feeling for Rob.

"Oh my gawd, Kelly, you are simply the best," Siobhan said. She was sloppy drunk, and she threw her expensive coat on over just one half of her body; the rest hung down and dragged along the floor. Her ankles leaned dangerously over her shoes. Her husband looked annoyed and frustrated. He gave her a look, and she said, "All right, all right, we can go now, you giant stinking party pooper." Siobhan turned to me. "He's pissed because he had tickets for a rock concert tonight at the ACC, and I ruined everything again with my job. Yawn. But he doesn't understand how busy and important *I* am. I am. I am." And then she hiccupped. I couldn't believe it—it was picture perfect and so ridiculous.

"Have a nice evening, Siobhan. The party turned out amazing. People will be talking about its success for years, I know."

Siobhan's husband pulled her off me. I could see him speaking angrily to her as they left.

In an instant, I saw how ridiculously drunk and stupid I must have been at the company party a few weeks ago, how unprofessional I'd been acting. It was hard to be Siobhan; it was hard to want to be so successful. The pressure probably made it all worse and so much harder to hold it together. But this wasn't the answer—getting so drunk that you were hugging your staff and talking down to your husband, who was standing right next to you.

Maybe my mother was right; I needed to take my life more seriously. I hated that she was *always* so very right—not because she knew
everything, but because she knew *me*, and maybe that was worse.
I did need to take myself more seriously. Staying on a course that I was
obviously driving hard against, like walking against the wind when
you could easily just turn around, was me wasting my life.

"Love will always change the direction of your life," she had said
last week. "But make sure, in this case, that you aren't using it as an
escape hatch."

"Rob is not a bus I'm trying to jump out of!" I'd shouted.

"Are you sure?" she replied.

I did love Garrett, but I loved him in the context of this life,
of this job, of the wonderful gift of a life that Rob had given me.
Would I have loved him outside of that if it was just the two of us
watching bad TV in our pajamas and eating takeout every night
because we didn't like the same food as each other? I didn't know,
but he couldn't be my escape hatch either.

When I got back to the table, Marianne was sitting with Garrett,
who looked absolutely miserable. She glared at me as I sat down.
I just ignored her. Garrett turned toward me and said, "Why won't
she go away?"

Marianne pretended not to hear him and started chatting away
about what a great party it was and how she hadn't been expecting
him to show up. "Where's Jen?"

"Marianne," I said, leaning over Garrett, "please take a hint and
for once in your life, shut up. Go and do something useful." I picked
up my walkie-talkie and buzzed, "Beth, I've found the purse and
handed it over, but Marianne's looking for something to do. I'm
sending her your way."

"I don't know what she has over you, Garrett," Marianne said,
"but you're pathetic, and Jen deserves better than being treated this
way by you. And you—" she said, pointing at me.

"Marianne," Garrett said, "I've never liked you, not back home, not now, and especially not at this moment when you're talking that way to one of my closest friends. Kelly's not perfect. The other night got out of hand. But right now, I need her, and I don't need you. In fact, if I never see, hear, or talk to you again, it won't be too soon."

Stunned into silence, Marianne slipped out of the booth and headed over to where Beth was standing. I saw Beth look back at me and shook my head. I didn't need her to come over.

Garrett leaned back. "I need another drink."

"Yes."

"But I shouldn't have another drink."

"No."

"Can we make out? I've wanted to forever, and I'm afraid I'll never get the chance to kiss you," he said.

"No." I laughed. "I want to kiss you, too, but I don't know for sure if Rob's broken up with me, and I can't cheat on him. I've hurt him enough as it is."

"I'm not going back out west. I don't want to."

"You don't have to. It's all right to break up. It'll just be hard."

He considered this for a moment. "No, I can't lose my job. I'll never find another one, and I don't want to freelance."

"It'll sort itself out. We're young."

"Not that young. I'll be thirty next year."

"You sound like Meg Ryan."

"It's true."

"Guy thirty and girl thirty are two very different things. At least you have the start of a career."

"True."

And then we laughed. An honest-to-goodness things are going to be okay between us laugh.

Garrett said, "I feel like myself with you, all the time. I don't have to pretend."

"Maybe we're a little too comfortable with each other."

"I can't believe that, I really can't. It has to mean something."

"It does. Maybe it means we're each other's ladders to the other side."

"No." His eyes were red rimmed, glassy. "No. He's a good guy, he didn't deserve me slobbering all over you. But fuck, Kelly, those shoes, that dress. And then seeing you together in that place, all grown-up and shit with real furniture. I wanted to punch him so hard."

"We haven't spoken in days. Rob talked to my mom and told her to come and get me. He couldn't even face me."

"Wow."

"Yeah."

"Is it that bad?" Garrett downed the rest of his whiskey. "And is it wrong that knowing you almost might be broken up makes me feel a bit better?"

"You're terrible."

"I'm not terrible. I never cheated on Jen. You never cheated on Rob. It's not wrong to fall in love, Kelly."

"It's all just coming to a head. With my drunken confessions the other night, yours tonight. We're being selfish. They're good people. We're hurting them, and that's what I can't live with. I love him."

"You're breaking my heart," Garrett said. "But I get it."

I nudged him, shoulder to shoulder. "Rob's too good for me, I'd say. But all the ways we're different, our families and everything—it all adds up to me liking the security only because it gives me an excuse to fail before I've even tried to change."

"There's safety in numbers."

"There's safety in the number two, that's for sure."

"I do love you, Kelly."

"I know," I said. "And I've counted on that for far too long. In my mind, you were the solution to everything. If you didn't have a girlfriend. If I told you how I felt. If we weren't just friends, then my whole life would turn in the direction I wanted it to. But what I'm just figuring out is that *I* have to turn it that way. I can't expect Rob to do it, and I certainly can't expect you to do it."

"What happened in the last five days to make everything so fucked up?"

Garrett paid the waitress for his scotch and offered me a slug. I shook my head. "We figured out that we have to grow up."

"Had to happen sometime."

"It really did."

I laid my head on Garrett's shoulder and felt the familiar calm. I wasn't angry. I wasn't feeling guilty because I didn't have to hold it in any longer.

"Are we okay?" I asked. "I mean, are you okay?"

"We're okay." He squeezed my hand under the table and didn't let go. "I don't know if I'll make it without completely cracking up, but I have to at least try."

"What time is her flight?"

"Let's not get all Hollywood."

"If there was ever a time in your life for you to get 'Hollywood,' it would be now, when you haven't said a proper good-bye."

"Shit. When you put it that way."

"Is she leaving tonight?"

"She's trying to get on a WestJet red-eye."

"You need to go, like now, because it's already eleven, and you certainly don't want to be trying to get a cab after the bells have chimed midnight and the whole world has decided New Year's Eve is rubbish and now they want to get home and eat a bag of chips."

"You're so romantic."

"It's my greatest hidden feature."

"Thanks, Kelly."

"You're welcome, and here, I'm scrawling this on a napkin—please give it to Jen. I know she'll probably never trust me—hell, she'll probably never like me, but at least I can say I'm sorry."

I took the Sharpie I had in my pocket from writing the VIP signs for some of the chairs and scribbled *Jen, I am truly, completely, wholly, incredibly, sorry. About everything.*

Garrett swallowed the rest of his drink and slid out of the booth. "Looks like a great party. Beth really kicked it out of the park."

"Is that a sports metaphor?"

"Mixed, now that I think it through. It's a mixed metaphor."

"Go now before you confuse any more words. And make your peace."

Garrett pulled me toward him and kissed me gently. It was a fitting end to my work-boyfriend obsession. We didn't let it go too far. And even though I wanted to pull him into a dark corner and slip my hands under his shirt to feel his stomach, slide them farther down, I also wanted to hold him close and let him know that I was sorry for how sad he was and that I was there for him, whatever he might need.

"This might sound clichéd, but if you need anything, call anytime. I mean it. We're not back at work for another few days, and if you go home, well, know that if you need to talk, I'm here."

Garrett tightened his arms around me while people milled around, growing drunker, growing bolder, already breaking their resolutions. We stayed there together, quietly ignoring the world.

* * *

After Garrett had left and the party was inching toward the bells of the New Year, I pulled up a stool at the far end of one of the bars and sat looking out at the crowd. Beth was dancing in the middle of the floor, laughing, her hair flying. With only fifteen minutes to go before the big countdown, I was glad to see her burn off a little of her stress on the dance floor. I was staring off into space when I felt someone standing a bit too close beside me.

"Now, this is a nice party," Evan said.

I was startled to see him there: crisp white shirt, great oxfords, impeccably tailored pants. He knew how to dress, I had to give him that.

"Oh, hey," I said. "I didn't think you'd show up."

"I told you I didn't have anything better to do," he said, and winked.

"Dude, you really need to cool it on the winking. It absolutely ruins all you've got going on."

He laughed. "Ruins it?"

"Completely."

"Point taken." He paused. "Do you need a drink?"

"Not really, but I'll take one. I am impressively sober right now, in truth."

"Rough night?"

"Not particularly—not for me anyway. But I was working, and I had to stay on top of things."

"Are you still working?"

Out of the corner of my eye, I caught sight of Beth, hands on her knees, shuffling her butt back and forth to some old-school Tribe Called Quest song I'm sure she requested.

"No," I replied. "I'm just about done. Countdown to a whole new me."

"A whole new you?"

"Long story," I said. "I'm not keen on shouting it out at a crowded bar."

"Let's go somewhere quieter."

I laughed. "Oh my god! The winks, the lines, how do you take yourself seriously? Do the women in your life fall for that crap?"

Evan laughed and held his hands to his heart. "I'm beginning to feel a little wounded."

"Evan, Evan, there's no way we're going to be friends if you get wounded by any measure of teasing."

He rested his hand on my shoulder and leaned in. "You're saying we're friends?"

"Boyfriend—let me remind you, I have a boyfriend. A serious boyfriend. We've been together for years. We own property together."

"I know, I know." He laughed. "Can you blame me for trying? Look at how spectacular your legs look in that dress."

"Go get yourself a drink. There are plenty of people here who will be more than happy to entertain your bad one-liners."

"Bam!" he said. "That's another shot straight through to the heart. Oh, ugh, I can't take it—rejection, it makes me feel like a mere mortal."

"Back down to earth, Superman, back down to earth. That'll be my role in your life. I'll consistently bring you back down to earth."

Evan slipped to the other side of me to try to catch the bartender's attention. When he came back with two domestic beers (that surprised me), I gladly accepted one and took a sip. When I looked up, Rob was standing at the other side of the room. The surprise must have shown, because Evan said, "What's the matter?"

"There he is."

"Who?"

"Boyfriend."

"Current?"

"Yes."

"In person?"

I laughed. "Actually, I think it would be better to describe him as the man I am most certainly not going to marry."

"What?"

"Another long story. Hey, thanks for coming. I'd better go, at least talk to him. Anyway, it is nice to see you, you're funny. I've enjoyed that."

"But not my winking or my conversation."

"No, neither of those things."

And then I winked.

* * *

Rob looked tired, drawn, and more than a little drunk. He wasn't swaying but he was having some trouble holding up his own frame. Steadying him, I said, "I'm so glad you're here. I'm so, so sorry."

"Aren't you always sorry, Kelly? Isn't sorry, like, your natural state or something?"

"Come, come over here and let's sit down where we're not in the middle of the party."

"What, you don't want me to *embarrass* you? At this job that you care so much about?"

I pulled at his arm until he stumbled toward me and brought him to the same booth where Garrett and I had been sitting just a little while ago. The ghost of that conversation still lingered. It was like a shared seat on public transit, that awkward feeling of participating in someone else's body heat a strangely intimate thing.

"I didn't think you were coming," I said. "But I'm glad you did. I'm happy to see you, to talk to you."

He spat out the words. "Where's Garrett?"

"On his way to the airport," I said.

"Well, good for him."

"It is good for him. I'm crushed that it took that horrible night at our place for me to understand it all, to understand myself, how I've been acting. I'm sorry that it was all so awful, but I'm not sorry to know what I know."

"What is it that you claim to know, Kelly? That you've been stringing me along like a proper gold digger for the last, oh, I don't know, umpteen years, shaming me into thinking that if I just hung on long enough you'd change and come around to it all?"

"Be as mean as you need to be right now, Rob. Let the dragon out."

"Are you being sarcastic?"

"No, not at all. You're mad. I don't want to say anything patronizing like 'You deserve to be,' or 'I've acted terribly, please forgive me.' I don't want to be forgiven. I've been thinking a lot this week, stuck at home at my mother's, talking, talking—you know she's never short on opinions—and I realized that I've been so miserable. Comfortably miserable, doing this job because it was easy but not taking it seriously, getting all caught up in drama that was just an excuse for me to act out. And I don't want to be that person anymore. It's not fair to you. Your mother said as much to me on Christmas Eve."

"What did my mother say to you? I've told you and told you not to listen to her."

"No, Rob, it's fine, she was right. In her own way. She was right all along. I always thought I was being so strong by being with you, staying together, proving to myself that I could be committed, that I could do something right. This week, I don't know, I figured out that I'm weak and scared and miserable, and I love you so much, but I don't want to get married. And I don't want to have kids. And it's not at all fair of me to hold you here with me, like a hostage, depriving you of the chance to find someone who might want those things with you. It isn't enough for me to think about it, to have that ring, that beautiful ring, your beautiful heart, and spend the rest of our lives together drinking myself to death because I'm so miserable."

"I'll go anywhere with you. Do anything. Don't, Kelly, I don't want—you just have to ask."

"I'm not going to. Ask, that is. I'm going to say right now that you should keep the apartment. I'll stay with my mom and Carl for a while until I find a place. And it's going to suck and be hard, and I can't believe I'm even this calm right now, but I am, and this is what I want, and I'm—"

"Come home, please. I can't do it here, I can't have this conversation here, now."

The countdown had begun—people were shouting numbers—and Rob pulled me close to him. There was a tenderness between us when they got to one, and cheers all around, and then we were kissing, and it felt like good-bye for me. I said, "I'll come home as soon as I can. I will."

But he didn't leave. He sobered up, helped Beth and me close down the party, and stayed close. He held my hand in the cab back to our condo, and we got in bed together side by side, not saying much, but both knowing that everything had changed.

Epilogue

THIS MORNING HAS been full of déjà vu. I slipped into old clothes and warm boots, and recognized that the grayness belonged to the last four months, not to the present hours as they move forward. The memory of that dinner is trapped like an earworm in my mind. I play and replay it. Would I do it all differently? Could I have been an adult about everything from the start? Balancing out relief and regret have gotten me through the long, cold winter.

I'm lucky. The moment Annie heard that I'd called it off with Rob she let me stay in her basement apartment. The rent is cheap, and I'm not often there, except to sleep. Annie's always traveling, and my stepbrothers are here now that university exams are done. It feels like a second home. My mother comes by, and Meghan's spent the night a couple times, pregnancy pillow in tow.

Today, I was knocked off kilter, first by the temperature—above freezing and holding—and then by a crocus, purple and bright, that I spied poking out of someone's garden as I walked to the bus stop on my way to school. I'm working on some extra film credits, putting together a portfolio. As I walked, the wind pushed into me with the force of a lover you know is wrong for you but whom you can't resist. Still, I persisted, aching, sore, exhausted, because I knew that we'll soon be rid of this winter. Soon I can welcome spring, just like I did that flower.

Rob bought me out of the condo. He was beyond decent, and the money sitting in my bank account gives me a freedom I never thought I would have. I could afford to go to school in New York. I've applied, but I don't know if I'll get in. I could finance my own film and get my start that way. Take that amazing camera Rob bought me for Christmas and head off to find my story. I could buy another place. It's nice to have options. Rob didn't have to be that generous.

Garrett didn't come back from the West Coast. As far as I know, he tried to resign over email but the powers that be convinced him to work out of the small Vancouver office until he sorted out where he wanted to live. Marianne packed up their place for them. He and Jen could be back together, or they might be split up, I don't know, and I'm trying so hard not to call or text him because I miss him with every inch of my body. But I promised myself I'd be alone, stand on my own two feet, for as long as I could possibly stand it.

I miss having them both in my life: the constant goodness of Rob influencing me in ways I didn't even realize, and though my own rebellion pushed back, it kept me in an odd sort of balance; and Garrett, who was the ever-present person to go for lunch with, to riff off in truly boring meetings, to make the hours fly by. They filled up my life. Being alone is scary. Rob keeps in touch, and I'm glad for it. It's only been four months, and we were always friends. I can't imagine my life without him, although I know it'll come to that eventually. He'll meet someone soon, I can feel it, and it'll be quick—a destination wedding, which would kill his mother. Then they'll take up residence in that house his parents are itching to buy for them.

Rob taught me how to love, but I didn't love myself. And falling for the wrong person won't ever turn out right. And then I found the right person, but the timing was all wrong. I haven't found the balance between the two that I hope is out there for me. Love is tricky. But now that I know I can stand on my own two feet, I can wait. It will happen.

If it doesn't, that's okay, too, because I can fill my life up with family, and traveling, and movies, and everything that means something to me. The trick is to be happy either way. To understand yourself is a win in life, to be your own person, to pursue your own dreams.

I resigned my publicity job so I could go back to film school until I could sort out whether I'd head to New York or not. I forced myself into the spring term with a lot of pressure and phone calls and help from the most unlikely of places—Evan. He's a producer, of all things. One of life's little pieces fell into place. I'm working for him part time, keeping him organized, and absolutely not allowing any kind of romance. No work boyfriend. No *actual* boyfriend. It feels good to fill up my own space. Who knows? I might have made the two biggest mistakes of my life in quitting my job and giving Rob back his ring. I guess I'll never know what might have been. But *this* is my fairy-tale ending: me standing on the subway in jeans and Uggs, heading to my editing class at Ryerson, a decade older than everyone else enrolled, and loving every minute of it.

* * *

A few days later, I'm about to leave for school when there's a knock at the door. I shout, "Annie, you know you can just come in, it's not locked."

"Hi," he said.

"Oh." Any further words were lost.

"I'm ready if you are."

"Garrett—"

"No excuses."

"I'm so happy to see you."

And that's where I'll fade to black and cut.

Acknowledgments

I F YOU, DEAR READER, are anything like me, then you've flipped to the end of the book and are starting here. Welcome.

I'm very lucky to have a number of amazing Rebeccas in my life: thank you to Rebecca Eckler for publishing this novel, and for being a tireless champion throughout the process. Next up is the wonderful and amazing Rebecca Mills, whose friendship and support have been a delight of my adult life. There would be no *The Work Boyfriend* without either of them.

Thank you to Heather Sanderson. Those five words aren't enough, but she knows the well-deep meaning behind them. Thank you to Kathleen Olmstead and Mose for Tuesday walks but also for reading the new draft and offering both advice and a space to talk about what was and wasn't working. Thank you to Allison Dick for reminding me that it's okay to keep going at any age. Ice cream later? Kristina Vayda. Je t'aime.

To my ride or dies: Amanda Ramdeen, Lesley Calvin, and Suzette Chapman, our group chat is everything. Thanks to my Alliance Atlantis friends Nadine, Sue, and Mia (who read the previous version—so, so appreciated). Nads, thank you for putting the idea of a work boyfriend in my head and for our obsessing over them back in the day.

To Fiona Simpson, this version of the novel is so much better because of your deft hand and the pointing out of Rob's flaws.

Thank you. Huge props to Jay Flores-Holz for agreeing to draw the cover and for simply being awesome. Thank you to the whole team at RE:BOOKS, including Chloe and Emilee.

Dad and Sue, and Jeremy, thank you. Also, thank you to Gerrè, Judy, and Marilyn. To my cousins and nieces and nephews, I love you. And Chloe, there are no chili peppers in here, totally safe for you to read. Jan, I still miss you. I think I will always miss you.

Brian and Ethan. You are the two best decisions I've ever made in my life, and that's true even when I'm grumpy and exhausted. I'm so lucky you love me even then. I'm even luckier to love you both so much it hurts.

This book is dedicated to my mother, who left us when she was far too young, but not before instilling in me a love of romance novels. Her "stories" littered my childhood and started me off on a career that's been nothing short of fulfilling. I hope her hand is turning these pages somewhere and that she's smiling that I've finally leaned into the romance I always knew was at the heart of my creative life.